# The Holder
# of Annanbourne

Tiggy Greenwood

GW00715402

MEADOWELL

Published in Great Britain in 2015
by Meadowell
Meyden Revel, Cheselbourne, Dorset DT2 7NP

A CIP catalogue record for this book is available from the
British Library.

Printed in Great Britain by Berforts Information Press,
Stevenage, SB1 2BH

ISBN: 978-0-99326-250-0

Paper used in the production of this book is a natural, recyclable
product made from wood grown in sustainable forests.

www.meadowell.com

Have you ever walked into somewhere and IMMEDIATELY felt good about it? You may not have seen him, but that's the Holder you're sensing. Every property ever built has one, and you've always known it really.

Edwin Mosstone (Mossy to his friends), the Holder of Annanbourne, may be a little clumsy, but his hopes, his goodwill and his love for his Dwellers is real. Your Holder is almost certainly like that. He can't stop your problems happening, but he's always there, willing you on.

The Holder of Annanbourne is NOT about witches and wizards and ghouls. It's about the true spirit of place, the actual being that is born when the first piece of a property is laid, embodied by the building, changing with the strange changes humans insist on making, sharing in their delights and their pains. The Holder wants to help you make your house into a home, if you let him. The only food he needs is your laughter and acceptance. So let Mossy into your life. Understand him, and he'll help you sense your own Holder trying to guide you. The best friend you could ever wish for is on your side.

Find out more at
www.annanbourne.com

'I liked it; a real page turner, that kept me reading. This is a cheery house spirit with a sense of humour, not like any others. It has a really good, believable family dynamic, with a subtle spiritual element that avoids being preachy, but is distinctively positive. You initially think the baddie is a good person, only realising, along with the characters, how deeply unpleasant he is. And it has a cracking ending.'
Tim O'Kelly, *One Tree Books – National Bookseller of the Year 2012 – Costa Book Awards Judge 2001*

'No sooner had we finished the book than the children were asking when we could get the next in the series. I just couldn't get over how visual it all was.'
Jo Scott, *Pagham, West Sussex*

'I loved the bit where the children blow up the neighbour's garden.'
Theo, *aged 9*

'So we must have a Holder in our house too… I wonder what ours looks like?'
Bella, *aged 11*

'I just loved it. The idea of a creature that looks after the house and all the people in it, who can pull nightmares out of sleeping people, and is improved as the house improves is brilliant. I liked the way it got faster and faster, and the whole trip up to London was great.'
Charity, *aged 12*

'I liked the fact that it shows that you don't have to be rich to have a good time. I loved the bicycle rides and the races. It was fun.'
Mimi, *aged 11*

To Jay,
guardian of my dreams.

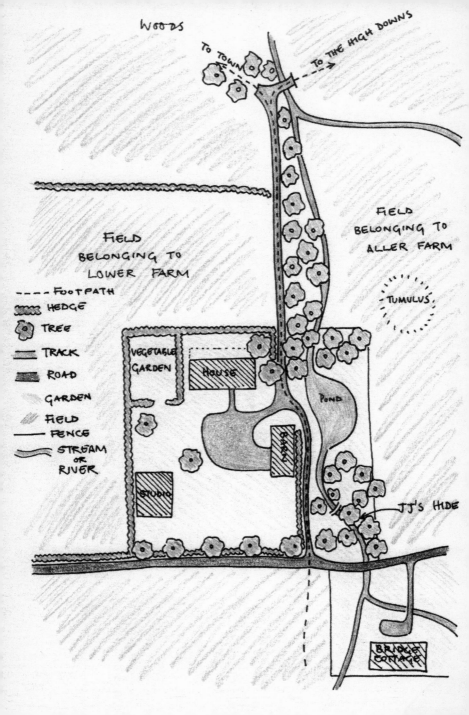

## CHAPTER 1

# Arrivals

'Look! Look!' exclaimed Cissy, jumping from the car. 'It's still here!'

'What's still here?' asked Rollo once he stood on the gravel beside her.

'The house,' explained his sister. 'Last night I dreamt it had fallen down, that we couldn't live here.'

My house! Fallen down? thought Mossy. Discretely tucked out of sight behind the iris at the water's edge, he stood on tiptoe, peeking round a yellow flower to inspect the new arrivals.

He sighed as he looked at Annanbourne, nestled comfortably at the foot of the downs, the fields around it rising to the high hills. The windows tried to sparkle in the early summer sunshine, but he could see where repairs were urgently needed. Previous Dwellers had saved them from disaster, but that was many years ago, and recently they had been neglected. The old timber frame creaked, flints were missing here and there, plaster was falling off and a strong breeze found its way too easily through the thin walls.

We need help, he admitted with a grimace, but we're not falling down yet. He stretched his aching back, rubbed tired eyes and pulled his ragged clothes about him. He was feeling his nearly six hundred years.

Nevertheless, concentrating hard, he tugged at his ears, pulling them up straight, ready to catch every word. I do hope you'll look after us, he sighed. The duck, with whom he had been passing the time of day, waggled her tail and set off for the far side of the pond.

'I'll let you know what they're like when I've had a chance to find out more myself,' he called after her.

'Annie, what time did the removals men say they'd arrive?' the children's father asked his wife.

'Any minute now,' she replied, looking at her watch. 'JJ,' she added, ruffling the hair of another boy who Mossy decided must be about seven years old, 'if you're going down to the pond, please be careful. We have nothing ready for drying wet boys.'

'Don't worry, Mum,' said Rollo. 'I'll keep tabs on him.' He ran with Cissy to join their younger brother at the water's edge. Mossy, now hidden behind a clump of watercress, smiled. He preferred it when there were children in his house. They usually brought laughter and fun, keeping him well fed and full of energy. These ones looked promising.

'I can't see any fish,' remarked JJ, examining the water that slid softly by.

'Maybe they've all been eaten by a giant fish eagle!' suggested Cissy, her eyes widening in alarm at the thought. Mossy stepped onto a stone to crane his head over the leaves of the iris for a better view. The stone wobbled.

'More likely to be a heron,' pointed out Rollo.

'Huh!' Cissy didn't agree with him. 'Just because you're older than me. You're not always right.' She shrugged her shoulders.

'Hey look!' JJ was pointing at something down by the water's edge. Carefully Mossy parted the slender leaves of a rush, his long, thin fingers silently opening a window between the green spikes, his nose catching a whiff of JJ's curiosity.

'It looks like a stone wall, under the water,' noted Cissy. 'An underwater house,' she decided this time. 'A ruined castle.'

Rollo looked across the pond.

'More likely to be part of an old water mill,' he suggested.

Now it was Mossy's turn to be surprised. He turned curious green eyes on Rollo, searching out every bit of information he could sense.

What had made him think that? There was no sign of the mill any longer. Those few stones were all that remained of the old building. It had fallen into disuse as the river diminished, turning into the stream it was today. The ruin had been demolished nearly a century before, leaving him as thin as a rake.

Checking that he was safely invisible, he leaned forward to catch a better smell of the boy. There was something about him... Someone he reminded him of... Mossy scrutinised him carefully. Rollo was tall for his age, fair-haired like his brother and sister, with bright eyes that clearly wouldn't miss a thing.

The stone beneath Mossy's feet rocked. He grabbed a leaf to keep upright, but his foot slid on the slippery surface. Suddenly it shot out from under him, flinging him into the water with a splash.

'What's that?' exclaimed Cissy, heading towards where Mossy lay, as still as possible, water seeping into his ears and tickling his nose. An old toad, annoyed by the sudden activity, crawled away between the stems, determined to find a quieter spot. JJ pushed past his sister.

'It's just a frog,' JJ told her, turning back. Cissy lost interest, but Mossy stayed immobile. Getting out of the water might make ripples that could be spotted, and, even though he couldn't be seen, he didn't want to risk further investigation. He dug his fingers into the mud to hold himself still.

'I bet this **was** a mill pond once,' Rollo decided. 'It would make sense out here. When Annanbourne was a farm they could use the water for power. It would have been dead handy.'

Ah, you should have seen it, thought Mossy. There was a time when it made all the difference, kept a family going when everything else failed. But you'll never know what it was really like, he realised. You had to have been there.

'Hey, come on everybody,' their father's voice called. 'It's time to choose bedrooms!'

'Wait for me!' called JJ, running up the bank and across the track.

'Me too!' called Cissy, racing Rollo towards the house.

With the children's attention diverted, Mossy hauled himself out of the water. He was soaked, but there was no time to waste. He had a job to do. Regardless of his dunking in the pond, a glow of warmth spread through him.

'Hang on a tick, Jack,' called Annie. 'I want to take a photograph.' She held up a camera.

The family arranged themselves on the path that led to the front door, giving Mossy time to hurry ahead of them. At the opening he turned, his arms stretched wide in greeting, his eyes now sparkling bright blue. His long fingers wriggled with glee and his spindly legs longed to dance. But he stood proudly, his ears pointing skywards, ready for The Greeting. Annie tucked the camera into her pocket and, with Jack holding her hand and JJ skipping beside her, they walked up the path towards him.

As Jack slotted the key into the lock Mossy bowed low, and when the door swung open he made a sweeping gesture with his hands and turned to lead them in.

'*Welcome to Annanbourne,*' he projected, directing his message to these new Dwellers. '*May you flourish and thrive here. May love surround you and joy sing in your hearts. We of the house greet you, our new Dwellers. As you open the door, so we open ourselves to you. While the house gives you shelter, warmth and a place of safety, I, the Holder of Annanbourne, will protect and cherish you. Long may you stay, and long may you play.*'

'Our new home,' sighed Annie. 'It feels so good, doesn't it?'

I'll say, agreed Mossy. It felt just right. He looked beyond them to where JJ had paused on the threshold.

'Mum! Dad!' JJ called out, beckoning them over. 'Look at this!' He crouched to examine the stone doorstep.

'It's just a bit of muddy water, sweetheart,' explained Annie.

Mossy clapped his hands over his mouth. Oh no! In his eagerness to greet the family and bring them safely home he had completely forgotten that he was still wet. As the water dripped off him, it had become visible, pooling on the stone.

'What's the excitement?' asked Rollo, joining them.

'Maybe there's a spring under the house,' suggested Cissy, cheerfully. 'Maybe it's about to burst out of the ground and flood everything and…'

'Don't be dappy, Cissy.' Rollo laughed. 'These are two patches of water on the ground. It hardly makes a flood!' Mossy checked that he'd left no more puddles on the floor and picked up a bit of pondweed that had dropped off his trousers. He rubbed away a tiny bit of mud with his sleeve. Time to dry off outside, he decided.

'If it were a spring the water would be coming from under the stone. It'd be around it, not two little puddles on top of it,' Jack told them. 'Still, I wonder where it came from…' he mused, looking upwards. 'Cissy may not be so wrong about floods. We don't know where the water pipes are, only that there are several that need replacing…' His voice trailed off as he and Annie headed anxiously into the house.

'I don't think it's a flood, not from anywhere,' said JJ. 'It looks like footprints.'

Mossy, who had been about to slip quietly past them, froze in his tracks and looked over to where his footprints were, indeed, wetly marked on the stone.

'I can see what you mean,' Rollo agreed with him. 'Narrow ones,' he pointed out. 'Something with long thin feet…' He paused, thinking.

'What kind of animal has long, thin feet?'

Mossy let out his breath again.

*'Just keep thinking about animals,'* he projected.

'But only two feet,' Cissy pointed out. 'Most animals have four.' Mossy gulped.

'Maybe it's a mini kangaroo,' suggested JJ. 'You know, a walla-whatsit.'

'No, even walla-whatsits are bigger than that,' Cissy corrected him. 'Maybe the front prints of whatever it is have dried off.' Mossy relaxed again.

'Unless,' Rollo pondered, 'we've got a House Sprite.'

What!

Mossy examined Rollo. I'm not a 'House Sprite', he almost said aloud, but it set him thinking. What was it that he'd heard about Place Readers? Could this boy be one? And if he were, would it mean trouble? He waved a hand at Rollo, just to check that he couldn't actually be seen. Rollo smiled, not at Mossy, but at his brother and sister. It looked as if Mossy was still safely invisible.

'That would be fun.' Rollo grinned at the two younger ones.

'Are they good things?' asked JJ. Things! Humph! thought Mossy. We're alive, as much as you. We have feelings and emotions. We can get bumped and bruised like you do, too. There are even times when we can be seen; if we want to let you see us, that is. His eyes sparkled at the memories of times when he'd surprised people.

'I thought they did naughty things like turning milk sour,' said Cissy. Mossy blushed at the memory, but that had only been once, when there was a girl who was unkind to the cows she milked. It had worked – she'd been kinder after that. '… and pinched people and made things go missing and…'

'Don't muddle them up with Gremlins!' warned Rollo.

Mossy chuckled quietly to himself as he folded his arms and leant back against the wall. We've been given all sorts of names over the centuries, he thought. Depends whether people like us or not. But this is more than that. Interesting, he decided, nodding his head. I've never had a Place Reader here before.

'Hey, look!' JJ pointed down at the stone. 'The water's almost gone!'

'No pipes that could have caused any trouble,' announced Jack, reappearing. He looked at the track where a removals van was reversing carefully round a corner. 'Here comes our furniture. I think it's time we got cracking. Come on you lot. Help me show them who sleeps where.'

## CHAPTER 2

# Meetings

The warmth of the late summer sun quickly dried Mossy's footprints and in the chaos of unpacking they were completely forgotten.

Cissy took a bedroom at the side of the house, sticking her head out of the window.

'Look, Rollo! I can see forever! Dragons, at the top of the hill – watch out! Hey, Mum, I can't shut this now.' Mossy nodded his head. That wasn't the only window that was beginning to rot.

As soon as he was dry, Mossy clambered into a small tree and warmed himself doing gymnastics, swinging from branch to branch. A robin perched beside him.

'I saw your missus earlier, on a worm hunt I think,' he told the bird. The robin cocked his head and chirruped.

'The new Dwellers? They seem OK, but it's early days as yet.' Mossy swung off the branch he was sitting on and leapt for the one above. He caught it with only one hand and after a bit of a struggle, hooked his legs over and hung upside down.

The robin hopped round to the other side and fired off another round of twitters.

'Not sure,' admitted Mossy, 'but they've already put a table on the terrace outside the kitchen. Why don't you go and fetch your mate, hop about on it and see if that gives them the right idea?'

As the bird flew off, Mossy turned right way up again and inspected another window. A well-worn teddy bear was looking out of the smallest bedroom, his darned nose pressed against the glass. It looked as if JJ was making sure that an old friend could enjoy the view too.

At the back of the house Mossy climbed a collection of flower pots and peered in through the kitchen window. Crumpled paper carpeted the floor as Annie added another plate to the pile on the table beside her. He leaned closer to see if any food had been unpacked. The pots under his feet rocked. Then they rocked a bit more. Mossy grabbed the sill too late as the whole lot rolled over under his feet. Annie turned a startled face towards the window.

'Oh dear!' she exclaimed. 'I didn't think those pots looked very safe.' JJ rushed out to check for any breakages, and Mossy only just managed to jump clear in time to avoid being stashed inside them as they were re-stacked.

'Nothing broken!' the boy called back. 'And look, the bird feeders are here too. All we've got to do is find the bird food and I can give that robin I was telling you about something to eat.'

Perched on the saddle of a bicycle propped against the wall of the old barn, Mossy watched as JJ hauled all sorts of things, that weren't bird food, out of yet another big box. They were interrupted by the clang of the doorbell.

JJ started to run out of the barn as Mossy launched himself from his seat. He landed with one foot on a tool box and the other in a bag of compost just as the boy caught his own foot under a curled hosepipe. As JJ sprawled forward he flung out both hands, knocking Mossy flying like a ninepin, so that he spiralled through the air, landing with the tip of his nose inches from JJ's.

'Weerff!' exclaimed JJ as his breath was knocked out of him. 'That was a good one!'

Not so sure about good, but certainly surprising, thought Mossy. It's not often that I meet someone as accident-prone as me. As JJ stood up, dusted the dirt off and headed for the door, Mossy staggered in his wake.

Outside, he spotted his neighbour Puddle, the Holder of Bridge Cottage, with two of his Dwellers.

'What's up?' whispered Mossy.

'Nothing. We're just being friendly,' Puddle replied.

'Nice one,' Mossy congratulated him. 'It's a long time since we've had gifts from your place.' JJ went to find a parent. Mossy, who had hardly seen Puddle's Dwellers since they had arrived a couple of years before, checked them over. The boy was tall, with shiny black hair, dark eyes and a bright, alert face. He looked the same age as Rollo. The woman was short, with curly brown hair and an easy smile. She had a plate in one hand and a jug in the other. He grinned at Puddle.

'Looks good,' he chuckled.

'Mum!' they heard JJ call in the house. 'Dad!' There was a pause. 'Anyone?'

Cissy galloped round the corner.

'Hello there! Who are you?' she beamed at the arrivals. 'Something the matter? Can I help?'

Annie and Jack arrived at the front door.

'Hello,' said the visitor, holding out the jug and plate. 'It's not long since we moved in over the way, and it was hungry and thirsty work. So we've brought something to keep you going.' JJ and Rollo arrived together.

'How kind!' exclaimed Annie.

'I'm Sue Raitata, and this is our son Jon,' added his mother.

'Annie Breeze,' said Annie, smiling warmly at her new neighbour. Introductions were soon made, and everybody shook hands, except for Cissy.

'Mucky hands,' she explained, holding hers up.

'Yours can't be any dirtier than mine,' Jon laughed. 'I was helping Dad build a wood pile earlier.'

'Well, in that case...' Cissy shook hands heartily.

Mossy and Puddle sat on the windowsill in the kitchen and watched as the two families enjoyed the brownies and lemonade.

'Well done, Puddle, this looks promising.'

'I'm getting the hang of things this time,' agreed the younger Holder, 'thanks to your advice, and I'm feeling better and better.' There was a burst of laughter from the group of Dwellers. 'Just feast on that,' Mossy reminded him, as he wriggled his toes in delight. 'Just what we need.'

Sue and Jon didn't linger.

'See you soon,' said Jon as they left. 'I'll bring my bike round and then I can show you the way to the quarry. It's ace riding.'

'Great!' agreed Rollo as he waved goodbye.

'Well, that looks good!' exclaimed his Dad as they all headed back into the house. 'Given those are our only neighbours, we seem to have fallen on our feet. And with a son the same age as Rollo!'

'No daughters the same age as me or JJ though,' Cissy reminded them. 'Jon said his sister was seventeen. Imagine that – ancient! And no good for games.'

'Don't worry, darling. I'm sure you and JJ will soon have friends of your own,' Annie comforted her.

'And meanwhile, come with me,' suggested Jack. 'I saw some logs we could use to light a fire to celebrate our arrival.' Brilliant, thought Mossy. This looks like a good start.

In the kitchen Mossy posted himself on the dresser, watching Rollo help Annie scoop armfuls of paper into cardboard boxes.

'We need to get it organised even though we'll have to change it when the kitchen is rebuilt.' Mossy's ears pricked up. Hmm, new kitchen, he thought. I wonder what else they might change. Whilst he was keen for repairs, he was well aware that some changes could have pretty far-reaching effects on a Holder, too.

Before he could find out anything further, Cissy burst into the kitchen.

'Mum, Rollo! Disaster!' Surprised that neither Rollo nor Annie seemed very concerned, Mossy looked over at her anxiously. 'My chest of drawers is all in the wrong place and I can't move it. Every time I try, the carpet wrinkles up, and now it's blocking the door so it's impossible to get out. I was nearly stuck there for ever, and I could have died of starvation.'

Starvation! thought Mossy, he'd seen that in the past, but

Cissy looked remarkably healthy. And what could a chest of drawers have to do with it?

'It takes weeks to starve to death!' laughed Rollo. 'We'd have noticed you missing long before you were even hungry.' Ah ha, thought Mossy, another of Cissy's imaginings.

JJ burst through the door, tripped on the corner of a box and cascaded across the floor. Mossy nearly toppled from his perch as he craned sideways to see if the boy was alright. JJ struggled back onto his feet.

'Look what I've found!' he exclaimed, waving a fist in the air. 'A lucky talisman hidden at the back of the alcove in my room!' Mossy leaned forward as JJ produced a smooth pebble. It was a beautiful stone, softly mottled, with a hole worn through the middle.

'*I remember you,*' Mossy silently greeted the stone. '*I remember when you were first found. When was it? Must have been a hundred and fifty years ago! You were a lucky talisman then, too. I hadn't realised you were still here all this time. I may be hundreds of years old,*' he smiled, '*but you are more than thousands of years old. I've gathered some knowledge in my time, but it's nothing compared to what you've been through.*'

He looked down, seeing the gentle glow that no human eye could see, as the stone nestled in JJ's hand; a glow brought by memories of ancient fires and ancient freezes, worlds of change and an understanding of time locked in its core. From deep in hidden rock, fractured by burning deserts that now bloomed, washed and worn smooth from tumbling in seas now dry, it carried its secrets still.

If you think your talisman brings you luck, then it will. He smiled as he looked at JJ. Maybe it'll bring us all luck, too.

## CHAPTER 3

# Changes

A couple of days later Annie helped the children prepare for school.

'You don't want to miss the beginning of the new term,' she told them firmly.

'Who says?' protested Cissy. 'I wouldn't mind.'

'I would. I want to get into the football team,' decided JJ, crunching round the kitchen in new football boots.

'Now's the time to make friends,' Rollo reminded her. Reluctantly Cissy agreed.

Jack was about to disappear for a couple of weeks.

'I'll call from America, and I'm sorry to leave you to sort this out on your own,' he said as he waved goodbye.

'It's OK,' smiled Annie. 'We're used to it.'

'Won't Dad see us on the first day of our new schools?' asked Cissy.

'You'll be able to tell him about it on the phone,' Annie reminded her.

'But he always rings at such weird times. We never get to

speak to him,' JJ complained.

'I'm sorry,' sighed Jack. 'I wish I could be there too.' Mossy felt Jack's sadness as he slammed the car door and drove off.

It wasn't long before Mossy noticed interesting developments. People came to visit, and he joined them as they walked about with Annie.

'Not a problem...' he heard one say.

'Ooh, tricky one that,' said a different man the following day as he looked up at the same bit of roof.

'It's not difficult,' a third man decided, 'but you'll need scaffolding.'

'Cupboards here and here, and here, and here,' declared a woman as she waved her arms about in the centre of the kitchen. 'Get rid of that for starters,' she added, pointing at Mossy as he perched on a shelf.

'*You can't get rid of me!*' Mossy projected firmly. '*You'd destroy the house!*'

'Dressers are so old-fashioned,' she declared. He disagreed. He liked the dresser, it suited the house and made a perfect viewing platform.

'Knock this out... Stainless steel...' Mossy shuddered and looked over at Annie. Fortunately she looked almost as horrified as he felt.

'Have to have all that out,' announced another man as he tapped on the plumbing in the scullery, 'there's lead in that, and it's your rising main.'

Mossy nodded. The pipework was old, but he remembered the excitement when water had first been piped into the house rather than having to be hauled in buckets. Not much had changed since then, and there were times when the system groaned with fatigue.

'Shower?' asked Annie. The man brought out fistfuls of brochures, and Mossy looked over Annie's shoulder to admire the pictures.

Mossy checked time and again that nothing major was being added to the house and smiled broadly at the thought of all the improvements being planned. His ears waved in alarm, however, when Jack returned from another of his foreign trips and Annie showed him pictures of conservatories.

'Imagine that at the back of the kitchen,' Annie suggested.

Oh dear, sighed Mossy. Glass extensions onto old houses were risky for Holders, particularly one who'd already had to cope with extensions before. Glass could be brittle and he knew he'd feel anxious if he had to cope with glass fingers, toes or however such an addition might change him.

'Think of all the light...' smiled Annie. Mossy shuddered.

Later that evening, as he was sitting on his bed, JJ suddenly remembered that he needed to add something to his school bag.

'Don't start the story without me!' he called, as he grabbed his slippers, pushed his left foot into one and hopped about, waving the other at his right foot.

'*Slow down,*' Mossy gently reminded him. '*More haste, less speed.*' But JJ's mind was full of other things and he wasn't receptive to Mossy's projection.

At the top of the stairs he bumped against the banister, his bare foot skidding on the worn carpet. He gave a yelp of dismay and tumbled forward, the slipper shooting out of his hand, hitting the wall and bumping down the stairs.

'**Arms round head**!' shouted Mossy, not caring who heard him as he flung himself down the stairs to JJ's aid.

There was a terrible series of bangs as JJ fell, head first, down three steps, and then tumbled onto his back before somersaulting wildly down to the stone floor at the bottom.

Mossy crept close to JJ's side. Gently he placed a hand on the boy, his long fingers slipping under the arms that JJ had wrapped round his head to protect himself as he fell. Mossy felt his pulse beating weakly. Quickly he ran the other hand over the boy's limp form. He could feel a serious pain in JJ's left leg and another at the back of his head. How bad they were he wasn't sure. Silently he stepped aside as the others crashed down around him.

'JJ!' cried Cissy, as Annie bent over him. 'Mum, what happened?'

'I didn't see, he suddenly fell,' her mother replied. 'Jack, call…' But Jack already had a phone and was dialling the doctor. 'Rollo, fetch a blanket. Cissy, bring a glass of water.'

'Oh, Rollo!' cried Cissy, her eyes awash with tears as she hurried into the bathroom. 'Is he going to be OK? Rollo, he can't die, he wasn't even bleeding. He won't, will he?'

'Mum and Dad are both here,' Rollo reassured her as he dragged the counterpane off his bed. 'Just do what Mum said, get water. Dad's calling for help. And you know JJ. He crashes often enough, but he always bounces back.'

'Just because he always has doesn't mean…'

'Cissy, shut up.' Rollo frowned at his sister. 'It's no good tizzing, and I don't want to think the wrong thing, so don't you dare say it either.' Hearing the sharpness in his voice Mossy realised how worried Rollo must be. Silently Cissy fetched a mug of water and picked up a damp flannel as she left the room.

'An ambulance is on its way,' announced Jack.

Although Mossy did his best to comfort the family as they waited beside JJ's unmoving body, all he could use was touch. They needed reassurance, words, knowledge that he didn't have. They needed someone to tell them that he was going to be fine.

As soon as the paramedics arrived they took charge, carefully lifting JJ onto a stretcher, explaining all the while what they were doing.

'He's unconscious, and we'll check him fully at the hospital. Not surprising after a fall like that. Well done for not moving him, and the cool flannel on his forehead will have done a power of good.' Annie slipped an arm round Cissy's shoulders.

'See,' she smiled down at her. 'You did the right thing. He'll be fine.'

'Oh, Mum, that's all I want. JJ better and bouncing around again.'

Annie went with her son in the ambulance.

'Thank goodness you were here, Jack,' she said, as she climbed in beside the still body. 'Not stuck abroad somewhere. I don't know how we'd have managed if you'd been away.' It was the closest that Mossy had heard her come to complaining about Jack's frequent absences.

Mossy tucked himself in beside Rollo as Jack read to him and Cissy that night.

'JJ hates missing the story,' said Cissy, her eyes welling up again. The phone rang.

'Rollo, can you get that?' asked Jack, his arms full of his daughter.

'Mum! Hi,' said Rollo. The others watched him closely in the silence that followed. 'OK...' Another pause. 'So then?...' Another longer pause. Rollo nodded his head and then a broad grin broke across his face.

Mossy could feel the warmth of his relief flood through the room, washing the anxiety out of the others.

'Mum, that's brilliant. See you later. And don't worry, I'll tell them.' He turned to face the family.

'He's OK. He regained consciousness in the ambulance. He told Mum it was really cool inside, and he loved the siren.'

'Typical!' laughed Cissy.

'He's broken his left leg and will have to stay in hospital overnight, but Mum will be back later when he's gone to sleep. Oh, and she said to say thank you to whoever shouted out 'arms over head'. The doctor said it could have saved his life.'

Jack and Rollo both looked at Cissy.

'Not me,' said Cissy with a shrug, 'I thought it was you, Rollo.'

'I didn't even see him fall...'

'Must have been JJ telling himself,' decided Jack. 'Odd, but maybe he's learning to take care of himself, a bit.'

'Not very successfully yet,' Rollo reminded his father.

No one saw Mossy's grin of pride. I got it right, he thought.

It was a several days before JJ arrived home with a plaster

cast on his leg and crutches to help him walk. Mossy looked at him and remembered extensions. He'd felt equally disabled when they had built on the new parts of the house back in the 1600s, but he hadn't had the help of crutches.

Extensions! he thought. In his relief at JJ being all right, he'd completely forgotten to persuade Jack and Annie to give up their plans for adding a conservatory. His time had been filled with keeping everybody calm when Jack had been called away on another unplanned trip.

Helping the boy get round the place without knocking things flying in all directions took patience. It was a full time task, and he collapsed into exhausted sleep each night. By the end of the first week they were both getting the hang of it and the boy could get about pretty well.

JJ, with Mossy close behind him, swung himself into the kitchen, leant his crutches against the dresser, grabbed a glass and hopped over to the kitchen sink.

'What are you doing?' called Annie.

'Just getting a drink,' he replied, turning his face towards his mother as he reached for the tap behind him.

'*Careful,*' warned Mossy. '*Remember, one thing at a time.*' JJ's hand landed on the wet washing sponge rather than the tap.

'Ergh!' he exclaimed, snatching his hand back and turning to see what he'd touched. His bandaged leg couldn't cope. He wobbled. Not again! Mossy's heart leapt into his mouth as the boy grabbed the counter with both hands.

'Be careful!' Annie's exclamation showed that she'd seen. 'We don't want to go back to the hospital again quite yet!' Cissy rushed in from the sitting room, a look of consternation on her face.

'Oops!' grinned JJ, sheepishly. 'No worries!'

'I can call an ambulance if you want!' laughed Cissy.

Mossy stared at her. Cissy was making a joke rather than building it up into a major drama. That was a change. If she could do that, then there was hope yet for JJ.

'Any chance you could carry my glass over to the table?' asked JJ. 'If I try to hop, all the water will come out before I can drink it.'

Mossy stared at him, amazed. Without any kind of prompt he'd thought about consequences. However, it didn't alter the fact that as the boy turned round to sit down his foot caught the crutches and sent them skittering across the floor.

'Sorry Mum,' he said, as he looked at the paint that had been knocked off the skirting.

'Don't worry, love, it'll all be sorted out when the work starts on the house.'

Mossy realised that he had to get cracking on preventing the conservatory. He spent the rest of the day still trailing after JJ, but his mind wasn't on the job. He was racking his brains for a plan.

Maybe I could…

What if I…?

I know! I'll…

But nothing seemed to be just right, and he couldn't find the solution. As a result, JJ tripped against a step and broke a flowerpot, and then shortly after left his crutches propped against a wall, where they fell over and sent Rollo flying when he came rushing back after a bike ride with Jon. Cissy was all consternation, proffering bandages, arnica and sympathy.

When the children were all in bed Annie sat down to wait up for Jack, who was due to return that night.

'What a day we've had of it,' Annie sighed when he arrived. Jack put an arm round her.

'Tell me about it,' he smiled at her. 'Problem shared and all that…'

'I don't know, it seemed to be just one accident after another. Dear old JJ is a walking disaster zone.'

'Nothing new there,' laughed Jack. 'What did I see on the way in? A broken flower pot, I think. And there seems to be a new scar on the skirting in the kitchen.' Mossy rubbed the scratch on his finger.

'Well, you missed Rollo going for six when he tripped over JJ's crutches. And it's made me think,' Annie carried on. 'You know that conservatory we were talking about?' Jack nodded his head.

Mossy's ears pricked up. He crossed his fingers.

'Maybe it's not such a good idea. It's not as if we haven't got plenty of space anyway, and somehow I just get the feeling that it wouldn't survive long.'

'Funny you should say that; Rollo mentioned it when I went to say goodnight. He seemed to think it would be wrong for the house, something about too much glass in an old building.'

Mossy grinned. So that's what a Place Reader was about. Good on him. No need to think up complicated plans, just get Rollo to help.

'We're not committed to anything there anyway, so it's quite simple, we'll just say 'No, thank you.' Jack concluded. Annie smiled up at him.

'We can always re-think when they're grown up,' she said.

That's fine by me, thought Mossy. By then you'll be so used to it as it is, and the way we've lived together all that time, that you won't need me, or Rollo, to tell you that we're best left as we are.

## CHAPTER 4

# Improvements

Autumn was well under way and a frost on the ground, when men arrived to wrap the house in scaffolding. Mossy inspected it carefully, worried by the long metal poles that swung about the place. He didn't want any more bruises than necessary.

JJ, now a dab hand with his crutches and hopping about with confidence, was back at school with the others. On their return they were impressed by the scaffolding too.

'Is it going to be there for long?' JJ wanted to know.

'Even if it is still here when your plaster cast comes off, that doesn't mean that you can climb all over it,' Annie warned him.

'How did you know?' JJ seemed amazed that his mother could have any idea what he was planning.

'Mums just do know, my love.'

'They're replacing my window soon, aren't they?' Cissy checked.

'Not just yours. There are several that need doing, and

while the scaffolding's here we might as well make the most of it.'

A couple of days later Mossy found JJ leaning out of his window and examining the boards outside.

'*Oh, no you don't,*' Mossy projected. '*Think it through. Come on, JJ.*' He was so busy trying to get him to think about what he was planning that he didn't hear Cissy come into the room behind them.

'Wassup, JJ?'

'I was just thinking… When this cast is off…' His voice was frozen quiet by the fire in Cissy's eyes. She took a deep breath.

'D'you know, when you fell down the stairs, I thought you'd died. You were so still and pale. And then I thought, that even if you hadn't died, you might. And I was frightened, **really** frightened. But Rollo said I wasn't to say it, because he didn't want to think it. He was scared too. Rollo, who's never scared about anything, who's clever as clever and knows everything. You didn't move and you didn't say anything and you were a horrid colour, like all the blood had gone. It was awful.' Sudden, silent tears, triggered by the memory, spilled over and ran down Cissy's cheeks.

'And then they took you off in the ambulance, and I still didn't know if you were going to be alright. But if you won't even **think** about what you do first, then I'm going to have to go through all that all over again. We're going to keep on being frightened like that. It's not fair. You've **got** to get it right.'

JJ and Mossy both stared at her wide-eyed. She had said all the things that Mossy had thought, all the things that JJ had never realised.

Silence hung in the air. Cissy rubbed the tears away with the sleeve of her jumper.

'Cissy, I'm sorry. I didn't know. I... I...'

There was a long pause. Mossy could feel JJ struggle. There was a longing to try things that wasn't going to go away, but he didn't want to make Cissy sad either.

'I'll learn to think first.'

Thank you Cissy, thought Mossy. I think you've really stopped him in his tracks. He won't always get it right, but I can feel a change.

'Maybe I'd better shut the window?'

As the tiles came off the roof, Mossy's head ached with the chill. But he loved it when they tucked in new insulation, thick layers of roof felt and replaced the tiles. His hair grew thick and lustrous, with a dark sheen that he admired when he caught sight of it as he leant over the pond.

'Have you ever seen such a fine fellow?' he asked the duck. She quacked loudly, waggled her tail at him and swam away with her head in the air.

'No, I won't get big-headed,' Mossy protested, admiring the roof instead.

A week later JJ was full of excitement.

'The plaster cast is coming off today!' he announced over breakfast.

'You hope,' Rollo reminded him. JJ took no notice.

'And I'll be able to ride my bike, and kick a football and....' Suddenly he caught Cissy looking at him. Neither of the children had said anything about their conversation, but Mossy had noticed a subtle change in the boy. JJ grinned at his sister.

'Tell you what,' he said. 'I think what I'd like first is to find a place to build a hide.'

Weeks passed, and JJ's limp became hardly noticeable. There was so much going on that everybody was kept busy, but his struggle with the scaffolding continued. He kept eyeing it until one weekend Jack beckoned him over.

'What is it with you and the scaffolding?' he asked.

'I look out of my window and I can see for miles,' JJ explained. Mossy, standing beside him, squinted his eyes.

Time was when he could see for miles too, but these days his vision was blurred. His eyes felt tired.

'And I wonder – if I can see so far from my window, what's it like from the top of the roof?'

Suddenly Mossy understood. It wasn't high jinks that JJ was after, it was just curiosity. Mossy knew that view. He'd sat by the chimney pot many a time, perched astride the roof ridge with his back resting against the warmth of the brickwork as he admired a fine sunset. His eyes misted over as he remembered a time a couple of centuries back, when he'd been on the lookout for his Dwellers returning. They'd needed careful tending that time. JJ was right, the view was amazing.

'Well, you've been surprisingly patient, and you haven't launched out on your own, which makes a change,' Jack commented. 'How about we go together?' His son's eyes lit up.

'Oh Dad, really?!'

'But we'll have to be extremely careful.' JJ already had a foot lifted, when Jack called him back again. 'We can't forget the others.'

It was quite a deputation that headed up the ladders, Jack leading the way and Rollo at the rear, while Annie waited at the bottom.

'Someone has to be here, just in case.'

'Mum!' exclaimed Rollo. 'Just what 'in case'?'

'Ambulances,' muttered Cissy darkly. 'Broken legs… stretchers…'

'You coming, or just dreaming up disasters there?' laughed Rollo.

They climbed upwards. Mossy swung himself up the rungs of the first ladder, slipped between their legs and ran ahead to check the route. In no time the whole troupe was right at the top.

'Hold tight and stay safe!' warned Jack. 'Watch out for each other.'

'Wow!' breathed JJ, his breath billowing about his head. 'It's amazing.'

'Hey, look – dragon breath!' said Cissy, blowing clouds of her own, lifting claws at her father's back.

'It's a perfect look-out point!' noticed Rollo. 'You could see anyone coming from miles away.'

'Friend or foe?!' Cissy called out, her hands cupped round her mouth like a trumpet. Annie, stamping her feet to keep warm, waved up at them from the garden.

'Friend, I hope!' she called back.

'Or people coming back from wars; the injured or missing,' mused Rollo. 'Imagine – from here you could see who was coming long before anyone in the rest of the house. You'd know the news first. I wonder if they had a look-out?' They always had me, thought Mossy, remembering times past. Just as you do.

Mossy squinted and peered into the distance. Although he couldn't see as well as in the past, it was good enough to be sure there were no disasters coming. It was just the detail that was fuzzy; not all the time, just when looking in certain directions.

Everyone arrived back beside Annie together.

'Amazing, Mum!'

'You can see for miles.'

'No ambulances!' laughed Cissy.

'See, all brought back safely to you,' smiled Jack.

'And I won't need to do it again, promise,' JJ reassured Annie with a hug.

Soon more men arrived, to tackle the windows. Several frames had rotten wood and others needed to be completely replaced. Sawdust flew about the place. Hammering echoed around the house.

'Ease it in, mate.'

'Nice one.'

'Another job well done!'

'What a difference!' exclaimed Annie, admiring the sparkling new glass.

Mossy was even more impressed. He rubbed his eyes. He looked across the field beyond the stream; the autumn leaves, dancing across the sky on a brisk breeze were crisp in every detail. In no time he was perched on the roof ridge again, looking out in all directions. The fuzz had gone.

Everywhere he saw bright, sharp objects gleaming back at him. Over by the pond the moorhen was stepping daintily through the watercress, drops of water like tiny, falling diamonds dripping from her toes onto the brilliant green. A thrush landed beside him, cocking her head on one side.

'No, just enjoying the view,' he reassured her. 'You have no idea quite what a difference those new windows have made. This is wonderful. I've never seen this clearly before in my life! This new glass – it's like having new eyes!'

No sooner had the scaffolding gone than another team of workers arrived, these ones armed with coils of wire and boxes of screwdrivers. Mossy felt a ripping sensation run through him as the old wiring was pulled out. He felt listless and tired. Annie indicated where the new wiring was supposed to go. Lines were drawn all over the walls.

'Can I draw on the walls too?' JJ wanted to know. I do hope not, thought Mossy looking down at his clothes, now streaked with dirty lines. But worse was to come.

As the men gouged channels into the walls poor Mossy's clothes simply shredded about him.

Sitting in a dejected heap beside the weed-strewn vegetable garden, Mossy buried his head in his hands. The robin and his mate landed beside him, hopping between his feet and peering up at him. A trill of birdsong broke the quiet.

'I know I could show them, but there's no point,' he retorted. 'And I really don't want anyone seeing me like this. They don't know what they've done. And anyway,' he added with a shrug, 'it's only clothes. I shouldn't grumble; after all, their work has already given me new hair and eyes.' He winked at the birds.

Suddenly he caught sight of someone cruising high in the sky.

'Speaking of which – sparrowhawk coming in over the wood,' he warned the others.

In a flash they were tucked discreetly into the shelter of the hedge. Whilst they waited for the danger to pass, a wren offered him a couple of dried privet leaves to line his shoes and Mossy found some wizened clematis petals to pad out his trousers.

'A bit crackly, but it won't be for long I hope,' he told his friends, setting off back to the house with a cheery wave.

Drilling, dust and wires seemed to wrap themselves round everything for the next few weeks. Room after room descended into chaos. Annie was puzzled by the number of crushed leaves she found scattered about the house, but Mossy struggled to keep them in place as his clothes became more and more ragged. Even his skin was becoming roughened now.

'If only it were summer,' he told the kingfisher as they sat beside the pond one afternoon. With a trill of laughter the kingfisher darted off down the stream chasing a snack, his wings flashing blue in the clear winter sun. 'Alright for some,' called Mossy after him.

And then suddenly one morning Mossy noticed a change. There was a tingling in his left hand. He looked at his fingers as he flexed them. It was like a surge of new energy, a surprising vibrancy.

'That's that section completed,' the electrician told his mate. 'Onto the next,' he grinned. By the end of that day, the tingle flowed through both arms. Mossy felt startlingly alive.

'We'll be finishing in a couple of days now,' the men announced. 'Just the final checks, last connections and you'll be rid of us.'

'That's wonderful news,' said Annie. You're telling me, agreed her invisible companion.

By the time the electricians left, Mossy felt like a new person. He fairly zinged with energy, and danced through the house.

'Watch out!' he told a startled spider who was preparing her silk behind the dresser. He skipped past her foot, and then cartwheeled over her legs, until she gave up in disgust and went to find a shadier corner where she could cast her web in peace and quiet. A mouse peeked through the old cat flap in the back door to see what all the noise was about.

'No food in here!' he laughed. 'Only dust and chaos, but I'll show you where there's plenty.' He dived through the cat flap, back-flipped across the terrace and raced up the steps to the vegetable garden. The mice were struggling to keep up as he pointed to the abandoned plot. 'Lots of pickings here,' he announced with a flourish. 'All yours!'

'You wouldn't believe it!' he told the deer excitedly, as she nibbled at some old grasses that tangled in the fence between the stream and the field beyond it. 'I can't really describe it, but it's like having new blood in my veins. I feel so strong, as if I could do anything.' He swung himself down from the branch on which he had perched, and settled between her horns.

'Who cares about shredded clothes?' he laughed, as he unhooked his trouser leg from her ear and slid down her nose to somersault through the air. He landed on a soft patch of fallen leaves at her feet. Gently she snuffled at him.

'Yeah, you're right,' he agreed, 'my skin is a bit rough, but I heard them saying that the plasterers would be arriving soon!'

As term ended the family packed for their trip.

'A whole month of skiing!' grinned Rollo, as he stuffed some trousers into a bag.

'And a month of Christmas holidays,' added Cissy.

'I know it's hard when Dad's work takes him away for long sessions, and you don't like it when he's too tired to join in all your games, but one of the perks of Dad's job is being able to afford to go away for the next stage of the house works,' said Annie as she helped JJ sort out his socks. Mossy realised that he'd miss their cheerful racket. He was enjoying having these Dwellers in his house, not only because they made him and Annanbourne feel so much better, but because their happiness also kept him so well fed.

He shuddered as the family departed. He remembered, all too clearly, another time when his Dwellers had left 'for a while', but had never returned. In their absence he had suffered terribly, and had it not been for a particular friend he wouldn't have survived.

'Pull yourself together,' he muttered. 'It's not as if there'll be no one here.'

Dust and dirt filled the house as teams of builders stripped old plaster from the walls. Mossy looked as if he had a bad case of chicken pox. His skin felt raw. It itched like crazy and he longed to scratch himself from head to toe, despite knowing that it wouldn't help.

'I just want this over and done with,' he sighed, rubbing his back against the rough bark of an oak tree. A blackbird sang a trill of song from a low-hanging branch.

'I know, I know. I should think myself lucky. They came in the nick of time. Without the work they've been doing on us, I dread to think what might have happened. We were in a bad way and close to collapse. It's just that some of this isn't much fun, and unlike them I can't just swan off on holiday.'

But a week later Mossy was laughing weakly as he staggered out into the chill garden. He clapped his hands together and then held them out, showing smooth palms to the squirrel that ran along the top of the hedge.

'It tickles so as they stroke the plaster on,' he giggled, doubling up in another burst of laughter as the smoothness spread down to the tips of his fingers and Cissy's bedroom gained even walls without a blemish.

By the time the Breezes returned from their holiday the plastering was finished, and Mossy glowed with a healthy sheen.

As the first daffodils scattered yellow across the garden, plumbers arrived bringing new bathrooms and showers; Mossy had a spring in his step and a sparkle in his eye.

At half term the family departed on another holiday. New kitchen cupboards arrived, with smooth sliding drawers to complement the old dresser. Mossy felt an inner glow spread through him.

'The giraffes were amazing,' Cissy told Sophie and Jon when their neighbours came round for a celebration meal. 'You should see them when they try to drink…'

'It must be wonderful to go on amazing holidays the way you do,' said Jon.

'We're lucky,' agreed Rollo.

'But your Dad doesn't have to go away for weeks at a time to American conferences and things,' muttered JJ. 'He's always there when you want him.'

'I'm sorry, JJ. It's tough on you sometimes, I know,' Jack apologised.

Finally decorators arrived with a palette of colours to paint both inside and out. Soon the old woodwork gleamed with new paint, the window frames sparkling brightly in the spring sun, and the front door shone a deep, moss green. As gentle colours warmed the rooms, Mossy admired his new clothes. Gone were the old tatters, the holes and rags. His new clothes fitted perfectly, snug and warm.

'It's been a long haul,' he told the Barn Owl as he sat one evening on the chimney pot, catching the last of the fading sun, swinging his feet in the fine shoes that had arrived courtesy of the new carpets. 'But they've done us proud.' Slowly she turned her head towards him, her amber eyes speaking volumes as she gave him a long look.

'You're right, I've never had such perfect attention, and I'll make sure that I find a way to pay them back.' Spreading her wings, she gave a small shake to settle her feathers before launching herself onto the evening breeze. Her harsh call pierced the twilight. What had she meant? Was that a warning? he wondered. 'Enjoy perfection while you have it.' He certainly would, but surely this would last for ages?

These were the best Dwellers he'd had in a long time. They were kind and loving, to the place as well as to each other, and he had benefitted.

As he watched her fly off towards the evening star he looked down to the garden, where the family were returning from an evening walk.

'Thank you, my Dwellers; with this we can face anything. We're strong, we're refreshed and renewed. And I owe you.' He smiled. He had never felt so good.

## CHAPTER 5

# Running Smoothly

With work on the house completed, life became more settled and calm. Jack was still often away for days, sometimes weeks at a time, but the rest of the family were busy.

Friends from school could now visit more easily. 'Drop-ins' between the Breeze and the Raitata houses were a regular event, and the friendship between Jon and Rollo developed and grew stronger despite them being at different schools. Jon's sister, Sophie, was preparing for major exams in the summer. She wanted to go to university and had to get really good marks, which meant a lot of work.

'She's dead clever,' Jon told Rollo and Cissy proudly. 'But even she has to work hard to get into Cambridge.' When Sophie did come round Cissy was enchanted.

'When I'm as old as Sophie, I want to be beautiful and clever too,' Cissy told her mother.

Mossy was pleased to notice that Jon was happy to join in with Cissy and JJ as well as Rollo, and the house seemed permanently to ring with the sound of laughter when they were home. Mossy had seldom felt so well, so full of energy, as he leapt and bounced around them all. Nothing could have made him happier than having this family in his house, and his face carried a permanent grin which stretched from one pointed ear to the other.

Annie had started using the old granary opposite the house as a studio. Mossy liked to sneak in and watch over her shoulder, enjoying the creative process, as the images flowed onto the paper and canvas. He had never seen anything like this before. It was a kind of magic, as if the pictures were being conjured out of the air.

He revelled in the process, trying to predict from the first few lines what it might be that Annie would spread out for him to enjoy. He loved the development of the colours and was constantly surprised by them. The energy that flowed through the studio as each painting emerged was as forceful as that of a new child being born. It was as if a sumptuous feast was being spread before him afresh each time. He had never felt so vibrant, and the whole space glowed in response.

Sometimes Annie worked on detailed images and drawings, constantly referring to photographs and notes. These she gathered up and carted off somewhere. Mossy was sad to see them go, but intrigued by what might arrive next.

Best of all, though, he loved the big paintings. Annie paced about the studio, sometimes close to the canvas, sometimes far away on the other side of the room, constantly moving, checking and adjusting her work. Sometimes a model came and they worked on building beautiful images of people. Other times she worked on landscapes, and Mossy smiled as he recognised places he had known for hundreds of years, delighting at their appearance in the studio, radiating unexpected light. And then there were what he thought of as the little gems, small paintings of familiar everyday objects, things he had simply taken for granted, until he saw how Annie turned them into jewel-like studies of light and shadow.

'How come I never realised how beautiful they are?' he asked himself, as he looked at a painting of a couple of eggs and a flowerpot.

When the spring holidays came the children were at home every day. Mossy perched on the side of the bridge watching the continued construction of JJ's hide in the copse nearby. Rollo had persuaded Jon to help him and some other friends in the meadow beyond the stream.

He had spoken to the farmer at the top of the hill who owned that land.

'You know the field with the tumulus in it? Can we use that strip by the edge to make a jump for our bikes?'

'As long as you make it so that everything can be taken away if I need to put sheep in there,' Farmer Will had told him.

'And as long as we can use it too,' said his son Andy.

Chatter and laughter drifted over from the meadow where Rollo, Jon, Andy and Nick, his brother, were working on an earth ramp that was supposed to launch them into the air when they rode over it on their bikes.

Cissy collected sticks while JJ swept the ground of his hide smooth, carefully picking out the stones and putting them to one side.

'I can use these to make a path,' he told her. There was a sudden shout from the meadow. Cissy's head whipped round, alarm spread over her face.

'Oh no!' she cried out. 'Come on! One of them must be hurt!' JJ jumped up, hit his head on a branch and collapsed in a heap.

'You go ahead,' he called back, rubbing the top of his head with a gritty hand. 'I'll catch up.' Cissy raced off. Mossy looked carefully at the boy. The earth that was making his hair stand up on end was streaked with red. Oops! he thought, wondering if it was his hand or his head that had been cut.

'*Get up carefully,*' he projected.

JJ stood up slowly as Mossy dropped silently to the ground beside him, and together they headed off towards the others. Cissy was already on her way back.

'No worries!' she called out. 'It was just Nick laughing when Rollo's bike landed sideways and he nearly squashed Andy. No one's hurt!' Oh, yes they are, thought Mossy. This time you need to see what really is the matter.

'Come on,' she continued, 'let's get back to your hide.' JJ turned and trudged silently in her wake.

'Wassup?' she called over her shoulder. Pay attention, thought Mossy, reaching out to tweak her trouser leg. She turned to look in their direction.

'What have you done to your hair?' she exclaimed, laughing. She stopped, looking more closely. 'JJ?... JJ!' Immediately she turned and shouted to the others.

'Come quickly! JJ's bashed himself. I think he's got brain damage. He can't talk!'

'Yes, I can,' he corrected her. 'You didn't give me a chance!'

'Sit down. No, lie down!' Cissy was all concern, waving her arms about and issuing instructions as the others arrived. Mossy stepped to one side as JJ sank down on the ground. He could see a trickle of blood snaking its way down the boy's forehead.

'Look! Blood everywhere,' Cissy explained to Rollo as she grabbed his arm. 'Don't let him die again!' Mossy caught the panic in her voice.

'It's not blood everywhere,' Rollo corrected her, as he examined his brother's head. 'And he didn't die last time, remember?'

'Heads always bleed a lot.' Jon put an arm round Cissy's shoulder to calm her. 'Even quite little cuts. It might not be as bad as you think.' Rollo was taking charge now.

'Jon, can you and Cissy go and warn Mum?' He turned to JJ. 'How about a piggy back?'

'It's OK, I can walk. It's just my head that hurts.'

Cissy ran towards the house as they got to their feet. Mossy decided that he could be more use keeping Annie from worrying, and hurried after her and Jon.

'Mum! Mum!' shouted Cissy. Mossy caught a foot on a poppy stem and stumbled, stubbing his toes on a stone that lay hidden in the grass. Come on, he berated himself, pull yourself together. Ignoring the pain, he took a shortcut over the stream. He grabbed a fallen willow stick and pole vaulted over the water as Cissy and Jon ran across the bridge.

'Mum, where are you?' Cissy called. But Mossy knew.

He'd spotted Annie entering her studio earlier. He sprinted across the garden, focussing his thoughts on her.

'*He'll be alright. He'll be fine in your care,*' he projected towards her.

'Mum, it's JJ!' called Cissy as soon as she spotted Annie. 'He's walloped himself and there's blood everywhere. He's coming,' she continued, waving one hand in the direction of her brothers, 'but he can't really talk properly and it's everso bad.' She paused to draw breath.

'It's not quite that bad,' Jon gently corrected. 'But there's a lot of blood on his head.'

'Thanks for the warning. Cissy, I'm sure he'll be alright. Bring him to the house and I'll get the First Aid box.'

Mossy sat beside Annie, his hand resting with the lightest of touches on her shoulder. She wouldn't notice it, but he could let his strength flow into her and keep her confidence strong as she checked JJ's head.

'You must have really whacked yourself, fella,' she said, as she sponged the blood from his hair. 'But I don't think it'll need stitches this time.'

'I'm sorry, Mum,' JJ apologised. 'I just didn't see the branch, and I did so want to help Cissy and Rollo.'

'Lie there quietly for a bit while it settles,' said his mum. 'How about a cool drink to pass the time?'

As she headed off to the kitchen, Mossy perched on the arm of the sofa beside him. Tentatively he reached out one long finger and gently brushed the boy's fringe from his eyes. JJ snuggled down, smiling at his mother as she returned with a glass of milk and a book.

'Thanks Mum, you're the best.' He grinned up at her as

she opened the book and started reading. Mossy stayed put. He liked stories.

It wasn't long before they were back out in the garden.

'Take it gently,' Annie called after them. Don't you worry, thought Mossy, I'll look after him. Feeling very pleased with himself, he neatly side-stepped a cow parsley that was bent across the path, grinned, and put his foot firmly into a molehill he hadn't spotted. By the time he had shaken the earth off his foot, apologised to the mole and adjusted his clothes, JJ was way ahead and about to cross the stream. Instead of using the bridge he was reaching for a low hanging branch to help him swing across.

Running to catch up, Mossy realised that the branch was more dead than alive. There was no way it would hold him safely. JJ was concentrating on balancing on a big stone, getting ready to launch himself.

'*Look up,*' projected Mossy. '*Look at what you're holding!*' JJ paused, and then looked up.

'Oops!' He grimaced, let go of the branch, wobbled and then stepped back.

'You OK there?' Cissy was on the far bank.

'Yeah, fine. I don't know why, but I just got this feeling I should look up. See? That branch is rotten. If I'd used it I'd have fallen into the water!'

'You want that big one, the one with the flat, round leaves,' his sister advised him.

In no time JJ and Mossy were on the other side, busy with Cissy on further building work.

They were so absorbed that Mossy was the first to hear the sound of a car coming down the drive. He glanced over, realised it was Jack's car and took no further notice. Cissy and JJ carried on working until Rollo and Jon came over.

'Feeling better?' Rollo checked his brother first. Mossy swung himself into the tree to keep out of the way.

'Yeah, fine now,' replied JJ. 'What do you think?' He stood back proudly to allow the others to see. 'Cissy's been fantastic, too.'

'You've done brilliantly,' grinned Jon. 'I've got to head home, but I'll be back to see further progress soon.'

The Breeze children waved the others off and headed down the drive towards their home with Mossy trudging in their wake, still keeping an eye on JJ.

'I thought Dad wasn't due home until the day after tomorrow,' said Rollo. Mossy's ears twitched. Was that a note of anxiety he heard in his voice?

'Dad's home early? Great!' JJ broke into a run. 'Come on Cissy, we can show him the hide.' Mossy and the others followed close behind.

As they rounded the corner and turned towards the house, a familiar sight met their eyes. Jack and Annie were sitting on the step outside the studio barn.

'Hi there, Dad!' called Cissy, running over to them. 'We've got lots to show you!' But Mossy was struck by an unfamiliar feeling that spiked the air. Beside him Rollo's walk slowed, his eyes fixed on his father's face. Then Mossy noticed Annie's unusual paleness. Jack smiled at them, but Mossy could sense something wrong.

'Hi guys,' said Dad, his voice low and still in the warm spring air. 'Come and join us. There's something we need to talk about.'

## CHAPTER 6

# All Change

'Dad? What's the matter?' Rollo looked worried. Mossy settled beside JJ as he flung himself on the grass at Annie's feet and Cissy leant against her father's knees. Rollo remained standing, examining his father. 'I'm not complaining, but how come you're home early?'

'Dear Rollo,' Jack ruffled Cissy's hair as he looked with admiration at his eldest son. 'There's no point in trying to hide something from you. You always spot it!'

Mossy was busy checking feelings; there was strain in both Annie and Jack; not between them, but something that left them uneasy. He could feel anxiety from Rollo, but as yet Cissy and JJ were unconcerned. He wriggled his fingers through the grass and into the earth. He had a feeling that he needed to be firmly in touch with the Old Things. This felt like bad news.

*'Earth keep me grounded and Sun give me warmth. Stream keep me flowing and Wind blow me free. All will be well, my Dwellers – we are with you.'*

'Good and bad news, my lovelies.' Jack looked round at his family as Annie took hold of his hand. 'D'you remember me telling you my company had been taken over?' Mossy didn't, but he saw Rollo nod his head.

'But that was ages ago, Dad,' exclaimed Cissy, twiddling a daisy stem between her fingers, 'before we moved. Don't say we're going to move again. I like it here.'

'No Cissy, nothing like that. The trouble is that when two companies join together, sometimes it means that there are two people doing the same job. They already had someone who was in charge of my section of their company, and they don't need two of us.'

'Is that the good news or the bad news?' JJ looked up at his father.

'Well, the good news is that I'm going to be around more, while I look for a new job. The bad news is that jobs are tricky to find at the moment, and it may take a while.'

Mossy looked round at all the faces. He loved having this family in his home, but when past Dwellers had faced these sorts of problems they had ended up leaving.

'So there needs to be a bit of belt-tightening for a few weeks,' added Annie.

JJ hitched up his shirt and looked at his tummy. He turned an anxious face towards his mother.

'I haven't got a belt, Mum. I'm wearing shorts.' Laughter broke out on all sides.

'Don't you fret, JJ. It's not a real belt. It means that we're all going to have to pull together and try to live carefully.'

'Pull what together?' JJ was still confused.

'Make an effort to live a bit more cheaply and look after

each other,' explained his mother.

'Are we going to be desperately poor?' Cissy looked anxious now. The tension in her voice tightened the muscles in Mossy's back. 'Are we going to be homeless? Oh, we are… We're going to have to live on the streets… and eat out of dustbins… and… and I don't think I like fish heads.' There was a catch in her voice.

'No fish heads, and no living on the streets. We should be able to carry on living here. We just need to be thoughtful about what we spend,' explained Jack. 'Mum's going to see if she can get more work with the ad agency she does illustrations for, and who knows? I might get a new job so quickly that you'll have only just got used to me being around when I'll be gone again.' Mossy looked at him sharply. There was an edge to Jack's voice that made it sound as if he were putting on a brave face for Cissy's sake.

'It'll be good having you at home more,' JJ broke in, his face lighting up. 'D'you want to come and see the hide Cissy and I are making?'

'Good idea, fella,' said Jack, standing up. 'Show me the way.' Mossy spotted him wink at Annie as he headed off, Cissy holding his hand and JJ skipping ahead.

What does that wink mean? thought Mossy as he eased his fingers free of the earth, stood up and went to Annie's side. He wanted to catch her feelings. The air felt brittle, crisp like frost. Hmm, he thought; she's keeping something back. Mossy glanced over at Rollo, who was still standing exactly as he had been from the very beginning.

'Mum,' Rollo sounded thoughtful. Annie looked up at him as he paused.

'Mum,' he started again. 'It's not quite as simple as you and Dad made it sound, is it?' Got it in one, agreed Mossy.

'Don't worry, Rollo,' his mother tried to reassure him. 'There's nothing for you to worry about yet.' Mossy could feel her trying to calm herself, but the air still juddered around her.

'Yet?' Rollo echoed her. 'So there will be later?'

'I'm sure it'll all be fine.'

'Look, Mum, I'll do anything I can to help. Remember I'll be thirteen soon. I'm not little like Cissy and JJ – I can help too.' As his mother stood up he gave her a hug. Mossy felt Annie ease and the air soften. Clever boy, he thought. You are already helping more than you know.

As Annie and Rollo headed towards the house, Mossy trailed behind them. The sound of JJ and Cissy's voices drifted over from the hide as they excitedly explained their building works. They seemed to have forgotten their anxieties already, but he could sense the growing stress in the older boy.

During the afternoon Mossy went from person to person. JJ soon settled back into his normal pattern, delighted to have his father around. Cissy, too, seemed to be completely relaxed. It wasn't until supper that she wanted another check on the change of lifestyle.

'If we're tightening our belts, does that mean no second helpings?' she asked, eyeing the fish pie. Annie laughed and offered her some more.

Mossy, tucked in a corner of the windowsill, noticed that Rollo, who was always hungry, turned down the chance. He carefully crept along the sill, until he came to the back of

Rollo's chair and stepped lightly onto the back rest. He placed one finger on Rollo's shoulder. Slowly he felt the tightness in the boy ease away. But he had to keep his wits about him as Rollo relaxed, and he whisked his legs out of the way to avoid them being squashed. He leapt for the safety of the sill, remembering not to grab the curtains to keep his balance. Rollo cast a glance over his shoulder and smiled.

'What is it, darling?' asked his mother.

'I'm not sure,' Rollo replied. 'Even though I know it's not great news about Dad's job, I just get the feeling that it's going to be OK. There's something about this place, something special. It's as if it's looking after us.'

Of course we are, grinned Mossy, you're our Dwellers. What else would we do?

That night when the children were tucked up in bed, Mossy sat with each of them in turn.

'Sleep well, little one,' Annie called softly from the doorway as she turned out JJ's light. He turned around, snuggled under the covers, one arm round his bear as he slipped the other hand under his pillow, his fingers curling around his lucky talisman.

'G'night Mum,' he mumbled, his eyes drifting shut. Mossy hummed a few bars of JJ's favourite tune, as he watched sleep gather around the boy and settle for the night.

Slipping through the doorway into the corridor, he spotted Jack heading into Cissy's room. She was standing by the window, gazing up the hill.

'Dad, do you really think you'll get a new job quickly?' she asked. Interesting, thought Mossy. She feels as if she's alright, but she's still thinking about it.

'Don't you worry,' her father reassured her as he pulled the curtains shut. 'I'm sure it'll turn out fine.'

'And we can stay living here always?'

'That shouldn't be a problem.' Not if I have anything to do with it, promised Mossy. You're the best Dwellers I've had in ages, and I want to keep you here.

'And certainly not if you get into bed right now, and keep your strength up.' Cissy was giggling and showing off her muscles as Jack scooped her up and tucked her into bed. Mossy gathered a sunny dream and tucked it under her pillow for her to enjoy later. Her eyes were drifting shut as her father left the room and headed towards Rollo. Mossy stroked the hair from her forehead and eased restful sleep over her before he squeezed out through the gap in the doorway to follow him.

Both the parents were with Rollo by the time Mossy arrived.

'But it's like I said to Mum, I'm older than the other two and you don't have to pretend with me,' the boy was protesting.

'As if that's ever been possible!' agreed Annie, with a sigh.

'At the moment we don't really know how long it'll take. So there might be no need,' Jack explained. Mossy looked from one face to another. Here he could see the tension again. The air felt tight and uncomfortable. What exactly was it that they were discussing? He hadn't heard them argue like this before, and the words felt sharp and troublesome.

'Jon started last month, and he said that they were looking for another boy to help out. If he's doing it, why can't I?'

'Well, for one thing Jon's at the local school and so he can carry on during term time. You're starting your new school in September. That means boarding, so you'll have to give up then anyway.' Annie sounded tired. Rollo slumped down on his bed, looking up at his parents.

'Well, I want to help, not just leave it all to you and Dad. If I can earn something, then there will be things I can buy for myself that you won't have to find the money for.'

'It's not that bad yet, old thing,' Jack was trying to sound reasonable. 'And getting all heated about it late at night isn't going to help. Can we talk again in the morning?'

'See what I mean!' exclaimed Rollo. 'You keep saying it's not that bad, but you're not even going to work at all, already.'

'OK,' Jack sighed, 'you want to be treated like an adult, so I'll fill you in. But this means that you've got to keep what we tell you to yourself. We don't want Cissy or JJ worrying.' Annie looked anxiously across at Jack as he sat down beside his son.

'The company have given me a good redundancy package, which means that we should be able to afford to stay here. But by using all the money for the house there will be nothing spare to go towards anything else. We'll be depending on what Mum can earn for a while, until I get something sorted out for me.'

'So it **would** be good if I got a paper round, even for a short time. Dad, **I** want to do my bit too,' pleaded Rollo.

Mossy felt that Rollo had a point. Over the centuries he'd

often seen boys Rollo's age working, helping in the fields when extra labour was needed. There had even been one who had taken over running the farm after his dad had died. A similar age to Rollo, he'd made a brilliant job of it. The farm had thrived; he looked after his mother and three sisters, and in due course had married and brought up a family of his own in the house. He was the one who'd built the mill and…

'Boys my age often used to work really hard in the past. Who knows,' continued Rollo, interrupting Mossy's thoughts. 'Maybe there was even someone like me who helped to look after his family here before.' Mossy's eyes widened in alarm as he clapped a hand over his mouth. Surely he hadn't spoken aloud? Could a Place Reader be a Mind Reader too?

'We won't make a decision either way tonight. OK? Just for now, love, don't stay up reading for too long, get some sleep soon, and we'll talk more in the morning. And remember – keep this to yourself.' Annie gave her son a kiss before leaving.

Mossy climbed the chest of drawers and, from the safety of a pile of books at the back, watched as Rollo prepared for sleep. Once he was safely tucked up with a book, Mossy jumped onto the end of the bed. He felt tired. Soothing anxieties was quite a drain on his energies and the softness of the duvet was very appealing.

He wriggled under the bottom corner of the covers until only the tip of his nose still stuck out. The occasional rustle of a page being turned was just what he needed to help him plan how to look after his Dwellers and keep them happy. It wasn't just the aches and pains he wanted to avoid; he was fond of this bunch. He was reminding himself how successfully he had helped JJ avoid falling into the stream, when Rollo turned out the light.

Mossy felt safe and warm in the darkness and had decided that further plans could wait until tomorrow, when Rollo's voice broke into his thoughts.

'Thank you for wanting us to stay here and for helping us. Whoever you are, whatever you are, I think we're going to need you.' Argh! Place Readers! thought Mossy, but even **they** can't see in the dark. He turned onto his side, tucked in his nose, pulled the duvet tight and disappeared into his dreams.

## CHAPTER 7

# A Close Shave

Mossy woke early in the morning and tiptoed down to the kitchen. He needed to commune with the house, prepare it for troubles, so they were not caught unawares. He checked every room, each corner, looking through the windows at the garden as it woke in the dawn light.

'At least we're in good nick,' he said as he sat down on his Starting Stone, the old hearth in the sitting room. 'They've done us proud and we haven't a single place of weakness.'

The smooth hearthstone gleamed under his hand.

'This is our chance to repay them for the good they've done us. We're going to need to stand strong for them.' He stretched his arms to ease a slight ache in his back.

'They're a bit worried at the moment, that's all.' The house eased itself yet more firmly into the ground with the gentlest of sighs.

Mossy joined the family consultation over breakfast. With his legs dangling off the edge of the dresser shelf he was well out of the way, but with a prime view.

'So, Dad,' started JJ as he reached for a jug. 'Now that you've given up work, will you be able to help me with my hide this morning?'

'I'm going to be busy in my study,' Dad replied. JJ looked crestfallen. 'But I can come out and help for a bit after lunch. How would that be?' A big grin spread across JJ's face as he poured milk onto his cereal.

'Yay!' he called out in celebration as he turned to Cissy and Rollo. 'And you'll help 'til then?'

Rollo turned to his parents.

'You said we'd make a decision in the morning.'

'What decision?' Cissy snapped to attention. 'Don't tell me – this is our last meal. Everything has run out and we're about to starve! It's OK. I can sing and dance to earn us a crust!' She leapt to her feet, waving her toast in one hand, and put her words into action, dancing over to the kitchen sink to fetch a glass of water. Mossy had to clap a hand over his mouth to keep the laughter in as she frolicked back, the water sloshing vigorously in her glass as she twirled into her seat.

Drama Queen you may be, he thought, but at least you keep everybody's spirits up!

'Nothing like that!' laughed Annie as she passed Cissy a cloth to mop up water scattered across the table.

'I'm getting a job,' announced Rollo. 'As a paperboy.'

There was a pause. Jack and Annie exchanged a glance. Mossy felt as tense as the atmosphere between them.

'We didn't...' started Annie.

'That's brilliant!' exclaimed Cissy. 'Jon's told me all about being a paperboy. I'm going to be one when I'm old enough.'

'Me too.' JJ was keen to join in. 'And you'll have to be a paper**girl,** not a boy – that's what Sophie said. She did it too.' Hmmm, pondered Mossy, three against two. He noticed Annie look over at Jack again.

'We're not sure it's a good idea,' explained Jack. 'As we said last night, you'll be starting at your new school soon, and there's going to be a lot of hard work.'

'But Dad, that's the whole thing,' Rollo argued. 'I've passed the entrance exam already and the rest of this term is just filling in time.'

'Yup, and you did brilliantly,' agreed Jack. Even Annie nodded. 'But…'

'Jon says it's easy, and he's saving the money to get new tyres for his bike.'

'And if they turn out to be real slave drivers,' Cissy interrupted, 'we'll all go in to fight on Rollo's side, rip the shackles off and bring him tottering out into the sun again.' Mossy, open-mouthed, stared at her as she carried on enthusiastically. 'And then we'll nurse him back to health, and soon he'll be able to walk again and his sight will come back…'

'Sight come back!' Annie was laughing again. 'I've never known doing a paper round mean that a boy loses his sight!'

'So you agree?' Rollo caught at the chink in his parents' determination.

'Well…' Annie sighed. 'It's almost impossible to change your mind once you've decided on something.' She nodded her head.

'But…' Jack joined in, fixing his son with a look. 'If it seems that it's getting too much, then we'll have to think again. And remember, you'll have to stop at the end of the summer holidays.'

Rollo was thrilled at gaining his parent's permission and rushed straight round to Jon's house to tell him. Soon the bikes were out as the children prepared to head to the village store.

'I'm coming!' announced Cissy.

'Me too,' added JJ. And me as well, decided Mossy in his role as guardian.

'Then we're counting on you two big ones to keep an eye on Cissy and JJ,' said Annie. 'It's to the village shop and then straight home, OK? No launching off into the great blue yonder unless Dad and I are with you.'

'Yup, yup, yup!' the little boy agreed. 'Anything you say.'

Mossy clambered up the back wheel of JJ's bike as it stood propped against the wall. There was space for him to sit on the small rack over the back wheel, and if things got a bit risky then he could duck under the saddle for shelter.

In no time they were bumping down the drive to the lane. It had been a while since Mossy's last bike ride, and he'd forgotten this feeling of being shaken to pieces, but soon they turned out onto the smooth tarmac.

'Stick behind me and stay close to the edge of the road!' he heard Rollo call from somewhere ahead.

'I'm behind you, JJ!' Cissy called out. 'And Jon's behind me!'

Mossy held his legs out to keep them well away from the spinning spokes and gripped the underside of the saddle with both hands. JJ wobbled slightly as they headed up the slope, and Mossy wished he could see better. He stuck his head out, peering round energetically pedalling legs to see what lay ahead.

In the nick of time he spotted a damaged section of tarmac.

'Watch out! Pothole!' he shouted, hoping, for once, that his voice would be heard above the rushing of the wind.

'Thanks!' JJ shouted, swerving violently as he dodged around the cavity.

Mossy was flung to one side, his left heel dipping dangerously near the whirring wheel. One hand lost its grip of the saddle as he slipped sideways. He clung on tightly with the other leg, hooking it firmly against the metal as he grabbed at the frame of the bike. Slowly he eased himself back into position. That had been a bit close for comfort.

'You OK there?' he heard Cissy's voice call out. Mossy nodded his head.

'Fine thanks,' JJ flung the words over his shoulder. Alright for you, thought Mossy, you aren't the one who nearly had his legs sliced off!

The cycles came to a halt by the post office store, where Mossy climbed, slightly shakily, to the ground.

'Thanks for the warning about the pothole!' JJ grinned at his sister. 'I'd have been a goner!'

'What warning?' Cissy looked mystified. 'It was only seeing you swerve round it that made me remember that it was there!'

'But I heard you. You shouted 'Pothole!" JJ paused. 'Didn't you?'

'Not me, must've been one of the others. Come on,' she added, hurrying after Rollo and Jon who were already inside.

'Well someone did,' he muttered, hurrying after her. 'I can't've just imagined it.'

Mossy paused for a second in the doorway to watch a large and enthusiastic dog who was towing a woman towards them along the pavement. Realising that the door was about to shut he turned to race for the narrowing gap.

Too late! As he slipped through the crack, the door firmly clamped itself on the sleeve of his shirt. Mossy tugged, but it was no good. He was caught. He desperately hoped that someone in the shop would open the door and release him before an outsider came rushing through, flattening him in the process.

Rollo strode up to the counter.

'Good morning, Mrs Taplin. There's a card in your window that says you're looking for another paperboy. I'd like to apply.' Mrs Taplin looked him up and down.

'How old are you?' she asked. 'And have you got a reference?'

'12, nearly 13,' replied Rollo.

'And I've come to give him a reference,' added Jon.

'A friend of yours will be fine, Jon.' Mrs Taplin smiled at them. 'Let me get the form. You'll need your parents' signature.'

Pleased that it was all going well, Mossy looked around to see what the others were up to. He spotted them watching a large lady struggle to pass a parcel over the counter.

'Can I help?' offered JJ. The woman looked down at him.

'Little boy, if I need help, I'll ask.' The woman frowned at him. Mossy scowled at her.

Suddenly there was a scuffle behind him, the other side of

the door. It sounded like a fight going on; huge heavy breaths and scrabbling feet. Mossy struggled to escape. Come on you lot, he thought looking over at the children. *'You've got the form; let's go.'*

But Cissy was lingering by the rack of sweets.

'Rollo, are we so poor now that we can't ever have sweets again?' she asked.

'Sit, will you? Just sit!' a voice pleaded outside. I can't sit, Mossy wanted to tell the owner of the voice. I'm stuck in the door, and I don't want you breaking through and turning me into a pancake.

'And don't chew that either! Digger!' exclaimed the voice. 'No!' The heavy breathing changed into loud sniffing. There was a nose checking him from the other side. Mossy didn't want the owner chewing him instead of whatever he had been chewing outside.

'Well then, you'll have to come in, but you're to behave.' The outside voice didn't sound as if it expected its companion to behave at all. Mossy stepped as far away from the door as he could. His shirt, his lovely new shirt, was stretched tight. He didn't want it damaged any more than he wanted to be damaged himself. Who knew when there would be any more decorating done on the house now? The door eased open; Mossy leapt out of the way and turned to face whatever was coming through.

In bounced the dog that he had spotted earlier, still towing its companion behind him, its tail merrily sweeping all the magazines into a heap at one end of the rack. Mossy fixed him with a fierce blue stare. Digger quailed and stopped in his tracks.

'I'm so sorry, Mrs Taplin,' said the woman as she tried to sort out the magazines. 'Digger kept chewing his lead, so I couldn't leave him outside.'

The children were trooping out through the door, heading for their bikes, but Mossy couldn't leave yet. He clearly had a job to do. Fixing Digger to the spot with his eyes, he walked over until they were nose to nose.

'What d'you think you're doing?' he whispered, so quietly no person would hear, but plenty loud enough for any dog to catch. 'You're supposed to look after your human, not make her life difficult. Hasn't your Holder explained that to you?' Digger's tail drooped.

'What's the matter?' The dog gave a small whine, its nose now hanging down too.

'Oh dear,' sighed Mossy, 'don't tell me, you live in one of those new houses.' The dog nodded its head. 'So your Holder's too young to know how to instruct you properly. Hmm.' Mossy thought swiftly.

'I haven't got time to explain in detail, but try to remember this. You're A Helper. Look after them; guard them and be gentle. Be good, and then you'll be A Hero. Get it right and they'll give you treats.' The dog's tail lifted, the tip giving the smallest of wags as he went and stood calmly beside the woman.

'Goodness, Digger!' Mossy could hear the woman's surprise as he ran through the door. 'You **are** being good!' There was a pause. 'Could I have some of those dog biscuits too, please, Mrs Taplin?'

Outside, the children were organising their bikes.

'If I get this form back today, Mrs Taplin said that I can

start tomorrow!' Rollo sounded pleased. 'Come on you lot, we've got to get home so that I can come back as quickly as possible.'

JJ had just turned his bicycle round when Mossy arrived, panting, at his side and grabbed a pedal. JJ stepped on the opposite pedal, whirling the Holder up into the air where he grabbed the bike frame just behind the front wheel.

No more sitting where I can't see, decided Mossy, reaching for the handle bars. JJ swung a leg over the saddle and started to pedal vigorously to catch up with the others who were already heading up the hill. Mossy, hanging on for dear life, wrapped his legs round the frame, rested his feet on the bicycle lamp and let the wind blow through his hair.

This is more like it, he thought.

## CHAPTER 8

# What's Brewing Now?

Rollo's new job was the first of many changes that Mossy observed. Each morning he stood next to Annie or Jack as they watched the boy hurtle off on his bike. At the end of the first week he admired Rollo proudly displaying his wages to his parents.

'See? I can do my bit too!' The pleasure in his voice eased the ache that had continued to grow in Mossy's back since the day of Jack's surprise return from work.

Soon Annie started her new job with the ad agency. Instead of working in her studio she was the one who, several days each week, headed off in the mornings while Jack stayed at home making breakfast and helping the children organise themselves. On the days that Annie was at home she went into her studio to work on drawings that she took with her next time she left. There seemed to be no time for her beautiful paintings any longer. Mossy missed them and sat by the idle easel, wondering when there would be more.

Despite Jack's assurances to the children that he was

working in his study, Mossy could see that this was a very different kind of work. Before, there had been papers all over his desk and the phone kept ringing. Now he was the one who made calls, and although he wrote letters and emails, there were very few that arrived. Mossy perched himself on the back of Jack's chair and read the computer screen over his shoulder.

'... Nothing at present... Keep you on our books...' What are Recruitment Agencies? he wondered.

The outings and treats that everyone had been used to stopped happening, with everybody spending more time at home.

'We can mend that,' said Annie when JJ came home with a tear in his trouser knee. Hmm, thought Mossy. They used to just go out and get a new one before.

Sometimes Jack just sat at his desk staring at the screen, his head in his hands. At times like those the ache in Mossy's back spread down to his hips, making his legs stiff.

But when the children were home Jack's face lit up, and any indication of his worries disappeared. Mossy's aches and pains eased when JJ invited friends to play in the hide that Jack had helped him complete.

Cissy, who had loved helping her Dad plant seeds in the vegetable garden during the holidays, carried on her work there every day after school, making the most of the long summer afternoons, carefully checking that her plants had enough water. The loud squeals that erupted from Cissy when she came home to find the first beans ready for picking, made Mossy's hair curl with delight as he danced in her shadow.

Rollo finished his homework in record time that day and came out to see what the commotion was about. Mossy ducked behind some lettuces that were fattening up nicely.

'Can I use them?' he asked.

'What for?' Cissy eyed him cautiously.

'Eating, you duffer,' laughed Rollo. 'What else would I use them for?' Mossy relaxed and sat on the warm earth as the robin hopped down from a nearby hedge to see if Cissy had dug up any worms recently.

'But these are for everybody to eat!' protested Cissy. 'You can earn money from your paper round, but growing things is all I can do to help.'

'No worries,' Rollo assured her. 'I just thought we could have a go at making supper for everybody from what you've grown. It'd give Mum and Dad a break, and you know how tired Mum is when she gets home these days.'

'Brilliant!' exclaimed Cissy, looking around the vegetable garden. Mossy's eyes lit up too. This was just what he and the house needed to keep them in top form.

Mossy abandoned the lettuces and sneaked off to the rhubarb patch. Standing underneath the canopy of the big leaves, he took a stem firmly in both hands and shook it vigorously.

'Rhubarb crumble!' shouted Rollo and Cissy in unison. In no time they had arms full of rhubarb, some broad beans, a handful of radishes, a couple of lettuces and were heading for the kitchen.

Mossy waved goodbye to the robin, who had successfully hauled out a fat worm to take home to his chicks, and ran to catch up with the children.

JJ was helping himself to a drink of water when they came into the kitchen.

'Just the person we need!' said Rollo. 'Can you find Dad and give him something to do to keep him out of the way for a while?'

'Why?' JJ looked dubious. 'Are you trying to get rid of me?'

'Not a bit of it, we need you back here as soon as you've sorted Dad,' Cissy reassured him. 'We're making supper, and we need all three of us to get it done in time.' JJ grinned, hurrying to find his father, with Mossy in tow.

They found Jack emerging from his study. There was a strained look on his face which gave Mossy's heart a twinge. What was it that so worried him? he wondered. Today in particular there seemed to be more than just the unsuccessful job hunt.

'Hi there, Dad!' JJ called out. Jack stopped, the look on his face changing to one of pleasure as he turned towards his son.

'Hello there!' he greeted him. 'What are you up to?'

'Um...'

*'Come on, think quickly,'* projected Mossy, standing close by his left leg.

'Umm…' The boy couldn't find an answer

'If you're at a bit of a loose end you can come with me. I need to check the mower; it's making a strange rattling sound. Then you could help me mow, maybe?' Normally he would have jumped at the chance. There was nothing he liked better than riding beside his Dad on the lawn tractor, hanging on tightly over rough terrain, helping to steer.

Mossy wondered if he was going to give up on the cooking and stay with his father.

'Actually Dad, I've promised to help Rollo and Cissy with something. Maybe after that?' Mossy fixed Jack with his mind.

*'Don't ask what he's doing.'*

'Well, if you change your mind, come and find me.' Jack grinned as he turned towards the shed. 'Have a good time!' he called over his shoulder.

When they returned to the others, Mossy swung himself onto the shelf above the counter top where the children were working and rested his back against the biscuit tin. Below him there was a flurry of activity. Cissy was busy washing lettuce, dumping the wet leaves onto a large tea towel.

'Can I shake it dry?' asked JJ.

'OK,' agreed Rollo, 'but hang onto it this time.' JJ gave a guilty chuckle. Last time the corner of the cloth had slipped out of his hand, and wet lettuce had flown all over the yard.

Mossy went to keep an eye on proceedings. Hopping down from the shelf, he avoided a large bowl that Cissy had just put down on the worktop. Using the handle of a drawer he lowered himself down, reaching with his foot for the knob on the door below it. The stiffness in his back made moving around hard, and his foot slipped so that he landed in a heap beside Cissy. He only just avoided being stepped on as she reached sideways for the butter.

Gathering himself together, Mossy gave his bashed knee a quick rub and ran outside to catch up. JJ, grasping the cloth bundle in both hands, raised it high above his head.

*'Hang on tightly!'* Mossy reminded him silently. As the

bundle swung down, a sweeping spiral of water droplets arched in its wake. Mossy was so busy admiring the beautiful pattern that he didn't notice that he was in the direct line of fire. Splashes of water sprayed all over him, soaking through his clothes.

'Whee!' called JJ, as he swung the bundle up again and then spun round on the spot.

It seemed that no matter where Mossy tried to shelter, the water always found him. As the lettuce grew drier, so Mossy became wetter and wetter. He hung his head and watched the water trickle along his nose and drop off the tip, hardly noticing JJ as he bounced back into the kitchen.

'See! Lettuce all safe,' came the proud announcement. 'But the yard's soaked!'

'You've managed to douse yourself fairly well too!' commented Rollo. Mossy, cheered to think he wasn't the only one who'd had a surprise shower, arranged himself on the shelf again and watched Cissy rubbing her hands through the butter, sugar and flour in her bowl.

When JJ picked up a big knife, however, Mossy snapped to attention again. Although he had made huge improvements in thinking before doing anything, JJ was still accident-prone, and Mossy decided that he'd better get the others in on the job too.

'*Rollo, pay attention!*' he projected. Rollo put his own knife down.

'OK, if you're chopping things, do it carefully. Help me with the rhubarb. One piece at a time, and concentrate.' Mossy concentrated too, focussing on the little boy as he worked.

'*Fingers,*' he reminded him from time to time, projecting his thoughts gently into JJ's mind.

Fortunately, Rollo was a quick worker and had done a lot of the cutting before his brother joined in. The job was soon completed. With a sigh of relief, Mossy relaxed against the biscuit tin and listened to the happy chatter below him. This was the best way to relieve the bump on his knee as well as his other aches and pains.

In no time, the crumble was cooking in the oven, and a big salad was in a dish on the table.

'We'll peel the eggs just before we serve it,' decided Cissy, passing her chopping board to Rollo for washing. 'It'll give them time to cool after being hard-boiled.'

'Mum should be home any minute,' JJ said. 'She'll be so pleased, and it's a really good surprise, too.'

Outside they caught the sound of the mower growling across the garden.

'I'm going to give Dad a hand,' JJ called, as he ran through the door.

'I'm going to finish watering the tomatoes,' Cissy announced, hurrying after him.

'Thanks for the help,' Rollo called after them. Left alone in the kitchen he stood by the sink and looked out of the window. 'If only it were all that easy.'

Mossy looked at him. He looked tired, not the kind of tired you usually saw in a boy, but the sort of tired that an elastic band gets just before it snaps. You're not the only one who feels like that thought Mossy, and wondered how to help.

The sound of a car pulling into the drive broke into their

thoughts, making them both look out of the window. There was Annie getting out of the car, as Jack and JJ came rocketing round the corner of the barn on the lawn tractor.

'Hello you two, I thought I heard something going on!' Annie greeted them. Mossy sat in the open window, kicking his legs in the warm evening sun and watched as Rollo went to join them. When Cissy had arrived from the vegetable garden the whole family headed back towards the house.

'… and we've got a really good surprise for you too!' he heard Cissy announce.

'Something we all did…'

'To give you a bit of a break,' finished Rollo with a broad grin as they came into the kitchen.

'Ta Daa!' sang JJ, spreading his arms wide to draw his parents' attention to the table laid with supper.

'Jack, you are brilliant!'

'Not me,' confessed the children's father. 'I'm as surprised as you. This is all their own work.'

'What a bunch!' laughed Annie. 'I'll dump my stuff and we can eat straight away.'

Happy chatter over the meal was a feast to Mossy, too. The children told their parents their news and talked about plans for the half-term holiday, now only a few weeks away.

The pain in Mossy's knee was soon gone, and he enjoyed the music of their voices so much that it was a while before he noticed that Jack had hardly spoken a word. The meal over and everything cleared away, it was time for the children to go upstairs to prepare for bed.

'It's so hard going to bed when it's still light,' complained Cissy as she headed up the stairs. 'Don't you just wish it were the holidays already?' Rollo laughed and said something that Mossy couldn't catch. The warmth of the evening and the children's enthusiasm made him feel relaxed and sleepy, so much so that he almost missed Jack's quiet words.

'Annie, we need some time. I've been checking things and we've got some serious talking to do and some hard decisions to think about.' Annie looked over at him sharply.

'Now this minute? Is it something to do with the children? Or can it wait 'til they're in bed?' Mossy racked his brains. He was pretty sure the children were all fine, except for Rollo being so stretched. Had he missed something?

'No, no.' Jack put a reassuring hand on Annie's shoulder, 'The children are fine. They're more than fine. They're glorious. It's me, it's all my fault.' Mossy looked closely at Jack's face. There it was again, that look of utter hopelessness, the one he usually kept hidden from the rest of the family. For the first time Annie saw it too.

'Jack, surely nothing's that bad. If the children are fine and we have each other, we can cope with anything.' A loud whoop of laughter floated down that stairs. 'Come on, my love, we need to get upstairs to those wonderful kids of ours, and we'll talk about it later.'

Mossy decided that he needed to be on hand for whatever it was. He could see they were going to need him too.

## CHAPTER 9

# A Change Of Life Style

Mossy was installed on the corner of the sofa when Annie and Jack appeared, having said goodnight to the children.

'Well?' Annie turned expectantly towards her husband. 'What is it that's bugging you?'

Mossy turned to look at Jack and saw the life drain from his face as he sank down on the sofa beside his wife. His hands hung limply by his sides. He seemed unable to look at her.

'Jack, darling!' Annie's voice sounded shocked. 'Nothing can be that bad.'

'Don't count on it.' Jack's voice was low, barely a whisper. Annie took his hand. Mossy felt a ripple of strength pass between them. Come on, you can make it through this, he thought. You know you can.

Everything stood still, even the house seemed frozen. Jack took a breath.

'When I lost my job we both thought that it would no time before I found a new one. I don't think that any longer. I've applied for all sorts of jobs, some of them so basic that I could do them with my eyes shut. Each time I draw a blank. I've been wondering why; whether there was something that was getting in the way. Now I **know** there is.'

There was a pause. Jack knotted his hands together as if trying to draw strength from somewhere deep inside him.

'Today I saw something my old firm wrote about me. A company who had just turned me down sent it on.' He pulled a crumpled piece of paper from his pocket, held it out towards Annie, still staring at the floor. 'Read that.'

There was silence while Annie read. Mossy crawled behind her, trying to find a position where he could read the words, but all he could see was her face.

She blanched, then turned towards Jack, flinging her arm across the back of the sofa and knocking Mossy not merely off it, but headfirst, scrunched into one of JJ's trainers.

'But Jack, that's not true!' she exclaimed. 'It can't be.' A sudden flash of doubt filled her eyes. 'It isn't, is it?'

'Of course it's not true. It's not even half true.' Mossy was heartened by the shout of protest from Jack. Whatever it was, it hadn't knocked all the fight out of him yet. 'But no one will take me on with that being said about me. I can probably prove it's wrong, and get it corrected, but it'll be difficult and will take ages, and we haven't got ages.' Now Annie looked puzzled.

'What do you mean?' Mossy was puzzled too. Having wriggled out of JJ's trainer, he was half way through unknotting one of the laces which had tied itself round his leg. He stopped to listen.

'It's the money too.' Ach! Money! thought Mossy as he

wriggled his foot free and crossly kicked the trainer under the sofa. He grabbed the arm and pulled himself upwards. Thank goodness I've never needed the stuff. It seemed to cause Dwellers no end of problems; not enough, too much, uneven shares. As far as he could see it was nothing but trouble.

'We used all our savings for the house. I know that,' Annie paused, her eyes still on Jack.

'Every last penny,' Jack agreed.

'But that means we're safe. We have a home here.' A glow lit Annie's eyes as she spoke, a smile that shone deep into Mossy's heart.

'I've been doing the sums.' Jack's face was still desolate. 'There are bills to pay, living expenses…'

'But that's why I'm working!' This time it was Annie's turn to protest.

'Yes, and that's great, but that was only supposed to tide us over, keep us going until I was earning again. Oh Annie, I'm so sorry.' Jack's head sunk into his hands. 'I've let you all down so badly.' Mossy ached all over. This feeling in Jack was so strong, so sad. It was almost as if he had given up hope.

'I don't get it,' Annie tried to comfort him. 'I know I don't earn what you do… did…' Jack's shoulders slumped further. She paused, 'but it should be enough to cover basics.'

'It is,' Jack reassured her. 'As long as we live simply and don't have any disasters, we can just about get by on what you earn.' Jack reached out and took his wife's hand, holding it tightly in both of his. 'It means no holidays, no treats, no trips to the cinema…' There was another heavy pause before he could bring himself to look up into her eyes. Mossy's heart ached at the pain he saw in his face. 'But in September Rollo is due to start at his new school.'

Mossy looked from face to face. He could see understanding growing in Annie, but he was still puzzled.

'Ah… Right,' she said, 'I understand now.' Silence fell in the room. Mossy edged closer, lightly resting a hand on Annie's shoulder. He felt a tightness in her. Reaching out with both hands now, he leant towards her and, with a touch as delicate as moonshine, he gently stroked her shoulders to ease her.

'He's worked so hard for that scholarship.'

'Rollo's done brilliantly,' Jack agreed. 'But the scholarship doesn't cover all the fees.' Suddenly Mossy understood. 'We simply won't have enough money to pay for the rest.' There was a pause. 'Unless there's some sort of miracle, he won't be able to go. And there are Cissy and JJ to think of too.'

Mossy listened as the talk carried on. Jack and Annie tried all sorts of suggestions, but it kept coming back to the same answer; there just wasn't enough money to do all the things that they had previously planned.

As lightly as possible, Mossy moved between the two adults, a touch here and there to calm them, to ease any tension that might build. By the time they went upstairs he was confident that he understood as much of the problem as they did. What worried him most was one idea that they had discussed briefly.

'What if we moved from here? Found somewhere smaller, cheaper? The money would cover some of the school fees for a while.'

Mossy felt distraught at the thought. Lose these Dwellers? Miss out on seeing the children growing up? He was so pleased with the progress he was making with JJ. He realised how much he would miss Cissy's dramas. And it was fascinating seeing a Place Reader at close hand. And somewhere deep inside him was a growing feeling that he needed them to stay here.

'Oh Jack, after all we've done here – my perfect studio?' Annie's face seemed to echo his feelings. Quite, agreed Mossy, realising how much he would miss seeing more of Annie's paintings.

'I know,' Jack agreed. 'And the children are so happy here. I just thought we ought to think about it.'

'*Forget it*,' hoped Mossy as he racked his brains. A frown lifted from his brow. Maybe he had a solution too, at least for part of the problem.

As they settled down to sleep Mossy leaned against the frame of the front door. The house eased itself on the ground with a slight creak. 'You're right,' agreed Mossy, 'we're well rooted, and I think these Dwellers will be too, with a little encouragement.'

Outside, the moon burst from between scurrying clouds; the windows glinted, a shaft of light slanting through to rest on the hearth.

'Mmm, that's a good point, too. We must keep their hearts warm and loving.'

He climbed up inside the chimney and perched, slightly sootily, on the top of the smoke stack, from where he gazed at the land around, admiring the trees that stood sentinel along the banks of the stream. His Dwellers would be safe here, he knew. Two bats swooped low over the pond, the stream burbling quietly on its way as it flowed over the weir. Mossy nodded his head in agreement.

'I'll remember that, too. We'll check that all the bad things are washed well away from them.'

Just as he was about to slip back inside, the white Barn Owl drifted by on muffled wings, the tips of her feathers rippling in the breeze.

'I promise,' he replied to her. 'I'll ask for advice when I need it, be safe, no rushing.'

Mossy wandered through the bedrooms, checking on his Dwellers. Annie and Jack were fast asleep, curled around each other, close together even in their dreams. So long as we can keep you like that, working together and supporting each other, then you'll cope with anything, he thought, a smile sweeping through him. Annie gave a gentle sigh, turning over and snuggling into Jack's shoulder, as he wrapped his arms around her and held her even closer.

In JJ's room chaos reigned. Half-worn clothes were heaped on his chair, toys scattered across the floor. JJ was sleeping with one arm thrown out, the other tucked under his pillow, his duvet slipping off the bed. That's good, thought Mossy, as he pulled the duvet straight. You hang on to your talisman. It's a good one, and it'll keep you sound and true so that you fly as straight as the best of arrows.

In Cissy's room there was more order, but already Mossy could feel her worry growing. She was restless, her legs twitching. I'd better keep a close eye on you, he decided. Gently he brushed the hair from her forehead.

'Sleep well, drama queen,' he whispered, scattering happy dreams across her. Cissy relaxed, a smile crossing her face as she slipped into a deeper, more restful sleep.

Mossy was always cautious in Rollo's room, even when he

was asleep. He climbed up and sat on the pile of books beside the bed. *Children of the New Forest*, he read, and looked at the picture on the front. Hmm, I can remember when people living here wore clothes like that; it was soon after they built our extensions. Mossy rubbed his thighs, remembering the pains of sudden growth that had come with the increase in the size of the house. Rollo stirred, his eyes opening.

'Ah, hello there,' he said, his voice thick with sleep. Mossy gasped. He had been so immersed in his memories that he had completely forgotten to stay invisible. Fade, fade, he thought, shimmering out of visibility.

'*Just a dream*,' he projected. '*Not here. You never saw me.*'

Annie was in a rush the next morning, skipping breakfast and hurtling off to the station whilst the others gathered themselves together.

'We'll talk this evening, OK?' she checked with Jack as she raced through the kitchen.

'That's fine,' he called as the door banged behind her.

'You'll talk, or we'll all talk?' Rollo asked, looking up from his cereal, his eyes searching Jack's face.

'Don't you worry,' Jack tried to reassure him, but Cissy was all ears too.

'What are we talking about? What's gone wrong?' she quizzed, stopping in her tracks, waving the milk bottle in one hand.

'Who says anything's gone wrong?' Jack laughed uneasily.

'Because if there was nothing the matter you'd tell us what it was,' Cissy explained.

She's got a point there, thought Mossy.

JJ stuck his head round the door and waved a trainer with one hand.

'Dad, I can only find one shoe. Where's the other?'

'Well, where did you take them off?'

'Been there; done that.' JJ called back. 'I left them by the sofa, but now I can only find one.'

'Come on, I'll give you a hand,' said Rollo, abandoning his empty bowl by the sink.

'Trainers don't walk on their own,' said Cissy, sounding rather smug, swinging her feet back and forth under her chair.

Mossy was smitten with guilt. Too right they don't, he admitted, and ran through to the sitting room where he wriggled under the sofa. In his hurry the previous night he had kicked the shoe rather hard and now it was wedged firmly underneath. He tugged and hauled. The shoe broke loose, shooting both he and it across the wooden floor, to land in a heap at the edge of the rug, just as Rollo and JJ entered.

'JJ!' exclaimed Rollo, pointing at the trainer. 'You'll be telling us you can't see the nose on your face!'

'Bu… But it wasn't there! Really it wasn't.' JJ looked puzzled.

Mossy, checking he was properly invisible, froze. Rollo reached down towards him. Oh no! That shoelace was causing trouble again. It had flicked across his ankle and hooked itself into his boot. Keeping the rest of his body absolutely still, he worked the toes of his left foot against the heel of his right boot, levering it off just in time to allow the lace to slip free as Rollo picked up the trainer and handed it to his brother.

'Next thing you'll be telling us that it got there all on its own,' he laughed. 'Unless…' Now it was Rollo's face that had the puzzled look.

'Unless what?' asked Cissy, joining them.

'Unless… Oh nothing. It was just a dream I had last night. Or a feeling I get sometimes. I thought I saw…' His voice trailed off.

Mossy let out a sigh of relief.

'You're as bad as Dad, you know,' Cissy grumbled. 'Starting to say things and then giving up.'

JJ, who had been sitting right beside the immobilised Mossy, got to his feet.

'Thanks anyway, and whatever you say, I know where I left my trainers, and I looked there, and all over, and there wasn't one in the middle of the room. Something shifted it and it wasn't me,' he grumbled, stomping off towards the stairs. Cissy shrugged her shoulders and pulled a face at Rollo.

'Come on, you lot, or we'll be late for school,' Jack's voice called from the kitchen.

As JJ raced back down the stairs, and Cissy and Rollo ran to find their homework, Mossy decided it was time to find a safer spot. He grabbed his boot with one hand and hopped about, trying to work his foot into it as he struggled out of the way.

Peace and quiet descended in the wake of their departure. OK, thought Mossy, standing on the threshold, time to draw breath and plan for the future. He sat down and rested his chin in his hands, a slight frown creasing his brow as he wondered how to manage it. After a moment he was decided. I'd better visit Puddle.

## CHAPTER 10

# Solutions and Disasters

Mossy ambled down the drive with a smile on his face. His visit had been a success.

'It's the least I can do,' Puddle had told him. 'After all the help you gave me with my new Dwellers I owe you a whole heap of favours.'

They'd sat on the bridge, swinging their legs over the rushing water, as Mossy explained what he needed. Puddle was full of ideas these days and had jumped to his feet, clapping his hands in delight.

'That'll be a piece of cake!' he exclaimed. 'They're so pleased at the moment, they've just had good news about Jon from school. It looks as if he might be doing as well as Sophie. That ought to convince them, shouldn't it?'

The two Holders had decided that they ought to be able to let the children do most of the persuading.

'Rollo's good at working things out,' Mossy had explained, deciding to keep quiet about being seen during the night. 'His parents know he's reliable. Best of all, he always sees things so positively. It's just a matter of them realising that it's the right solution.'

After discussing a few more details, Mossy decided to head home and find out what Jack was up to. He ducked under some cow parsley that was hanging over the drive, spattering the gravel with white petal freckles, and then paused to sit for a while by the stile, enjoying the sun. His left leg was stiffening, and an ache had spread across his shoulders. The sun would do him good. He was still there when the robin flew down, cocked his head on one side and chirruped.

'Just feeling a little tired. My Dwellers need looking after at the moment, but I think it's nearly sorted out now. I'll soon be back on form, don't you worry.' The robin ducked his head twice and turned to look at Mossy from a different angle.

'He's always in his study at this time of day,' Mossy replied. 'All I need to do is sit quietly with him until the others come home. He's a bit stressed.' The robin gave a short burst of song and flew away.

'That bird always knows how to make me feel better,' Mossy chuckled, pushing himself back onto his feet and continuing slowly on his way.

Near the house his attention was caught by a strange sight. Instead of working in his study, as he had usually done since being at home, Jack was sitting outside on a step. In the same way as the evening before, he was hunched over, head in hands, eyes cast down. Mossy hurried towards him.

How long had he been like this? Even though he was discreetly invisible, he was aware that in this state Jack was unlikely to notice him, whatever he did. This Dweller was becoming too withdrawn and despondent. He had to get him going again.

Ignoring his aches and pains, he hurried to the pond and quacked loudly across the water to catch the duck's attention. As she swam over, Mossy spotted her ducklings swimming in her wake. Just the thing! He explained the problem and then hurried back. On his way he checked over his shoulder and grinned at the sight of the duck waddling across the gravel towards them, her ducklings scurrying to keep up with her.

As she arrived in Jack's line of vision, she gave a loud quack. Jack glanced up and, seeing the ducklings clustered around her, a fleeting smile skimmed across his face.

'Ready?' checked Mossy. He stuck his toe in front of the smallest one. The small, fluffy bundle tumbled and crashed to the ground. Beak outstretched, it gave Mossy a wink as it struggled to its feet. Then it tripped again, this time bumping into its neighbour. They both squawked and crashed about, flapping their stubbly little wings, staggering sideways and knocking over two of their sisters. Mossy had both hands clapped over his mouth to stop any noise escaping, but his ears caught the sound he was most hoping to hear – a chuckle from Jack. The mother duck fussed around them, rounding up her team of acrobats and herding them back towards the water with loud warnings about too much tomfoolery. The youngest duckling gave a final farewell waggle of its tail as it hurried after the rest of the family.

Jack stood up and gave his shoulders a shake.

'Who am I to be sitting here in a heap, uselessly worrying, when I ought to be doing something practical?' he asked no one in particular as he looked over towards the pond. 'You ducks go and perfect your swimming, and I'll... I'll...' Mossy crossed his fingers. There was so much Jack could be doing, even if he wasn't going to be job-hunting for a bit.

*'Cissy wanted you to check something in the vegetable garden,'* Mossy silently projected in his direction.

'Mmm,' pondered Jack, turning away from the pond and looking over the hedge. 'I know.' There was a new purpose to his step as he headed off.

Mossy enjoyed trailing around with Jack gathering bits and pieces together; an old tap from the shed, some blue piping left from the water main repair, plenty of tools and a spade.

He sat on the edge of the odds-and-ends box while Jack rummaged through it, fishing out a variety of plumbing equipment. He watched him measure distances and hammer pegs into the ground and then dig an experimental hole. When Jack flagged for a bit, a vacant look taking grip of his eyes, Mossy nudged a screw so that it rattled across the ground, bringing Jack's attention back to the matter in hand.

This is more like it, thought Mossy. You seem better than I've seen you in ages.

Before he went to collect the children, Jack had everything ready, and Mossy was happy to let him go on his own. When the children returned they would all be busy with homework and then preparations for supper. Time to put his feet up.

He was still busy taking life easy, sprawled along the top of a bookshelf beside Rollo, who was struggling with some rather tricky maths, when he heard Jon knock at the door. Ah ha! It looked as if Puddle was getting on with his part of the plan.

'You ready to come on that bike ride?' Jon asked.

'I've just got to finish this,' said Rollo, waving a hand in the direction of his work, 'and then I'm more than ready.'

'What is it?' asked his friend. 'Anything I can help with?' In no time the two boys were putting the completed work into Rollo's school bag and heading towards their bikes.

'Hang on, boys, where are you going?' called Jack

'Out to the field to practise on the jumps,' called Rollo. 'OK with you?'

'Homework first,' Jack reminded him.

'All done!' grinned Rollo, 'Jon gave me a hand. There was a bit I didn't understand, but he explained where I was going wrong. I just hadn't got the hang of it in class.' The sound of their feet running down the path faded as Cissy looked up.

'I wish someone would explain this so it makes sense,' she grumbled, looking up from her science. Jack sat down beside her. Mossy relaxed again and closed his eyes.

I knew I could count on the children, he smiled to himself.

By the time Annie arrived home all work had been put away, supper was ready and Jon had been invited to stay and join their meal.

'I cooked it!' announced JJ. 'Dad helped!'

'Only a bit,' agreed Jack, 'and it was all his own idea.'

'So that explains the menu,' laughed Cissy, passing baked beans, cucumber and anchovies. 'JJ's favourites!'

Supper was a happy affair. JJ entertained them with a story about a friend who had caused complete mayhem by smuggling his hamster into school in his book bag. When it had escaped, they discovered their class teacher was scared of 'mousey-type things'.

Jon, in turn, had them in stitches describing how his friend, Matt, had made the most of their rather short-sighted physics teacher, Dr Longers, being called from the class. Matt had leapt to the front of the room and performed a brilliant impression of the teacher in full flow, using two fifty-pence coins taped in place as makeshift glasses. Matt had been standing dramatically, with his arms spread wide, calling everybody's attention.

'Splendid, **splendid**, girls and boys. **So** right! In the final analysis it **all** comes down to **how** you look at the detail.' He had peered blindly at them through his fifty-pence pieces. They had all been laughing when Dr Longers had suddenly returned, standing silently behind him.

'Detail **and**… your **times tables**, boys and girls,' Matt had continued.

'**So** very right, Matthew,' said their teacher in the sudden silence that had fallen across the room. 'But you won't be seeing much detail through **those** particular spectacles.' And he had relieved Matt of the money.

'I wish I were at your school,' said Cissy. 'It sounds fun!'

'It's not always like that. We have to work hard, too,' Jon pointed out.

'You must do,' agreed Rollo, as he turned to his father. 'He understood my maths better than I did, and I'm in the scholarship class!'

'Oh, that's because we have all sorts of after-school clubs. I go to one for maths extension, and a science one too, where we do stuff that isn't in the normal classes. Sophie used to do them. They're fun, and they really make a difference.'

'How is Sophie?' asked Annie.

'She's fine!' Jon grinned. 'She's just doing the last revision for her exams now and has arranged to start a job at the garden centre as soon as they're finished. She won't be going to Cambridge until October, and she wants to save some money first.'

'Cambridge!' Jack sounded impressed. 'I hadn't realised she'd been offered a place there. Mind you, she still has to get the right grades.'

'She will,' said Jon confidently. 'She's really clever.'

Mossy was watching Jack and Annie's faces and caught a glance that passed between them. Brilliant! His plan was working and he'd been right; the children were the ones to make it work. Rollo's voice broke into his thoughts.

'It sounds like a cool school. It's a pity it's already decided that I have to go away to be a boarder. I think I'd really like it there.' Mossy spotted another look flash between Jack and Annie, but nothing was said.

The conversation moved onto other things when JJ announced that he needed suggestions for how he should dress up for Book Day the following week. Cissy had already worked her character out.

'I'm going as Pippi Longstocking. I just need some orange wool for making plaits, and a pair of Dad's shoes.'

With supper over, it was soon time for Jon to return home and for the children to head towards their rooms. Annie,

Jack and Mossy lingered in the kitchen.

'What do you think?' asked Jack.

'About what?' Annie seemed more intent on drying up the big bowl in her hands.

'Rollo's school. Well, Jon's school actually. Maybe we should think about it? Or at least talk to Sue and Rajesh.' Mossy held onto the sink tap to keep himself from jumping up and down. He had to resist the temptation to scoop some of the foam from the washing up and throw bubbles into the air in celebration. This should stop them thinking about leaving.

'Mmm.' Annie still wasn't really paying proper attention. What's up with you? Mossy wanted to know.

'Annie!' Jack seemed almost as exasperated as Mossy. 'Don't you think that we should at least talk about it?'

'Yes, of course,' Annie agreed, putting down the bowl and dumping the drying cloth in it. 'It's just… that I've got news myself.'

Mossy and Jack both looked at her curiously.

'My boss, Dirk, well, actually he's the head of the whole company, called me into his office. He's really pleased with what I've been doing. 'Impressed,' is what he said. He wants to promote me, give me more responsibility. It'll mean I'll be properly full time, so I said I'd talk it over with you and let them know tomorrow. It's good news: more pay. I think I should go for it, Dirk seemed really keen.'

'Annie! That's great news.' Jack gave her a hug. 'And what a way of saying that they like what you're doing! But are you sure? This means that you'll have no time for your own work, and I know that matters to you too. Since we've been here your painting has become even better. Are you sure you want to put that on hold?'

Suddenly Mossy saw a flash of anger shoot through Annie. She pushed Jack away, her eyes hardening. Mossy felt the pain of it dart through his arms like an electric shock. What was going on here?

'How can you, Jack? You know that's the one way to stop me! I'm trying to do my bit, trying to make sure we have enough money to be fine, and you just don't want me to be successful. One of us has to earn a living.' Mossy saw Jack wince as the words flew like daggers across the room.

That's not fair, he wanted to cry out.

*'Jack's right. Your paintings are the most beautiful things I've ever seen. They are vibrant with life. They're a feast for everyone. He's trying to protect that, not trying to stop you. Your paintings are your glory.'*

But Annie couldn't hear Mossy and wasn't listening to Jack either.

'OK, so what I'll be earning won't match what you used to get. It won't pay Rollo's new fees, but at least it means that we can stay here. We'll be able to eat and be warm and… and…' Tears spilled over, running down her face, draining the strength out of both Jack and Mossy.

'Oh, Annie, my Annie, I'm so sorry.' Jack's voice was barely a whisper as he reached out a hand towards his wife.

'For goodness sake, stop saying how sorry you are!' Annie was shouting now. 'It doesn't make anything any better. I'm going to take the job and that's that.' She was glaring at Jack now, the air between them as sharp and dangerous as broken glass. Suddenly she turned on her heel and stormed out of the room, leaving Jack and Mossy gasping behind her.

Where did all that anger come from? wondered Mossy. He watched Jack leave the room and head for the stairs. That's right, he thought, go and check the children. They'll have heard shouting and be worried.

Cautiously he reached into the water, found the last spoon in the sink, lifted it out and laid it on the draining board. He rolled up the dish cloth and walked up and down on it to squeeze all the water out, before finally diving down with both hands to find the plug. As he sat and watched the water gurgle down the plughole, he dried his hands on the tea towel and pondered what to do next.

He had felt so sure that his plan to persuade them to let Rollo go to the big local school with Jon was right. It sounded like a good place, and it was free. Rollo would be happy there, and they wouldn't have to think about moving because they wouldn't need the extra money. Annie said that even with this new job she wouldn't be able to pay the fees, so maybe that was a plan he should still follow.

Dumping the dish cloth into the bowl again, he turned his thoughts to Jack. He was going to feel even more hopeless after Annie's explosion.

'And just as I had got him busy doing things again,' muttered Mossy under his breath.

He eased himself over the edge of the worktop, feeling for the knob on the drawer with his foot. Carefully he dropped to the floor and then slowly walked out of the kitchen towards the stairs. There would be a lot of comforting to do tonight. Even though his Dwellers would never know, he was going to be there with them to help them through.

## CHAPTER 11

# Nightmares

'But Dad, why was Mum shouting?  Mum never shouts unless I've done something really bad, and I wasn't even there.'  JJ, hunched up in his duvet, rolled over as his father sat down on the side of the bed.  Mossy lurked in the doorway, feeling the emotions that were trapped in the room.  Jack put an arm round his son.

'Don't you worry, chum.  There are times when **you** shout about something and it all turns out to be no big deal in the end.'

'But I'm just a boy,' reasoned JJ, shaking his head.  'That's what boys do.  Mum's are different.'  Mossy was shaken by the confusion that spread out around him.  Whatever else he was, JJ was seldom confused; he was either happy or sad.  Mossy could feel the little boy struggle as he tried to understand the changes around him.

Jack was explaining about work, stress and decisions as Mossy crept down the corridor to Cissy's room.

'But if they're going to get divorced, we'll have to go to live somewhere else, and I love it here.' Cissy was looking tearful already.

'Who said anything about divorce?' Rollo asked.

'My friend, Poppy, said that's what her parents did – they shouted and then they got divorced. Her mother said that her Dad was a useless waste of time and…'

'Hold on there, Cissy. You didn't even hear what they said. None of us did.' Rollo gave his sister a hug. 'You're going too fast. Lots of parents argue and they don't all get divorced.' But Cissy wasn't listening. Mossy could feel the fear in her. It vibrated through the room, winding into tight coils of bad imaginations.

'…And we'd have to choose who to live with, and I want to live with all of us, just like now, here.'

Mossy heard footsteps on the stair. Glancing over his shoulder he caught sight of Annie as she paused on the top step. The anger had gone from her face and now she simply looked drained.

'I'm so sorry,' she said, as she gathered Cissy in her arms. 'I'm tired after a long day.' Rollo rubbed his mother's shoulder.

'I told her it was nothing to worry about. See, Cissy? Mum's just tired.'

'Please Mum, don't get divorced.' Cissy's eyes glistened with tears as she rubbed her face against her mother's arm. Even Mossy could feel Annie's surprise.

'Where on earth did you get that idea from, sweetheart?'

Cissy explained about friends at school and the stories they told. Rollo quietly left the room with Mossy limping behind him, shadowing his steps and timing his footfalls.

He had to be careful with this one; a Place Reader who had spotted him, even though he had convinced him into thinking it was a dream, needed careful treatment.

Slowly Rollo walked about his room, pausing to look out of the window before he sat on the chair in the corner with a sigh. He turned his head and looked straight at Mossy. Mossy looked down at his hands. It was OK, the carpet glimmered faintly through them. You might look as if you can see me, he thought, but you can't. I'm still here for you too, though.

Rollo gave a faint smile, shoved his hand through his hair and then got up, giving himself a quick shake. Humming quietly, he picked up his towel and headed for the bathroom.

'I'm grabbing the bathroom first,' he called out as he headed for the door. 'Thanks,' he whispered, passing inches from where Mossy stood. Despite all his aches and pains, Mossy stood bolt upright, his eyes bright yellow in surprise. He stared after the boy.

Mossy took extra care after that, lurking in the corners of rooms, hiding in shadows as the preparations for bedtime continued. He sat, propped against the pillow, to listen in on JJ's bedtime story. He loved being read to as much as JJ did and was longing to hear what happened next to the group of children on their journey through France. Were they going to escape their pursuer?

He lingered after Annie turned out the light. Although the little boy looked more cheerful, Mossy sensed that he needed the comfort of his lucky talisman. Reaching under the pillow, he tweaked it gently so that it would be remembered. JJ's warm hand wriggled its way in, curling round the stone, which responded to the warmth by easing its age-old wisdom into his palm.

'*Give him comfort and protect him from bad dreams,*' instructed the Holder. Soon JJ was safely asleep, his arms wrapped tightly round his teddy.

Mossy slipped into the corridor that led to Cissy's and Rollo's rooms. Their voices were lively again, it sounded as if the worry had gone, so Mossy climbed the bookshelf under the landing window and looked out into the garden.

Suddenly he felt a draught. Where from? He patted round the edge of the window. There it was! Trouble! A tiny crack by the edge of the window frame.

'I can't say I'm surprised,' he muttered under his breath, even though it had only been one row. He was all too aware how quickly anger could damage the house. He rubbed his long fingers over his shoulders to ease them. '*Don't worry, we'll get this sorted,*' he promised, and decided it was time for a Nightwatch.

By the time the parents were back downstairs the sun had sunk low in the sky, and Mossy decided to check they were OK before settling to his night's work.

They were in the kitchen when he arrived. The sorrows and anger of the evening were slowing him down already.

'I just don't know what came over me,' Annie was saying as he entered the room. 'Suddenly it was if I'd been grabbed by complete anger. I've never felt anything like it before.' Jack leaned towards her.

'*Be gentle,*' warned Mossy.

'You're tired,' said Jack. 'You're working hard, and when you get home, we're all rushing about with things going on.

And then there are all the decisions too, about Rollo and what we need to do.'

'You're right,' said Annie, nodding her head. 'The work and this job seemed like a good idea. I've got to take it.' Mossy looked from face to face, trying to read what was going on behind the words.

'You must do what you feel is right,' agreed Jack, but Mossy felt sure that he wasn't happy.

'*What about the paintings?*' lamented Mossy.

'I'll hold the fort here,' Jack continued, 'and make sure everything is OK. It's such a change for us all; it's bound to take getting used to.'

As the conversation continued, Mossy worked out what he needed to do. Annie would be working during the day, so he needed to make sure that she got good rest and sound sleep at home. He would check that Jack was busy, so that he didn't sink into worries about 'not pulling his weight'. If the parents were fine, then he was confident that the children would be fine too.

He and the house would hold them safely, and the centuries of happiness and love would enfold them and see them through this muddle. Thank goodness there were children here again. They always helped. Mossy smiled to himself at the thought of the three unwitting helpers upstairs.

'So we'll talk to the Raitatas about the school and then see what Rollo thinks?' Annie was checking. At least that's one worry mostly out of the way, thought Mossy. Rollo would enjoy being in Jon's school, so he could relax on that front.

By the time Jack and Annie were in bed, the house and its

surroundings seemed to have settled into night calm, but Mossy knew that looks could be deceptive and started out on his patrol.

Rollo was fast asleep, his book propped open where he had stopped reading. Everything seemed fine there.

Cissy was another case altogether, however. Anxiety still rattled around the room, ready to jump on any crack in her defences.

'Right, I'll get you sorted,' he declared, with a grim look. Carefully he hunted through the room, gathering up the shreds of worry, scooping them into his hands from all the little corners and hidden places where they lurked.

'Come on out of there! Leave her alone!' He herded it all over to the open window, and with a mighty push shoved it out into the darkness.

'Not wanted here,' he announced, as he stood on the windowsill to make sure it was completely gone. Behind him in the warmth of the room Cissy sighed and turned over, the faint crease of worry on her forehead smoothed away. The Barn Owl glided silently by.

'Keep guard for me,' called Mossy. She tipped a wing at him, and a white feather floated down to rest at his feet. Gently picking it up, Mossy climbed back down to Cissy's bed and laid it by her pillow.

'There you are. Sleep well,' he whispered as he tiptoed out.

But JJ's room was a battlefield by the time Mossy arrived.

The little boy tossed and turned in his sleep, his fingers twitching as he fought a nightmare. His bear had been flung from the bed and lay on its back in the middle of the room.

'Oh no! I should have come sooner,' gasped Mossy. It was always easier to prevent nightmares than to get rid of them. The talisman had slipped loose and was lying on the floor, by the bed. Mossy picked it up and rubbed it. It glowed gently in return.

'Work to do,' Mossy reminded it as he dropped it gently onto JJ's damp palm and saw the boy's fingers close around it. A frown settled above his tightly closed eyes, as if he were trying to shut out the sight of something. He waved an arm in the air, fighting an invisible foe.

'No! No! I can't do that. Stop it!' Now he sounded really frightened. Mossy placed both hands on the boy's head, his long fingers curling so gently into place that there was no risk of him waking. JJ thrashed from side to side. Mossy followed every movement with his hands as he braced himself for a struggle. Now, with his mind, he dug deep to find the nightmare.

'Ha! Got you!' he said through gritted teeth. 'Out of there!' He pulled with all his might, his eyes glowing orange with the effort, as he hauled the terrifying images away from JJ's sleeping form and wrestled them over to the window. The Barn Owl was waiting for him, her claws ready.

As she carried it away in her talons, he turned back to the bed. The air had changed. JJ was sleeping calmly now. Mossy stroked the damp hair from the boy's forehead, and watched a smile of contentment spread over his face as his fingers relaxed around the talisman.

It took me ages to learn to do that, he mused, heading down the stairs, but it's worth it every time. The trick lay in making sure you got the nightmare out without waking the sleeper. When he was successful, all memory of the nightmare was gone. This had been a particularly nasty version, and he wondered if something might still linger in the morning.

'Don't worry,' he reassured the sleeping family, 'I'll keep an eye on your dreams.'

As he passed Annie and Jack's room, he cast a quick glance through the door. Everything seemed quiet and calm. No worries there he decided with relief, carrying on down to the sitting room.

Now he had dealt with it, he needed a rest himself. These new aches and pains were going to take a while to go, he realised, and he settled down on the hearthstone for a good, long dreamless sleep of his own.

## CHAPTER 12

# Gully Reports

Mossy was ready early the next morning, before anyone else arrived for breakfast. Jack was the first, making cups of tea to take upstairs. Annie rushed through soon after, dumping her mug on the kitchen worktop as she ran out to her car. Mossy raced after her, catching whiffs of stress, but also a feeling of determination.

Then he caught something else, a feeling he didn't recognise. What was it? It wasn't the creative flow that he felt when Annie was painting in her studio. He wasn't sure what it was, and something about it made him uncomfortable.

Funny how things change, he thought, standing by the track. It used to be Jack rushing off in the early hours, or disappearing for days, and though there had been times when he had sensed a similar determination, he had always understood what happening.

As the car disappeared down the drive, Mossy sat on the staddle stone and wondered if Jack had ever really enjoyed his work the way Annie loved her painting. Maybe he had at first, but by the time he came to Annanbourne it had become something he just did, rather than something he loved doing. Mossy knew that he had been good at it, just as he was sure that Annie was good at her job. Maybe what Jack needed was to see this as an opportunity. How do I get him to think that? he pondered, slipping off the stone to amble back to the house.

Sometimes things have to change, he thought as he passed the pond. The duck pushed her way out of the watercress and, followed by her entourage, paddled to the far side.

'Thank you,' he called out after them. The youngest one, trailing at the back, waggled his tail. Their mother quacked.

'Yup,' he called back, remembering how Jack's face had brightened. 'It worked a treat.' She waded up the bank and set about showing her little ones how to eat grass. Mossy paused to watch them, remembering when it had been the mill pond.

The water had flowed more strongly then, turning the huge horizontal wheel that powered the grinding stones. When the water stopped running so freely, the river dwindled to a stream and things changed. It was hard at the time, and the loss of the mill meant his Dwellers had had to change their way of living and working. But now he was glad.

The new river that had taken so much of their water flowed through the town, which had grown rapidly. A century later an industrial estate had spread into the fields. Houses he had known long ago had disappeared, their Holders vanishing with them. He shuddered at the thought.

That could have been him. Instead, the fields around him remained. His house had thrived and his Dwellers had been happier in the end, glad to keep their home. Nothing remained of the working mill. Only Rollo had spotted the memory of the buildings.

So how to help these Dwellers discover that change can be good? Mossy was still racking his brains as he slipped through the door into the kitchen where the others were gathering.

Cissy was full of beans, rushing about, laying the table. Jack gave her a hug.

'You're in fine form this morning!' he remarked.

'I slept like a log last night. I was really tired, but I feel like new today,' she explained.

Mossy beamed. His vigilance had been well worth it.

'And guess what?' she continued. 'Look! White and beautiful! I found it by my pillow.' She held up the feather like a lamp, to illuminate the room.

'Where did you find that?' Rollo asked, joining them.

'I said – by my pillow. Goodness knows how it got there. Magic,' she decided.

'You're right about magic,' Rollo agreed with his sister. 'I was reading about it the other day. White feathers have been thought of as magic for centuries. Some people say they're to do with 'the wee folk'.'

'What're 'wee folk'?' asked JJ.

'I guess you could say that they're the spirits of a place. White feathers are somehow connected to them, and some people think that they are special in themselves. Particularly ones that are just 'found'.'

'It's like my talisman,' said JJ, wandering across the room with a glass of milk. 'Suddenly, there it was. Maybe this feather is yours, Cissy. I needed mine last night. I had a horrid nightmare.' A look of concern flashed across Jack's face.

'What was it about?' he asked.

'I dunno,' replied JJ. 'I could feel it getting really frightening, and then it just sort of... went. And I can't remember anything else about it.'

Good, thought Mossy, he had won that battle too.

'And my talisman was under my pillow. See? It must have been that.' Mossy didn't mind what JJ thought. All he cared about was having successfully banished the nightmare.

As the family prepared to head off to school, Mossy decided to go along for the ride to check what it was like these days. He jumped in beside Cissy and climbed onto the parcel shelf at the back. The view was splendid!

He had always wondered why the children went by car when it was so close, so he wasn't surprised when they headed past the village school and onto another one, further away.

He remembered this school too. This was the place where one of his Dwellers had been beaten.

He could hardly believe his eyes as the children rushed into the playground ahead of him. Portly Mrs Baker, with her dyed hair, long sweeping coat and cane, had been replaced by a tall, thin man with smiling eyes, who greeted the arriving children. Mossy wondered if Mrs Baker had known how to smile. He tried to imagine it and shuddered. It would have been like seeing a grinning snake.

'Oh, Mr Goodman, I've done that homework you set us already!' announced Cissy, waving her English book in one hand. 'And it wasn't half as hard as you said!'

Inside Mossy's eyes grew ever wider. The dull, green walls had been painted with bright, lively colours. Children's work was pinned up all over the place. Mossy was just climbing some shelves to get a closer look at The Nature Table beside them, when he was startled to hear a voice in his ear.

'What do you think? Quite a change, eh?'

He'd been spotted! This was the problem when you strayed from home, he reminded himself as he spun round in alarm. A cheery face was beaming at him from the shelf above.

'Gully!' he exclaimed, with a sigh of relief. 'Thank goodness! I thought I'd had it! But shouldn't you keep your voice down? If I can hear you, so can the others.' Gully chuckled, folded his arms and settled down on the shelf beside him.

'Just listen to the racket around us. Everyone's talking fit to burst at the moment. There's no need to worry.' In the ensuing pause Mossy nodded at the loudness of the chatter around them. 'We only have to watch it when they go off to lessons.'

Seeing Jack head towards the headmaster's room, Mossy knew that he and Gully had time to catch up.

He was impressed at how well Gully knew all the children in the school.

'Oh, your Dwellers are fine,' he reassured Mossy. 'Rollo's won his scholarship, and Cissy's doing well, despite all her theatricals. JJ's a kind little chap, sensitive to the needs of others.'

'That's what worries me about him,' Mossy explained. 'He seems to feel others' emotions very easily.'

'So what's the problem?' Gully enquired.

'Their Dad's lost his job and things are changing at home. They're all unsettled, and it's beginning to have an effect on us too.'

Gully commiserated with Mossy about aches and pains.

'You remember Mrs Baker, don't you?' Mossy nodded his head. 'A right tartar she was. Unhappy children and unhappy teachers too. And all because she was basically lazy; couldn't be bothered to run things properly, always leaving it to others and then claiming the credit. I was a wreck. How are we supposed to do our jobs when we can barely move round the place? Good riddance to bad rubbish, I say.'

'So things are better?' Mossy checked. Gully did a quick back-flip off his shelf, caught the edge of the one Mossy was standing on and then somersaulted across to the table.

'As you can see – we're all in tip-top form these days!' he grinned. 'Happy, busy children, who feel pleased to be successful, a team of staff who get on well, and Mr Goodman's the best head we've ever had. We get the occasional hiccup when someone has to leave; parents moving house, can't afford it, whatever. But I can handle that OK.'

'Can't afford it?' echoed Mossy. 'So they still have to pay to come here?'

Things around them were beginning to calm as children headed into classrooms and parents left. Mossy glanced around and spotted Jack emerging from Mr Goodman's office.

'Why don't you think about it?' suggested Mr Goodman. 'Of course there are the police checks to be done, but it could be really useful.'

'How long do they take?' Jack was looking thoughtful.

'Only a few weeks, once we have a definite response from you. But I'm afraid I need to go now – assembly calls.' The head smiled warmly as the two men shook hands. 'I'll wait for your call.'

As Jack headed out of the school, Mossy bade Gully a quick farewell, slid down the leg of the table and hobbled after him as quickly as possible. He didn't want to be left behind. It would be a long walk home, and a difficult one in his present state. He was in luck. The car door stood open as Jack paused, looking back at the buildings. Mossy scrutinised Jack's face, questions racing through his mind.

What had the two men been discussing? And all that about 'police checks' – what did that mean? Was one of the children in trouble? He shook his head – he couldn't believe that. And anyway, wouldn't Jack look more worried if that were the case? He seemed to be just standing there, as if carved in stone.

Maybe it was another thing about money. Mossy hadn't realised that this school was yet another thing that needed to be paid for. If they couldn't afford the fees for Rollo's new school, what about the ones for Cissy and JJ? Mossy shook his head. He had no answers.

Gripping the lip of the door frame with both hands, Mossy heaved himself upwards, hooking a leg over to pull himself in. A pebble fell back to the ground with a loud clink. The sound brought Jack into action again, and he sat down, swinging his legs into the car, knocking Mossy into the darkness under the pedals.

Desperate to get out of the way, Mossy scrambled towards the centre. He was just about to clamber round the gear stick to safety when Jack grabbed it, gave it a wiggle and flicked Mossy back down towards his feet, which were getting in on the action too.

As the engine roared into life, the whole car vibrated in response. Mossy didn't know much about cars, but he knew enough to realise he was in just about the worst place, ripe for being squashed in half a dozen horrible ways all at once.

Jack's feet leapt about, first to this pedal, then that. Mossy whipped his toes from beneath one just before Jack slammed it flat to the floor and pulled on the gear stick, making the car jolt backwards.

In his panic, Mossy grabbed Jack's trouser leg to keep from being crushed. The car jerked to a halt again, now flinging Mossy under Jack's seat, where he discovered an old tennis ball wedged in place. At least this was safer!

Mossy now crawled, commando-style, under the seat as the car shot forward again. It was a bit of a squeeze getting past the tennis ball, but a hefty nudge from his elbow knocked it loose. Phew! he sighed as he emerged safely by the back seats. The car swung round a corner, rolling him and the ball over each other until they bumped up against the far door.

This was worse than the time when he'd been in the pony trap and the horse had bolted. At least he could communicate with a horse. Cars were deaf. He braced himself for an uncomfortable journey and settled down for a careful thinking session.

By the time Mossy heard the sound of the gravel drive crunching under the wheels he was feeling decidedly sick. His route to the door lay under the seat, but he also needed to be safe from Jack's feet. The tennis ball seemed keen to follow him, so he lay on his stomach, holding the ball in place with his toes. As soon as the car stopped, he wriggled forward to be ready for the door opening.

Suddenly Jack was out, and Mossy leapt up only to find that the ball had indeed decided to follow him and was now tangled in his feet. Mossy tripped, and the door slammed shut in his face. There was a loud clunking of locks.

What was Jack doing? Mossy felt a chill run through him as he realised what had happened. He was imprisoned in the car.

## CHAPTER 13

# A Way Out

At first all Mossy could feel was panic. Then he was cross. The ball rolled towards his feet. He kicked it. It bounced across the footwell and then rolled back again.

'It's all your fault!' he shouted, picking it up and throwing it over the seat. 'Get lost!' The ball hit a window, bounced onto the back, then down onto the floor again, out of sight. Mossy sat by the gear stick, his head in his hands, his eyes shut, and sighed. He needed to be in his house to look after people. Jack might get himself into all sorts of muddles.

'Who am I to think I can keep anyone out of trouble?' he asked himself. 'Look what I've got myself into now.' Something nudged against his foot and he looked down to find that the ball had managed to trickle back through to the front again. He picked it up.

'I'm sorry. I guess it's not really your fault; you just want to be played with. After all it's what you were made for, isn't it? I'll put you up here, and then the next time someone gets in they'll spot you and you'll be found again. OK?' The ball rocked gently as it settled, ready to wait.

The sun beat down on the car, and with all the windows shut it was hot. Mossy perched himself on the top of the driver's seat, his legs dangling down the back, his chin on the head rest, so that he had a good view of the drive and the courtyard, ready for anyone coming his way.

Hours passed and the temperature in the car rose. At last he spotted movement by the house. His eyes lit up as Jack emerged from the side door.

'This way!' he called. But Jack couldn't hear him and turned towards the vegetable garden. Mossy slumped back down again and ran a hand through his hair. His mouth was dry.

A mouse scuttled out from the side of the barn. Mossy thumped on the window, but that only made the mouse hurry faster. He gave a sigh as its tail whisked out of sight into the long grass. It looked so cool out there in the shade. Silence fell as the garden baked in the sun. Mossy took off his jacket and hung it beside him. His hands hung limply by his sides. The tips of his ears drooped.

Two wagtails landed on the gravel and started to dance around each other. Dip, dip, wag, wag. Mossy banged on the window again. The male stopped mid-wag and looked up at him briefly before calling his mate and leading her off into the sky.

'What's up with you?' Mossy shouted as their tails bobbed out of sight. 'I've helped you before. Never heard of pay-back?' He couldn't believe his eyes.

'Any minute now I'll turn into Roast Holder. It'll do something terrible to the house. I just need help.' He was running out of strength, his eyes pale grey and wanting to close. But a sudden flash of movement caught his attention. The wagtails were back, with the robins in tow.

'Oops. Sorry,' he apologised sheepishly. As the robins landed outside on the bonnet, Mossy slid towards the steering wheel, grasping it with both hands and pulling himself over to the dashboard.

There was a lot of cheerful chirruping from the other side of the glass.

'It's all very well for you to laugh,' said Mossy ruefully, rubbing the sweat from his forehead. One of the robins hopped onto the windscreen wiper and peered at him carefully before a short burst of song.

'No, he's locked it. I can't think why, I've never seen him do it before. Normally I'd just let myself out. Any chance you can get him back here?' The birds held a hurried conference before turning back to him.

'I know, I know. 'Patience is a virtue' and all that. It's just that I don't want to spend all day in here. If it gets much hotter I don't know what'll happen to me.'

The robins headed off, skimming over the hedge and disappearing out of sight towards the vegetable garden. Mossy eased himself out of direct sunlight, back onto the softer fabric of the seat. His throat was so dry he felt it might split. He was panting. Would it be any cooler in the foot well? He shook his head. This was no time to give up. He had Dwellers to look after. Send out a message, he decided, wondering why he hadn't thought of it before.

'I know it's a long distance, but try,' he told himself.

He leant against the door, chin resting on folded arms,

forehead pressed against the glass of the window, and focused on Jack. He knew where he was, could see it in his mind. The robins had been with him in the vegetable garden, collecting worms from his digging.

'*Please,*' he begged, '*Please, come to the car. There's something you need.*' Time and time again he sent out the message. Nothing happened. Maybe it was too far. Maybe he was already too weak.

Mossy sank back on the seat in despair. His eyes closed as he slipped into a state of blankness. A sharp tapping on the window brought his eyes open with a jolt. The robin ducked her head twice and chirruped loudly.

With a huge effort Mossy pulled himself up to peer out of the window. There was Jack by the house again. Gathering his remaining strength he called out as loudly as he could.

'Come to the car. Please come. Open the door!' he croaked. Jack went indoors. Mossy needed all his strength to keep upright; there was nothing left for calling out any longer.

Then suddenly Jack was back, hurrying towards him. The locks sprang open and Mossy summoned his last shreds of energy to dive through the door.

'Wow! What a blast of heat! It's like an oven in here!' exclaimed Jack.

Mossy slumped to his knees, slithering onto the rough gravel of the drive as Jack stepped over him, slammed the door shut and turned on the engine. Mossy had just sufficient strength to twitch his toes away from the wheels as they crunched by, carrying Jack off at speed, leaving him lying on the ground, gulping great breaths of fresh air.

As the sound of the engine faded into silence, Mossy lay

still. He knew he would have to move before Jack returned, but for the moment all he could do was focus on breathing, his eyes closed. A loud quack snapped his eyes open just in time to avoid the ducklings draping soggy watercress across his face.

'What's this?' he croaked. The mother duck quacked again as she organised her troupe.

'Full of iron, you say?' smiled Mossy as he sucked water from one of the leaves. 'It's just lovely to have something to drink.'

A flash of brilliant blue skimmed past their heads as the kingfisher swooped low, shaking his feathers and flicking a shower of tiny droplets onto them. Mossy lifted a finger in greeting.

'Aah,' he sighed, 'that's perfect!' His voice was already gaining strength.

As the ducks headed back to the pond, a quiet rustling in the long grass beside the barn caught his attention. Long ears twitched at him as the rabbits came over, nudging him with their soft noses, rolling him into the shade of the hedgerow before they slipped quietly out of sight again. The coolness of the grass that draped itself over him was wonderful; the dew that lurked at its base refreshing him as the strength of the earth flowed back into his body.

'Thank you, thank you,' Mossy murmured, slipping into a deep, restorative sleep, his head resting on a rose petal brought by the mouse.

By the time Mossy woke, long shadows lay across the

garden. He stretched out his limbs. A few aches and pains lingered, but he felt much better.

That was a close shave, he thought. I think I'll keep well clear of cars for a while. A gentle evening breeze rustled his hair as he got to his feet and headed for the house.

'Right then!' he exclaimed, rubbing his hands together. 'Things to do and plenty to think about.' Being roasted alive was no excuse for not looking after his Dwellers, and he needed some useful advice.

At the house all seemed to carry on as normal.

'... so that I couldn't possibly find any way of mending it!' Cissy was telling Annie, waving part of her gym kit at her. 'Not ever! And he says it has to be sorted by tomorrow, or I'll be skinned alive! Mum, I'm going to die!'

'Don't you worry, darling. It'll only take minutes to repair,' Annie soothed her as she took the shorts in her hand. 'It'll be fine by tomorrow morning. Just get yourself off to bed.'

'Mum, you're a life-saver,' grinned Rollo, looking up from his book.

'Isn't she always?' added JJ, as he raced Cissy for the stairs.

Mossy breathed a sigh of relief. Even though he'd been out of action they were OK. But that didn't mean that he could take things easy.

Despite listening carefully, Mossy didn't hear any of the children mention anything that could possibly explain why their headmaster might want a police investigation.

JJ was still caught up in whether his friend Jezz was going to be in the swimming team or not. Cissy was very impressed by all that Jack had done during the day.

'That's great, Dad. It'll make it so much easier.' Mossy was pleased. Clearly Jack's work was bearing fruit.

With the children settled and calm, Jack and Annie returned to finish putting away the dishes.

'How did it go at work?' asked Jack.

'It's settled.' Annie smiled at him. 'Dirk was really pleased. He says I'm the best artist he's had working on this team in ages, and the plans for the next project are really exciting. It's going to mean long hours sometimes, but I'm sure it'll be worth it.'

'I never needed Dirk to tell me how good an artist you are,' Jack assured her. Mossy caught a wistful sound to his voice. Neither did I, agreed Mossy. It seemed odd that Annie couldn't see it too.

'And you?' asked Annie. 'Did you ask them at school?' Mossy's ear tips vibrated in anticipation. Now he'd find out.

'I went in, as you suggested…' But Mossy's ears, stretched to catch the slightest nuance, had caught something else, too. Was that another nightmare he heard rattling at the windows upstairs? Catch the nightmare, or catch the information? What do I do? he pleaded with himself.

But he already knew the answer – he had to keep the children safe. Ducking out of the way as Jack reached towards the dresser with a stack of plates, he ran from the room to catch the nightmare before it ensnared one of the sleepers upstairs. As he raced up he heard Jack's voice carry on.

'… and he said that…'

It wasn't even a nightmare either. A bat that had lost its way and tangled itself in the gutter. Mossy gave it a firm piece of his mind, but by the time he returned, Jack and Annie had turned on the television and weren't talking any longer.

Although he lingered, the topic of school never came up again, and he was no further on in his investigations.

I need help, Mossy decided.

Once everyone was settled and the house was quiet for the night, he crept out to find his advisor. Nothing was moving. What if she were hunting elsewhere? The star-spangled sky was as clear as it had been during the day, warmth still hanging in the air as Mossy inspected the vegetable garden. Stepping through a crack in the gate, he wandered up the path between the beds. Cissy was doing well, he realised. She had a real knack for growing things. He was so busy admiring the tower of runner beans that he nearly fell straight into the hole. Ah ha! So here was Jack's work.

A long trench ran from the house, crumbled earth heaped beside it. At the bottom lay the bright blue pipe Jack had found the previous day. It looked as if it was about to be re-buried soon.

An iron post, with a lever tap attached three-quarters of the way up, stood at the top of the middle bed. Mossy put an ear to the pipe and listened carefully. He couldn't hear any water yet, so it wasn't connected, but he could see why Cissy was pleased. As he stood back to admire the length of the trench a flicker of movement up in the darkness caught his eye. There she was, his advisor, cruising in on silent wings.

Mossy waited patiently as the Barn Owl settled, tucking each feather neatly into place before she turned her great, golden eyes on him.

'Thank you for asking,' he replied. 'Much better now. A good rest and plenty of cool made all the difference. But I need another kind of help, please.'

He filled her in with his worries; school fees again, police investigations, how could he help? Slowly she turned her head, gazing at the land that lay around them, before turning back to him, her look sinking right into the core of his being.

'Hmm,' Mossy nodded his head. 'Keep them grounded, I can see that will help. But what about the investigations?' The owl turned from him again, this time her vision piercing the night, as she stared out over the fields towards the distant school.

'Must I?' Mossy didn't want to go back. It wasn't the school that worried him, but the journey that was of concern.

'Surely there must be some other way?' The glowing eyes swivelled back onto him, and he shrugged his shoulders, lifting his hands to defend himself from her sharp response.

'OK, OK. If I don't want to listen to the answer, I shouldn't ask the question. Point taken. I know you're right. I'm just not looking forward to it.'

By the time she left, he had his list of questions sorted out.

## CHAPTER 14

# Advices and Queries

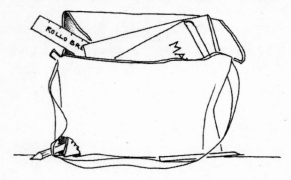

Mossy soon had a plan. The children took bags into school every morning and brought them home every evening. If he were prepared to spend the whole day with them, they could simply carry him there and back!

JJ's book bag was clearly too small to fit books and a Holder without risk of serious injury. Cissy's was stuffed to bursting with all sorts of things, including an old jersey that he remembered her wearing but hadn't seen for several months. Rollo's had the most space, but it was worn, and there was a hole in one corner, just the right size for a Holder to fall through. Several times, Mossy had watched Rollo's pencil case making a bid for freedom.

He had just decided that the safest mode of transport would be with Cissy when she came rushing in.

'Dad! Panic stations! I can't do my homework!'

'Bring it over here and I'll see if I can give you a hand.' Jack was calm and unruffled.

'No, Dad. You don't understand,' wailed Cissy. 'I can't do

118

it because I've left my bag at school. I haven't got it here, and I've got to hand it in tomorrow. You know what Mrs Tudor's like. She'll eat me alive!'

Mossy's shoulders drooped; there went his plan.

No way was he going to risk spending the night away from home, stranded in abandoned transport. He would have to travel with Rollo after all.

While Jack organised Cissy into phoning a friend to find out what the homework was, Mossy checked Rollo's bag again. At least it was organised. No soft jersey to snuggle into, but if he kept the books between him and the hole, that should stop him falling through.

He needed to get into school and find the answers. Half-term was coming up and he couldn't waste any more time. Tomorrow was the day.

Next morning, while the children had breakfast, he settled himself into the bottom of Rollo's bag with a book firmly wedged against his back. As Rollo's footsteps approached he braced himself, but nothing had prepared him for the sudden lurch as they were swung into the air.

Everything slid sideways, Mossy too. He landed with a thump against Rollo's back. Then there was another jolt. Everything swung the other way and then dropped a huge distance. Jack's voice was calling something as the top flapped open.

'I'm just checking,' Rollo said. His hand dived down beside Mossy, who leapt to one side as Rollo rummaged about, finally fishing out an envelope.

'Yup, got it!' The hand was back, stuffing the envelope beside Mossy's knee. They swung into the air again. Mossy hung onto the canvas wall and tried to right himself. His foot slipped and he looked down. There was a glimmer of light by the other knee. His heart plummeted. He had already slid too close to the hole. Frantically he hauled with both hands, kicking the pencil case down to block the gap.

Sudden jerks flipped him from side to side. Books slid cheerfully around, scissoring past his arm before finally squashing him firmly against the canvas wall as they crashed to stillness. The car's engine roared into life, announcing that they were on their way, but he no longer had any idea which way was up and felt carefully around with his hands for some indication of his whereabouts.

The seam from the side of the bag ran along his thigh. That meant… Frantically Mossy looked around for some glimpse of the light that would show him where the hole was. There was none, confirming his worst fear; the sharp feeling below his shoulders was the edge of the hole. It was his own back that was blocking out the light. Part of him was sticking through!

The smooth canvas walls gave no handholds as he tried desperately to find a safer position. Carefully he reached back with one hand to find out what was behind him. It felt firm and had a fabric covering, so, crossing the fingers of his other hand and hoping it was the car seat, he gave a tentative push.

'Rollo, don't poke me!' exclaimed Cissy.

'I'm not,' protested Rollo. 'I'm not touching you!' Mossy froze.

'Well, tell your bag to stop poking me then.'

'Oh no,' groaned Rollo. 'It'll be something sticking out of

that hole again.' There was a series of violent judders as Rollo gave his bag a hearty shake.

Mossy rattled to the far side, somersaulting round the pencil case. He narrowly escaped having an eye scooped out by a book and landed with his face squashed against the canvas, his neck bent at a strange angle and his left arm twisted over his right knee.

'Better?' he heard Rollo check with Cissy. No, Mossy wanted to howl, realising that he had no option but to stay still and silent.

By the time they arrived, Mossy's leg was numb and his ears felt distinctly odd. Voices came and went, and there were more jolts and bumps while he waited for a chance to escape. Pins and needles raced up and down his leg as it gradually returned to life.

There was a sound of scraping chairs as voices suddenly fell quiet.

'So, hand in homework first,' said a voice he didn't recognise. Mossy braced himself. Homework travelled in bags as well as Holders. This would be his chance.

A blast of light flooded over him as Rollo opened the bag. Mossy grabbed the edges and hauled. He swung one leg over, but the other was stuck. He looked down and grimaced. His toes had caught on the lip of that rotten hole. Rollo flipped the top shut, but Mossy wasn't missing this chance. He flung it open again and vaulted through the gap, ignoring Rollo's startled expression. Of course he was surprised at his bag opening itself, but Mossy had no alternative.

'Rollo Breeze!' a rather stern voice called as Mossy crept

under the shelter of Rollo's stool. 'Stop playing about with that. Pay attention, and bring me your homework.'

Mossy pulled at the tip of his nose to check it hadn't been permanently bent, and tugged at the top of his ears to ensure they were in full working order. He needed his senses in tip-top condition in this unfamiliar environment. When Rollo returned to his seat, he bent down and looked under it, his eyes briefly flitting past Mossy.

'Lost something Rollo?' asked his neighbour.

'No, not lost,' Rollo replied, straightening up. 'I thought something fell out of my bag, but I must have been mistaken.'

Taking advantage of the general mayhem as everybody milled about, Mossy climbed the legs of the stool and leapt across to perch briefly on the table, from where he could scan the room.

There was no getting out. All the doors and windows were closed, but they wouldn't stay that way all day. At some stage the door would open, and he needed to be ready to nip through, avoiding the crush of dozens of feet. Silently he made his way to the door and, hidden behind the bin beside it, he settled down to watch proceedings.

He enjoyed the lesson, liked the strange smells that Mr Suart made as he mixed chemicals, and was somewhat surprised when the children divided into groups and started cooking their own chemical concoctions. School had certainly changed since the last time he'd sat in on a lesson!

When everybody started clearing up, Mossy took it as a signal to prepare for the next part of his plan. He needed to find Gully and enlist his help. As the children rushed from the room, Mossy dodged about after them.

The corridors were hectic, people hurtled in all directions, and there were several times when Mossy had to flatten himself against the wall to avoid being trampled. Rounding a corner, he found himself in the reception area, close to the Nature Table where he had last met Gully. Even faster than the children had poured out at the end of the lesson, they disappeared into new classrooms. At last he was on his own.

'Back again already?' he heard a whisper in his ear. A broad grin broke across his face.

'That's who I need,' he exclaimed, spinning round to find his friend at his side.

'Keep your voice down, they'll hear us,' Gully hissed at him, waving a hand at two teachers hurrying past. Lowering his voice to the same level, Mossy explained his worries.

'Remind me who your Dwellers are?' Gully asked. 'Rollo, Cissy and JJ?' he continued after Mossy had told him. He shook his head.

'No, they're not in trouble. JJ spends time visiting the sick room and being patched up – he tends to bash himself about, walking into things, accidents, know what I mean? Although it's been a while since he did himself damage. But none of them are in **serious** trouble. Quite the opposite really.' There was a pause while Gully racked his brains. 'What exactly did you hear Mr Goodman say?' Now it was time for Mossy to think hard.

'I can't remember exactly. Something about 'police checks'?'

'Oh, that's OK.' Gully looked relieved. 'Police checks aren't for children, they're for adults. One of your Dwellers' parents must be a teacher.'

Now it was Mossy's turn to be puzzled.

'Teachers? No, neither of them.'

'Remember that Mrs Baker with her cane? She'd never have passed the checks these days. No one's allowed to beat children now. We still get lazy ones, but not the child haters we used to have. Every adult here has been checked – cooks, gardeners, nurses – everyone. I'm probably the only not-child in the place who hasn't been checked,' he chuckled.

'So if one of my Dwellers wanted to help in the school...' started Mossy.

'...she'd have to be police-checked,' Gully finished off for him.

'Even if it's a parent?' Gully nodded his head.

Mossy felt a huge burden had been lifted. The stiff neck, bent ears and slightly wonked nose were well worth it if this was the answer.

'Any way we can find out?'

'Follow me,' grinned Gully as he set off with a swagger. 'Mr Goodman keeps records of everything. If someone has asked him for a handkerchief, it'll be written down somewhere.' Mossy followed with a spring in his step.

Unlike the classrooms, the doors to offices were all left ajar. Gully slipped into the staffroom with Mossy close on his tail.

'There's a big diary in here where everything's written down. So long as there's no one here, we can check through it too. See if your Dweller has been in.'

'I know he came in,' explained Mossy. 'I was there. It's just what they were talking about.'

'It might say in the diary, but otherwise we can check the files,' Gully reassured him. 'We'll find out.'

He hurried across the empty room to a big table by the window, jumped onto the chair beside it, shinned up the arm and then launched himself at the table. Mossy followed close behind. There was the diary, open at that day's date. The two Holders leafed through the pages.

'Back several days,' Mossy suggested. 'Remember when I last came in?' They found the day alright and there in clear, black writing was the entry. 8.30 – Jack Breeze. But there was nothing to say what it was about.

'No worries!' said Gully cheerfully. 'There'll be a file in the office.'

Mossy had seen the office. It bristled with bustling people, and there was always someone coming in or out.

'Piece of cake...' Gully reassured him. 'We need to be there just before lunchtime. Time to spare. Why don't I show you around first?'

The two Holders passed a lively morning as Gully took Mossy round the whole school, proudly showing off various improvements. The playgrounds were best inspected while pupils were in classrooms, he advised, and Mossy could well understand when he saw the children burst out at the end of a lesson like water through a broken dam. He spotted JJ with a bunch of friends as they organised themselves into a game of tag. Cissy was busy with some girls in a group of trees where they had built camps. But search as he might he couldn't see Rollo. I'll find him in the end, he reassured himself. There's plenty of time between now and going home time.

Only once the children were safely tidied into classrooms again did Gully launch the assault on the office.

'Right – you watch the door and count the staff out. They eat before the children so there's someone here if help is needed during lunchtime. We have to count three out before we can get in safely.'

Gully headed off to check on a child who had been taken up to the sick room after break time, leaving Mossy leaning nonchalantly against the wall, watching the office doorway like a hawk. One out. Another out. Oh no – one back in again! Two out together. That looks like everyone gone, he decided. He was about to set off for the door when someone hurried back in again quickly followed by another. Oh, for goodness sake, he thought.

*'Go and have your lunch!'* How many were in there now?!

'Lunchtime. I'm off!!' he heard a voice announce, as another person left the room. Mossy crept towards the door. The brisk clacking of heels on the hard floor warned him to skip out of the way as the last of the office staff marched across the hall toward the dining room. Quietly he peered round the door. The office was empty.

Mossy stepped in softly with Gully at his side.

'My chap's fine, so we can concentrate on this now.' Gully led the way across the room. 'OK, the files are over there.' He pointed at a large cabinet on the far wall. Mossy's heart sank; the cabinet was shut. But Gully read his mind.

'That's why we needed them out. The drawers are easy to open, but it spooks them if we do it when they're here.' He chuckled. 'Got rid of one I didn't like that way once! Made her think there was a ghost – opening the doors when she was on her own. Serve her right, she was stealing stuff!'

The two Holders curled their fingers under the edge of the door, braced themselves against the frame, and heaved. Silently the door swung open. There were the racks of files, neatly organised in sliding drawers.

'Breeze, you said?' checked Gully, as he set off up the racks. 'They'll be somewhere up in the top ones.' Mossy followed him.

'You take that side. I'll do this. Hold on tightly when they start to slide,' Gully warned him.

Mossy was so amazed at the speed with which it slid open that his foot slipped off the rail, and if he hadn't been warned to hold on tightly he'd have fallen right off. Even so, he swung by his hands as he struggled to find a foothold.

'First time catches everybody out,' Gully was laughing at him. 'I fell off several times when they installed them.' He reached down a hand and pulled Mossy up to sit beside him, before pointing at a label.

'There you are. That's your lot, where it says Breeze. Pull it out, and the latest information is on the top sheet. I'm going to keep guard by the door.' He disappeared.

In no time Mossy had the file open. There it was on the top sheet: *Jack Breeze to discuss helping in the school. Police checks to be organised – once confirmed.* Mossy's heart gave a leap of delight. Everything was fine. It was all as Gully had suggested.

Quickly he flicked through a couple of the other pages. There was a sheet for each of the children, and it was quite clear that they were OK too. All his worries had been unnecessary.

So, if Jack was thinking of doing some work in school, at least that would keep him busy and stop him brooding...

'Quick! Close up!' Gully's voice shouted. 'Someone's coming.'

Mossy slid the pages into the folder, which he snapped shut and stuffed in the general direction of the files.

'Hurry!' Gully sounded worried as he scrambled up the drawer fronts. Mossy was still struggling.

'I can't get it in!' he protested, his grip loosening.

'Never mind,' hissed Gully, giving the drawer an almighty shove as he leapt for the safety of the desk beside it. Mossy's foot slipped at the sudden jolt, and he toppled headfirst into the files, his legs waving goodbye as he disappeared down amongst the pages.

## CHAPTER 15

# Finding A Way

As Mossy struggled to turn himself the right way up he heard a voice below him.

'What on earth…?' And suddenly the lights went out. Someone had shut the doors and he was stuck inside.

'Not again,' he sighed in despair. He had to get out before the end of school.

'*Gully?*' he projected, but silence blanketed him thickly. Where was his friend?

Feeling with his hands, Mossy found the top edge and pulled himself upright. All too soon his head bumped against the roof of the cupboard, but he was sure there was just enough space for him to crawl along the top of the files, if he could only get himself up there. He scrabbled and hauled, twisting himself to hook a leg over the edge. With a fair bit of puffing and panting he pulled himself horizontal in the narrow space. Commando-style, he crawled along the spiky tops, carefully working his way between the labels.

At the front a faint glimmer of light pierced the crack

between the two doors. It was just enough to show a narrow space down which he could climb. Hand over hand, he lowered himself to the floor.

'Mossy?' Gully's voice hissed through the crack. 'That you?'

'How many other Holders are there in this place?!'

'OK. OK. Hold your horses. They're all coming back.'

'…was wide open. It simply can't be left like that. Even if all the children are in classes. Anyone could have come in,' a voice complained.

'As I said, I haven't opened it today, so I simply don't understand,' a second voice protested.

'Maybe it was Mr Goodman,' suggested a third. 'He sometimes comes in to add something to the files when we're not here.'

'I'd better check,' insisted the first voice, and Mossy caught the sound of footsteps leaving the room. Had they all gone? Carefully he braced his feet against the bottom drawer and placed his shoulder against the door. Taking a deep breath, he gathered his strength.

He needn't have bothered. Just as he was about to put all his effort into it, the door swung wide, causing him to cascade onto the floor, where he lay spread-eagled in front of a pair of sharp-toed, high-heeled shoes. He held his breath, tucked his fingers in to keep them safe, and hoped that no one would tread on his nose.

Somewhere over to his left he caught the sound of stifled laughter.

'It all looks fine to me,' someone said. 'Hang on!' There was a pause. 'What on earth has happened up here?'

'Clear it up quickly. Pass me that file and I'll straighten it before Dilys gets back. It's probably just Mr Goodman not paying attention. You know what he's like.'

While they were occupied, Mossy stretched out an arm, put his hand palm down on the floor and pulled himself flatly forward. Cautiously he slid past the feet and into the relative safety of the open floor.

'*Mossy,*' he caught Gully's projection. '*Over here!*' Glancing to his left, he spotted his friend lurking under a desk.

'Boy, are you a sight for sore eyes,' he whispered once he was tucked in beside him.

'You should have seen yourself. You burst out of the cupboard like popcorn out of a pan.'

Making the most of the office staff being occupied, Mossy and Gully snuck out of the room and headed for the main part of the school. They raced between safe zones, avoiding the hurly-burly of children with their minds on lunch. Mossy's toes were trodden on once, abruptly jerking him to a halt, but otherwise their journey was without incident.

'I just need to find Rollo's bag and get myself settled into it for the journey home,' he decided.

'Cloakrooms,' suggested Gully. 'They often leave their bags in there.' But Rollo's bag was nowhere to be seen.

'Never mind,' Gully comforted him. 'There's plenty of time. Come on, I'll give you a treat to calm your nerves,' he continued, heading off to another part of the school.

'These are the music rooms,' he announced. 'Careful who you choose to listen to. The beginners can really mangle your ears, and I wouldn't recommend it. But there's a new boy, who started this term, who's quite amazing. I've never heard a child play the way he does, and it'll do you a power of good after what you've been through. Here he comes. Stick close to his heels and enjoy it!'

With a cheery wave of his hand, Gully headed off.

*'Things to do, people to see to! I'll find Rollo's bag for you,'* he projected as he disappeared round a corner, leaving Mossy to follow the boy into a small room with nothing in it but a piano, a stool and a chair.

He had a sinking feeling in the pit of his stomach as the boy seated himself on the stool and fiddled about with some knobs to adjust the height. But once the boy's fingers touched the keys Mossy understood what Gully had meant. It was like being in the studio with Annie when she was painting.

I suppose all great musicians started as children, he realised, letting the music float his aches and pains away, and build beautiful pictures in his mind that filled him with joy.

Refreshed and revitalised, Mossy left the room in the wake of the boy and headed back to find Rollo. He wandered the corridors, becoming ever more thoughtful.

He had so much to sort out. Jack needed settling, but it looked as if there might be something in the pipeline that would help with that for a while at least. Rollo, Cissy and JJ were fine for the moment, but he still needed to keep an eye on them. Annie was the one he was worried about. Heaving a sigh, he sank onto the floor and put his head in his hands.

'Can't be that bad!' Gully's cheerful voice broke into his thoughts. 'And I've found all their bags, so you can choose how you travel on the way back home.'

After much discussion, Mossy let himself be persuaded into travelling in Cissy's bag for the journey. At least that way he wouldn't have to battle with The Hole.

Gully marched him down the corridors to the girls' changing rooms.

'She's at sports at the moment, but she'll be back shortly. Get in now and you should be fine.'

'I don't know what I'd have done without your help,' Mossy admitted. 'Things are a bit hectic with us, but you've made a huge difference. Any time I can help you, just ask.' Gully put an arm round Mossy's shoulder.

'Any time, mate,' he grinned. 'And remember – no matter how good, no matter how bad, it soon passes in the longer story.'

Mossy had just settled himself into Cissy's bag, safely tucked into the old jersey, when he heard the doors bang open. A torrent of voices flooded the room.

'...never let's me get the ball!'

'... since Phoebe passed her...'

'Here, mind my fo...' Which one was Cissy?

'Anyone seen my skirt? I know I left it on my peg, and...' Mossy smiled quietly in the darkness. That sounded like her.

The bag was jostled and bumped as the girls changed, and then the chatter started to fade away.

'Hold on, wait for me!' he heard a voice call as footsteps hurried away from him, followed by a final bang from the door. Wait for me too, he wanted to call. Where was Cissy? Why hadn't she taken her bag with her?

As silence gathered again, Mossy's heart sank down to his

boots. What now? Where to next? He had to get home that night, even if it meant walking all the way. He couldn't leave the house and his Dwellers. Who knew what might happen if the Holder was missing too long? He was struggling free of the jersey and preparing to climb out when he heard the changing room door crash against the wall again. He froze.

'Hang on there!' It was Cissy's voice! 'I've just got to get my...' There was a sudden jolt as Cissy grabbed her bag and raced from the room. Mossy didn't really care how much he bumped and bounced as she swung it over her shoulder and chased after her friend. He was on his way again!

Another sudden swing was followed by a stomach-churning drop. Thank goodness for the protection of the jersey, thought Mossy. Light flooded in briefly as Cissy plunged a hand in beside him to grab a book. Then voices around them quietened as children concentrated on their work and Mossy relaxed into the safe darkness.

He was just beginning to feel that being a Holder in a school must be an easy way of living, when chaos erupted again. The bag shot upwards, banging down on a hard surface before more light washed over him. Cissy's hand rummaged about again, grabbed the remaining book and disappeared.

A voice mumbled something that Mossy couldn't catch.

'I think I've got it somewhere in here,' came Cissy's voice in reply. Mossy dug down into the jersey. Again he was swung upwards. Mossy grabbed a seam fiercely as he suddenly tipped upside down. Odd pencils, some scrumpled paper, the jersey and a rather well-chewed rubber collapsed onto the desk.

'I'm sure I saw it yesterday,' said Cissy as she gave the bag, and Mossy, a hearty shake. That was it. Mossy and a final, crumpled piece of paper cascaded onto the desk.

'How come that made a thump as it landed?' asked Cissy's neighbour. But Cissy wasn't paying attention. She pounced.

'Here it is!' she called, turning to the teacher at the front of the room and dropping her bag back on the floor.

'Cissy Breeze, you are a shambles. You need to get better organised. One more day and you'd have been too late to go on the trip.'

With Cissy occupied, Mossy tucked himself under the sleeve of the jersey and then peered over the edge of the table. Should he shin down and head for the bag, or stay put? All around them other children were gathering their possessions and heading for the door. But before he had the chance to move, Cissy was back.

'Dragon,' she muttered under her breath, as she bent down to scoop up her things. Mossy decided that his best chance was to hang onto the jersey and wait for her to put it back with all the other bits and pieces on her desk.

In went a pencil case, three books, the rubber and a writing pad. Cissy hung it onto the back of her chair and then stomped off to the wastepaper basket. Mossy's eyes widened in alarm. Surely she would add the jersey? Making the most of her absence he crawled into the sleeve instead of under it, and, with just his nose and the tips of his ears sticking out, watched for her return

'Hurry up!' The Dragon's voice rang out again. 'I'd like to go home too.' She and Cissy arrived together at the desk, where the girl slung her bag over one shoulder.

'*Your jersey!*' Mossy projected. '*Remember your jersey.*' But The Dragon got there first.

Mossy cringed as she pounced and shook it out. Gripping tightly to the cuff of the sleeve, he hung on for grim death as he swooshed through the air. I've had enough of being shaken, he thought, his teeth clenched. Briskly The Dragon folded the jersey in half and then half again, smoothing it down with one hand.

'What on earth have you got in here?'

'Nothing!' protested Cissy, pulling it from her. 'It's just a jersey. It's been there for ages.' She stuffed it into her bag. Mossy bit his lip to stop a squeal of pain as his head bashed against a book, his arm was folded behind his back and his nose was squashed to half its normal length.

'Are you sure?' The Dragon checked. 'I felt something…'

'Please, Mrs Tudor, Dad'll be waiting…' Cissy's plea hung in the air.

'Hmmph!' huffed the Tudor Dragon, but she must have relented. Mossy was almost relieved to feel the bumps as Cissy ran out of the class and then down the steps that led out of school.

The sound of the car's engine was like music to his ears. Secure in the knowledge that no one would pay attention anymore, Mossy wriggled into a comfortable position and breathed a sigh of relief.

Lulled by the children's chatter in response to Jack's enquiries, and wrapped in the soft wool, he began to relax. Police checks were simply part of a person wanting to help in a school. Maybe, at last, life could return to a more normal state.

When the engine stopped, he prepared himself for a final jolting journey. He would soon be home and safe. He felt movement around him.

'What's for tea, Dad?' JJ asked. Jack's voice was faint as he answered.

'Can I help cook?' asked Cissy. Mossy's brow furrowed as concern began to creep up on him once more. Cissy's voice was almost as faint as Jack's. A door slammed. And then another. Then silence.

Mossy couldn't believe it. Cissy had forgotten her bag! He was shut in the car again! He slumped back in despair, rubbed a hand across his face and sighed heavily. Slowly he pulled himself upright and placed his hands against the top. First step – get out of the bag.

Hang on though, what was that sound? Footsteps! Someone running across the gravel? He paused. A door clicked open.

'Oh, thank goodness!' Cissy sounded as relieved as he felt. 'I knew I couldn't have left it at school again!' Rollo's laughter rang out in the background.

Soon, standing on the hearth in the sitting room, Mossy could stretch out his hands and rub the familiar stones. He arched his back, grinned and ran one finger along the length of his nose, checking its full, fine length, while with the other hand he reached up to the tips of his ears. Yup! They were standing straight. Everything was back to normal.

## CHAPTER 16

# Decisions

A few weeks later the children were home for half term. It was great having them around all day, and Mossy feasted on the fun and games.

Annie left early in the morning, returning late in the evening. Rollo, Cissy and JJ made sure that they helped Jack have everything sorted out, so that she came home to a prepared supper and plenty of stories about what they had done during the day.

'Mum, you must see my new water supply that Dad made,' said Cissy, and then filled a bucket and dunked some radishes in the water. 'Here, try this.' As Annie munched her offering, Cissy poured the now muddy water on the rhubarb.

Rollo did his paper round before breakfast and then helped Cissy or joined JJ, adding to his hide. If they were busy, he dug out one of his books.

'Have you seen this, Dad? I reckon those are hazels in that bit of wood by the stream. I think it must have been a coppice in the past. It's the sort of thing they would have had,' Rollo explained, walking his father into the small piece of woodland by the stream.

Mossy remembered the coppice well. These days it was hardly recognisable, but he recalled when the wood was cut and used regularly. He was beginning to enjoy having this Place Reader living in his house.

'D'you think if we asked Will Earp he'd let us coppice it? It's only a tiny scrap of woodland, and he never goes there. We could use the wood to make things.'

'And then we could sell them and make pots of money!' beamed Cissy.

'We'll have to see what he says, but there's no harm in asking,' agreed Jack.

Mossy was delighted by all the activity. With everyone busy, there was no time for Jack to muse on his difficulties, and he was much more cheerful.

The Saturday before term restarted, the family gathered after supper. Mossy lounged along the mantelpiece above the fireplace. He was still chuckling at a joke of Cissy's and he felt relaxed. He was glad to be able to take things easily again, now that their problems were resolved.

'Dad and I need to talk with you about a last couple of changes,' Annie announced as she settled onto the sofa. Cissy snuggled up beside her.

'Don't say you've been made redundant too!' exclaimed Cissy, her face creasing into a frown.

'No, love, nothing like that,' laughed Jack. 'Your mother's too good at her work for that. Dirk thinks the world of her, doesn't he?' he added, giving Annie a broad smile. Now it was Annie's turn to frown.

'He certainly keeps me busy,' she said, shrugging her shoulders, a little uncomfortably Mossy thought.

'No. It's... It's things to do with school,' Jack rushed on. 'What with one thing and another...'

'Dad losing his job and his difficulty with getting another one,' added Annie. Mossy looked at Annie. There was a sharp edge to her voice that seemed to cut into Jack.

'Mum's right, it's my fault, and I'm sorry, but it means that we still have to cut back further. We've had long talks about this, and we've spoken with Jon and Sophie's parents too. We wanted to have a last discussion with you before we make a final decision.' Rollo's face creased into a smile.

'You mean that I'm going to be able to go to Jon's school, after all?'

'How come you're so keen?' asked Annie. 'Darden's is one of the best schools in the country. You worked so hard to get your scholarship.'

'I know Mum. But it means boarding, and I like coming home at the end of the day. I don't know anyone else who's going there. If I'm at Jon's school I can stay here with all of you. I know lots of people here now, and as for Darden's being one of the best – well – Sophie went to Jon's school and now she's going to Cambridge University. I couldn't wish to do better than that, could I?' He grinned at everybody. 'And I can carry on with my paper round,' he finished, as if that decided it.

Annie sighed.

'It's not what we wanted for you.'

'Maybe not, but I'd prefer it. Remember that play we

went to at Jon and Sophie's school last term? It was really good, wasn't it? And I'd be able to do things like that there, too.'

'And we could go too?' suggested Cissy, waving hands at herself and JJ. 'Two girls from my class are going next term. We've only been in this school for a bit, so we might as well change now as later. Most people start at the beginning of next term, and it would be so much better to be there from the beginning…'

'We weren't even thinking about you and JJ yet,' interrupted Annie, abruptly, her voice cracking sharply across the room.

'Sorry I asked.' Cissy apologised, shrinking away from her mother. Mossy frowned. What was up with Annie? JJ plunged a hand into his pocket.

'And I could go to the village school 'til I'm old enough. I could even walk there, you know,' JJ added, undaunted, and Mossy noticed his talisman glowing softly as he turned it over and over in the fingers of one hand.

'Aren't you happy where you are?' asked Jack.

'It's school, Dad.' Cissy shrugged her shoulders. 'It's OK as far as any school goes, but I'm with Rollo on this one. I'd rather go to school from home than be a boarder. So why not change schools now?'

'You never know, in a couple of years we might have got something sorted, and Dirk says…' She broke off. There was an uncomfortable silence.

'Dirk says…?' prompted Jack.

'Nothing.' Annie waved a hand as if to brush something away. What's Dirk got to do with it, anyway? wondered

Mossy. He's nothing to do with you. He's just Annie's boss.

'We'll keep thinking, but meanwhile, there's something else I wanted to mention,' added Jack, his voice brisk and cheery again. JJ stopped twiddling his talisman and stuffed it back into his pocket. 'And this is news for Mum, too.' And me? wondered Mossy.

'I've been talking to Mr Goodman.' JJ pulled a questioning face at Cissy and Rollo. Silently, Rollo shook his head and Cissy shrugged her shoulders. 'Not about you lot,' Jack reassured them. Cissy sat back. Ah ha! thought Mossy. I know where this is going. He decided to watch Annie instead.

'At the beginning of term, Mr Goodman sent a letter asking for parents who would like to volunteer to help with school trips. Do you remember?' Annie nodded her head.

'I asked if there was something more that I might be able to do,' Jack continued. 'He has suggested that I might like to help out in school in other ways too. How do you feel about me coming into school to be a class assistant sometimes?'

'In school. With us?' Cissy looked amazed. 'In what way?'

'A classroom assistant?' Annie looked at him blankly.

'That to begin with, but maybe all sorts of other jobs too.' Mossy's eyes flicked between the faces. So, he thought, the police checks must have been OK.

'Secretary?' asked Annie. Everybody laughed.

'Hardly!' laughed Jack. 'My secretarial skills aren't anywhere near good enough for that.'

'Nor your dragon skills,' added JJ. 'Mrs Bander is so cross if we come in late.'

'And all she has to do is tick our names off,' pointed out Cissy.

'Come in late?' Annie frowned at Jack.

'Only a couple of times when I first started taking them in,' explained Jack, 'and I've got the hang of it now.'

'So, not secretary,' said Annie, walking to the window, her arms tightly folded over her chest. 'What exactly?' she asked, turning to face them again.

Mossy looked at her anxiously. She seemed pinched, as if something hurt her, but the others didn't notice it.

'At the moment I'm not quite sure. Helping out in the classes mostly, I think.'

'Cool,' decided Rollo. 'You can give us the answers in advance.'

'Will you be able to help me with my maths?' added JJ. The children seemed excited by the prospect.

'I can't help you cheat,' Jack reminded them, 'but there might be times when I am in your class, and I wanted to check you wouldn't mind.'

'Why should we mind?' asked Cissy, giving Jack a hug. Mossy agreed with her. What could be wrong with it?

'So what do we call you?' wondered JJ. 'Mr Dad?'

'We can't call you Mr Breeze when everybody knows you're our dad,' agreed Cissy. 'That would be too weird.'

'You know Bob in my class?' asked Rollo. 'His mum is Mrs Warwick, and he just calls her 'Mum.'

'Poor guy,' Cissy was all sympathy. 'Having to call Mrs Warwick 'Mum'.'

'You won't turn horrid like Mrs Warwick, will you?' Now it was JJ's turn to look anxious.

'I'll still be Dad, just like now, and right now I'm Dad saying that it's time to head up for bed.'

As the children trudged up the stairs, Mossy swung off the edge of the mantelpiece, hung for a couple of seconds by his hands and then dropped lightly into a crouch on the hearth. As he rose to his feet and dusted off his hands, he noticed Annie turn from where she had been gazing out of the window to look at Jack.

'And what about pay?' she asked.

'No pay, I'm afraid. I'm there as a volunteer.'

'No pay?' Annie looked aghast. 'What do you mean? How can you take work with no pay, when we need every penny? Even Rollo's getting paid. We've all made sacrifices, some of them huge ones, and now even the children are talking about changing schools because we can't afford it. It's hitting them hard too, and yet you take work with no pay? You need a proper job.' Annie's voice was rising. Mossy looked from face to face. Could he calm this before it got out of hand?

'You said you couldn't stand me 'hanging around, doing nothing'. I thought this would please you. I'm going to be doing something. And if another job comes up, the kind you think is a 'proper job', I'll be able to change. Not that plenty of people don't think teaching is a proper job.'

'Oh Jack, you know what I mean – a job that earns something. How do we afford to stay here otherwise? We'll have to move, and then what will all these sacrifices have been for?' Mossy caught the sound of real anger.

'I'm doing my best,' Jack began. 'But if I can't get someth…'

'Mum? Dad?' JJ's voice called down the stairs, interrupting them. Oh thank goodness, thought Mossy. JJ stuck his head round the door. 'I can't find my pyjamas.'

'Remember the washing I did this morning?' asked Jack, his voice softening as he smiled at his youngest son. 'There are clean ones in the airing cupboard. I'll be up in a tick.' As JJ disappeared, Jack took a step towards Annie, but she turned her back on him, shrugging her shoulders, shutting him out, and stared out of the window. Jack stopped in his tracks.

'Oh, never mind,' Annie sounded as dismissive as she looked. 'I've got enough on my plate without worrying about that as well. You go on. I'll be up soon.' But she wouldn't turn to look at him.

This was so unlike her that Mossy decided that he had to investigate. Without making a sound he headed over to Annie's side, grabbed the edge of the curtain and swung himself onto the windowsill. With his back to the glass he looked up at her, carefully scrutinising her face.

He was surprised. Where he had expected anger he saw instead tiredness; tiredness and something else. And what was it that she was looking at so intently?

Turning his back to her, he too looked out of the window. There was the path that these Dwellers had trod so lightly when they first arrived, so happily, so light of heart. Beyond it lay the drive. To the left the old barn that now held cars, bikes, gardening tools and much more. Beyond... Of course! That was it! How could he have been so stupid? Mossy could have kicked himself.

Beyond it stood the old granary that Annie had turned

into her studio, abandoned since she had started to work full time away from home. Suddenly Mossy understood what else he had seen in Annie – it was sorrow. She was missing her painting, missing her creative days. No wonder she was so brittle.

Very softly he put his hand on her arm.

'*You will get there again,*' he silently reassured her. '*You will make your beautiful paintings again. We all love them, not just you, but Jack and the children too. And me.*'

Annie sighed, a great sigh from deep within her, and she brushed a weary hand over her eyes as if trying to rub the tiredness and sorrow away.

'Mu-um!' Cissy's voice drifted down from upstairs.

'Coming, darling,' Annie replied, tearing her eyes from the window and heading up to her family.

CHAPTER 17

# The Wrong Kind Of Food

Despite listening and watching carefully, Mossy never heard Annie and Jack return to that conversation. Somehow, though, the possibility of them leaving hung in the air. It made him feel nervous. He felt in his heart that this family belonged in Annanbourne and that he had to make everything all right again, make sure they stayed.

It was almost as if Annie and Jack couldn't bear to talk about it. In fact Mossy noticed a strange politeness between them that seemed very odd. What else where they not talking about? Listen as he might, he never heard Annie mention her work anymore, although her mind didn't seem to be on home life either.

Mossy perched himself on the stack of wood that Rollo and Jon had cut from the trees the farmer had said they could coppice. Helped by Jack, they had made three hurdles from some of the younger wood, and Jon had come round after school to give them a hand to weave some more.

'Can we use them to build a fence round the vegetable

garden?' Cissy asked. 'It'd help keep the rabbits out and stop them eating the spinach.'

'And if you made a little hurdle it could be a gate,' suggested JJ. 'But you'd need a gate post too,' he added. While Cissy admired their work, JJ headed towards the wood pile. Mossy jumped off it into the soft cushion of dead leaves from the previous autumn.

'Sounds like there's a mouse down there.' JJ ran round to investigate. Mossy froze. 'I can't see anything.' The boy gave up looking at the ground and turned to the heap of wood. 'This bit would do fine,' he finished, pointing to a particularly sturdy post.

'That would impress Mum, wouldn't it?' Cissy looked up at her dad. Had Cissy noticed Annie's detachment recently too? wondered Mossy.

'I hope so,' Jack replied, coming to join them. Hope so? thought Mossy. You know it would, don't you? I thought you knew all about her. Quietly he stole away, gently lifting an ivy vine as he nipped through a hole in the hedge. Hmm, how to get him on the right track?

A couple of days later Jack didn't return to the house after taking the children into school. Gone shopping, Mossy decided, and took the opportunity to check out some things.

He headed over to Annie's studio. At the side was a hole where some mice had made a private entrance, and the board above it was a little loose. Using a stone as a hammer he knocked at the board, slowly shifting it a bit higher. Two mice popped their heads out, and another came scurrying along the board above.

'Sorry about the noise,' Mossy apologised with a broad smile. The largest mouse sat back on his haunches and twitched his nose. 'I just need a look inside.' A short squeak above his head made him chuckle.

'Of course I'd rather use the door, but can you remember last time it was open?' The mice waited until he had raised the board up enough to make a space for him to squeeze through, and then jumped in front.

'OK, lead on,' he agreed.

It was almost completely dark, but there was enough of a glow for him to see the slender tail whisk through another crack ahead. Carefully he wriggled along behind, taking tiny breaths to keep as thin as possible, stretching his arms ahead.

The space widened, and he found himself between the outer and inner walls. Bright eyes twinkled at him briefly through the gloom before the mouse sprang round and scampered on again.

Mossy ducked after him and soon spotted light flooding in ahead. The mouse shot through, but Mossy paused.

'Skinny I might be,' he mused. 'But even I'm not thin enough to get through that.' Two little noses peeked back at him and then teeth got to work. In a matter of moments the hole was big enough. Mossy squeezed his way into the studio.

'Thank you. I'd never have managed on my own,' he said, as he dusted himself down.

They sat beside him as he looked around.

'Mmm.' he pondered. 'She really is very good, isn't she? These paintings are something special.' The mice ran across the open space, up one leg of an easel and on up the side of the half-finished painting, where the smaller mouse's tail hung down over the corner.

'You're right,' agreed Mossy. 'It needs to be completed.'

Before he could blink an eye the mice were back down again, hopping from the easel to the table and running across some tubes of paint. The older mouse was just about to sink its teeth into a corner of a tube when Mossy realised what they had in mind.

'No! No!' he called out. 'Not **you**! We've got to get **her** back in here. **She**'s the one who needs to finish it.' The mice stopped and turned to look at him, their noses twitching.

'I know. She hasn't been in for ages. I'll have to think of a way. Before I leave though, are there any other pictures in here? I'm sure I've seen her painting others, but I can't see them now.'

In no time the mice were down again, beckoning Mossy with their ears as they skittered across the room to the far corner. Following them, he spotted stacked canvases leaning against the wall. Gently easing one forward so that he could see the image, Mossy let out a sigh of delight. There it was! He remembered Annie working on that one; he'd stood at the back of her table and watched it gradually flow from her paintbrush. Next to it was another, another and a whole lot more of what he felt were his old friends. For a while all he could do was feast on them in delight.

His attention was caught by the sight of a small flake of white drifting down from a stack of sketch books on a bookshelf.

'What's that?' he asked, glancing up at the mouse balanced unsteadily on the top of a painting leant gently against its neighbour. The mouse glanced over its shoulder and gave a short squeak.

'You what!' exclaimed Mossy. 'You can't eat her drawings! Oh, for goodness' sake!' An eager little face popped out from behind the sketchpads.

'What are you thinking of? You aren't house mice! You're wood mice. Wood mice don't damage things.' A flurry of squeaks came flying back at him.

'I don't care if it **is** only the corners! Come out of there, and not another mouthful, d'you hear me?' Two very small mice crept out, their heads hanging in shame as one brushed a last remnant of paper from its whiskers.

Having checked all the paintings were intact, Mossy made the mice promise they wouldn't take another mouthful of anything inside the studio.

'I know your ancestors used to eat the grain in here, but this isn't grain, or even like grain,' he explained, scowling at them. The mice looked at each other. They could have told him that. 'These are precious, really precious. I think they might even be valuable.' He pointed out of the window. 'There's plenty of food outside. The meadow grass is in full seed, and if you stash some of that away now you'll have plenty to see you through the winter. You've got stacks of storage space between the outer and inner walls, as well as under the floor.' The oldest mouse looked over his shoulder.

'There isn't a cat any longer, hasn't been for years. Someone's been spinning you a yarn.'

By the time Mossy, now accompanied by six mice of various sizes, wriggled his way out of the studio again, he had managed to persuade them that they had an important new role. They had become Studio Guardians. Their job was to alert him if there was any risk to Annie's work during her absence, to warn him of any dampness or problem there. Although it was a separate building the old granary was still a part of his Holding, but because it had mainly been used for storage Mossy wasn't as tuned into its needs as he was to the house's. Having the mice on hand would help.

The sun shone warmly as he ambled back along the hedgerow, having left them busily occupied with collecting fresh grass shoots with juicy, new seed heads.

So, he mused, the paintings are safe, the drawings too, if a little gnawed at the some of the corners. All I have to do now is get Annie back in there with them. Jack should to be on hand to help too. Somehow he had to make him realise that Annie needed her painting in the way that most people needed fresh air; in the way that he needed their laughter and happiness – it was what he lived off.

Above him a wood pigeon cooed, her soft voice lulling him into pausing, enjoying the soft grass underfoot, the stillness in the air.

Hang on, Mossy's eyes widened in alarm; it was uncannily still. No sooner had the realisation entered his mind than he noticed that even the wood pigeon had fallen silent. Frantically he looked around him, his legs crouched, his arms spread wide. He was right out in the open! Too late he heard the swoosh of wind as the talons grabbed his shoulders, piercing his skin, and the ground disappeared beneath his feet.

'Put me down!' he yelled, kicking at the empty space beneath him. He reached an arm up and grabbed wildly for the yellow leg. His long fingers closed on emptiness as they lurched through the air.

'Put me down!' Were those black talons digging in a little less sharply? he wondered. He looked down. His house, the barns and garden lay far below him now.

'OK, you win,' he admitted. 'Just don't put me down from up here. Please,' he added as an afterthought. The barred wings beat firmly through the air as their flight calmed, and they tilted, swinging round, descending towards a telegraph pole.

The sparrowhawk landed lightly on the top, still holding Mossy firmly under one foot. She looked down at him with her sharp yellow eyes.

'Alright, message received loud and clear,' Mossy admitted, 'but not all mice are your lunch, and these ones have been particularly helpful. You know you can't eat me,' he added, through gritted teeth, as her other foot hung poised over him, 'so don't even think about trying to pluck me.' He glared back at the bird, his jaw set. The one thing you couldn't afford with a sparrowhawk was to look intimidated.

After a tense moment she flexed her legs, spread her short wings wide and, with a final shriek, leapt into the still air, abandoning Mossy rather precariously atop the pole.

He looked down. It was going to be a long descent, and a splintery one too. He looked across the fields towards Annanbourne and sighed. It would be an even longer walk back to the house. As he sorted out his arms and legs, straightened his nose and tweaked his ears, it crossed his mind that maybe he was losing his touch. He almost always spotted her arrival. After all, he was the one who usually put out the warning. If he'd missed seeing her coming, was there something else he'd missed? Something else as lethal as a sparrowhawk?

## CHAPTER 18

# Ups And Downs

After the long walk home, Mossy wasn't surprised to find that his Dwellers had returned before him. As he pushed his way through the final hedge into the garden he could hear Cissy's voice.

'Please Mum, please come and look. It's really good, what they've done.'

'Sweetheart, I'm tired today. Maybe tomorrow?'

'You're always saying that,' complained JJ.

'There'll be plenty of time tomorrow,' came Jack's voice, and as Mossy peered out from under the shelter of a low-hanging branch he was in time to see him put an arm round both Cissy and JJ's shoulders. He gave them a reassuring hug.

'Tomorrow's the weekend, and we've got two whole days of Mum at home. Let's show her what we've made for supper.'

Mossy was hungry after his trek and hoped that the suppertime chatter would give him a good meal too. As the children put the food on the table, he climbed onto the dresser and settled himself beside a big teapot.

'So much to tell you, Mum,' grinned Rollo.

'I've got good news too,' Annie smiled at them all. 'The big presentation I did worked well and all my ideas have been taken up. Dirk is really pleased and was saying something about some special new project with a huge client. I'll know more in a few weeks. But it might mean promotion.' Everybody was full of admiration and Mossy sat back to enjoy the feast. This is more like it, he thought.

By the time Annie had answered all their questions, making them laugh with her impressions of various different people during her meetings, it was time for the pudding.

'Wow! These strawberries are delicious, Cissy! You've really got the hang of the vegetable garden.'

'I helped pick them,' butted in JJ. 'And I hardly ate any!'

'So that's not a strawberry smudge on your T-shirt?'

'He did say hardly any,' pointed out Rollo.

'And you haven't seen the mark on the bottom of his trousers where he sat on one!' added Jack. By the time JJ sat back down again the walls of the room were warm with laughter. Mossy beamed; even better.

'But Dad hasn't told you his news yet!' announced JJ. Annie turned a glowing face towards Jack.

'Good news?' she echoed, looking interested.

'I had my first day in school.' Ah ha! thought Mossy, so that's where Jack had been all day. But Annie's face fell.

'Oh, I thought it was going to be news about a job, something like that.' Mossy caught the chill in her voice and glanced from one face to another to see if he was the only one. Only JJ seemed to feel it, and Mossy spotted the young boy reach across under the table to squeeze his father's hand.

'Dad came into school, and then all through the day we kept on seeing him about the place,' explained Cissy.

'He came in for Maths with us,' JJ told them.

'And French with us,' added Rollo.

'And I did some athletics with the year 7s. That kept me on my toes, I can tell you.'

'Doing what exactly?' asked Annie, drawn in by the children's enthusiasm. This time it was Jack's turn to make them all laugh.

'Oh Dad! I didn't know you taught Matt Pellow!'

'I didn't say it was Matt Pellow,' protested Jack.

'You don't have to when you make it sound just like him!' Mossy watched the glow in Jack's eyes as he talked about his day.

It was clear that he had really enjoyed himself in school. There was something new in him, as if someone had switched on a light deep inside. Interesting, thought Mossy, leaning forward, shifting away from the teapot and swinging his legs over the edge of the shelf. He's always been good with his children, but I've seen lots of Dads be like that – as many as the Dads who aren't. I wonder if this is something more? Like Rollo is a Place Reader, and JJ picks up on people's feelings, maybe...

The ring of the telephone broke across the chatter. Annie answered it as the others started to clear the table.

'I'll just call him,' she said, turning to Jack and holding out the phone. 'It's for you.' She paused. 'Mr Goodman.'

Cissy glanced from Rollo to JJ, but neither of them seemed to know why their headmaster might be wanting to speak to their father. 'Are we in trouble?' she asked. 'I didn't think I'd done anything wrong...'

'He didn't say it was trouble,' said Annie, as Jack took the phone and headed into the sitting room.

'Right you lot – washing up. Rollo, here's a drying-up towel. JJ, Cissy, you can put things away.'

Mossy made the most of everybody being distracted to swing down the shelves and onto the main worktop. He jumped nimbly out of the way to avoid JJ dumping a bowl on top of him and then had to skip backwards to escape knives Cissy was about to drop on his toes.

'And hundreds... thousands of people died.' Rollo was explaining something to his mother. 'Even in the country. And all because they didn't realise it was the rats. They just thought rats were, you know, one of those things.'

'Is it horrid dying of plague?' asked Cissy, looking intrigued. I'll say, thought Mossy with a shudder. We were lucky. We were far enough away.

'It might have been OK here,' Rollo almost seemed to echo him. 'It's far enough away from anyone else. But I bet the village had families that died. Anyway, that's what my project's on.'

'Fun,' commented JJ, looking rather glum.

'Gruesome,' added Cissy pulling a face, but looking delighted.

'Gruesome?' repeated Jack, returning. Mossy, standing on one foot on the handle of a cupboard and about to drop to the floor, froze as the room fell silent. Everybody wanted to hear what Jack said next. He grinned.

'All fine at school. All of you – and me too, it seems. Ian was just letting me know that everyone was really pleased with what I've done today and asked if I could come again in a couple of days.'

'Yay! Dad! That's good!' JJ gave his father a hug. 'I like you being in school.'

'Whoa.' Rollo raised an eyebrow at his Dad. 'It's 'Ian' now, is it?'

'Not for you, my boy,' laughed Jack, ruffling the boy's hair.

'Mr Dad rules!' Cissy joined in.

Mossy was sitting on the hearth, making plans, when Jack and Annie returned from saying goodnight to the children. He looked at their faces. The animation he saw in Jack made him even more aware of the taut tiredness in Annie. She needed to get back into her studio. That was the place where she could regain strength, through her wonderful paintings.

*'Come on Jack, you've got to get her painting again. Painting,'* he projected, as strongly as possible, carrying in his mind the vision of the half-finished painting he'd seen earlier on the easel.

'It's really good news,' Jack was saying.

'Hmm?' Annie didn't seem to understand.

'Your presentation going so well.'

'Thanks.' Annie smiled. 'I wish I could be so enthusiastic about you in school. But I just can't get over the fact that you're doing it for nothing. Of course they like it. They're getting it for free. Jack, if you were stacking shelves in the supermarket, at least it would be paid.'

'If only I could get you to see – to understand.' Jack

stopped, putting a hand on Annie's arm, trying to keep her attention. 'I'm with a whole bunch of people who really enjoy what they are doing. And the kids – they're brilliant. They really seem to want to find things out.' But Mossy could see that Annie wasn't listening.

'Dirk says there's a possibility that I might get taken on for that American deal I told you about.' Jack's hand dropped to his side.

'Well, that would be great for you, but...' he paused, took a breath, and then carried on. 'There's just one thing. When you first took this on, you said you were just going to do it to keep things going. That it'd stay low key. That you'd still be doing your painting, too. What happened to that?' That's the question to ask, agreed Mossy.

The room erupted.

'What happened to that?' Annie exploded, spinning to face Jack. Her hands clenched. 'I'll tell you what happened to that. **You** did.' She pointed an accusatory finger at him. Her voice sliced through the air like a knife.

'**You** losing your job, that whole mess of **you** getting it wrong, **you** doing nothing, and then **you** taking work that isn't paid.' Now the words flooded out of her. 'Paint? When? I don't have any option but to make this job work, and sometimes it's exhausting, and then at the weekends there are the children needing things done, all the things that **you** can't do.'

Jack was stunned. He looked as if the words cut right through him. Mossy put his head in his hands. This was all wrong; this wasn't what he had meant. How come he hadn't realised it was this bad?

But now that Annie had started she couldn't seem to stop. 'How can I paint? It isn't paid. I can't do something that isn't paid. That's what **you** do. Yes, I miss it. I miss it terribly. But it's a luxury. I've never sold any of my paintings. Can't you understand? One of us has to earn something and **you** aren't even trying. So don't you **dare** ask me about my painting!'

Suddenly her voice caught, and tears came pouring down her face. Mossy could feel the heartache. His ached too. Jack reached out towards her.

'Don't you come near me,' sobbed Annie, her voice low as she held her hands in front of her like a barricade. 'Just leave me alone.'

She stormed out of the room, leaving Mossy and Jack in shocked silence.

## CHAPTER 19

# Starting Over

It was as if a chill settled on the house, even in the heat of summer. The hurtful, angry words hung in the air, making Mossy shiver. He was puzzled too. Annie wasn't a hurtful person. This wasn't like her. It was as if someone else was talking.

The following morning, straight after breakfast, JJ hurried into the garden, returning with a bunch of flowers.

'For you, Mum.' Annie looked surprised.

'Why?'

'Because I love you, Mum, and you're special. And because I don't like it when you're sad and I want to make it better.'

'I'm not sad with you, my love,' Annie gave him a hug. 'Just tired. Sometimes work makes a person tired, you know.'

'Does it make you cross too?' Cissy was worried. Mossy found her in Rollo's room.

'They're doing it again, you know.'

'I heard it as well,' said Rollo. 'But Mum says it's because she's tired.'

'Why does being tired make her shout at Dad, though? He's not 'no good'. And he does lots of stuff.' Mossy nodded his head in agreement. That was what had him puzzled. What was making Annie think like this?

During the next weeks, Jack was more and more frequently in school. Mossy noticed that new lightness in him each time he came back, and listened happily as he and the children swapped stories.

'Mary said that she had you for Geography again,' said Cissy, as she walked up the path to the house.

'Yep.' Jack nodded his head. 'I was in their class for a lot of the morning. Mrs Arnold wasn't well, so I was covering her lessons. We had fun.'

'That's what Mary told me,' Cissy continued. 'She said Geography with you was brilliant.' Rollo joined them, swinging his bag over his shoulder. No wonder I nearly fell out of that, thought Mossy as he spotted a rubber bounce onto the path.

'Jim said he likes your lesson too,' he added. 'He says you're cool. That's not bad. Jim doesn't go a wow on school, but he said it was OK with you.'

'Good.' Jack looked pleased. 'I hadn't realised how much I'd like it, too. I'll miss it during the holidays.'

'Oh Dad, come on,' Rollo laughed. 'School's never that good! And anyway we've got lots to do during the holidays.'

On the days when Jack wasn't in school he was busy at home. Mossy came across him on the phone in his study.

'… no, I'm her agent.'

What's he talking about? he wondered, lingering by the door. Jack nodded his head and scribbled things down on a piece of paper. Mossy was too busy clambering up the front of the bookshelf to follow the rest of the conversation, but from there it was an easy jump over to the table to see what had been written.

'That's great, and I'll get back to you,' Jack finished off, standing up as he put the phone down. Mossy just had time to see the listed words – Dimensions, Media, Photographs, Dan Bartholemew – and an address, but there was no time to read it before Jack headed out of the door. Anxious not to be trapped inside anywhere yet again, he leapt from the table, landing with a distinct bang on the floor. Fortunately, Jack was in too much of a hurry to notice as Mossy chased after him.

This was more like the man that Mossy remembered when these Dwellers had first arrived. There was a purpose and energy in him these days that had been missing ever since he had lost his job. However, he was surprised to see Jack head into Annie's studio.

Peering cautiously round the door, he spotted Jack by the stacked paintings. Quietly he entered and, lurking in the shelter of the easel, watched with wide eyes as Jack began to leaf through the carefully stacked paintings. First he pulled one out, looked at it and then jotted something down on a piece of paper. Next he pulled out a tape measure, measured the picture, then added more notes. Dumping it on the ground, he carefully slotted the picture back into its place in the stack and proceeded to the next painting, starting the whole process again.

What are you up to? wondered Mossy, creeping up behind him to take a peek at this new list. *Still Life with eggs* – 25 x

38, *Smacam Down* – 45 x 70, *Misty sheep grazing* – 55 x 90, he read.

Mossy was still frowning in confusion when Jack stepped back, causing him to jump sideways to avoid being trodden on. Looking up, he paused, remembering when Annie had painted the picture now displayed. The frown disappeared, a smile taking its place as he gazed in admiration.

'You are brilliant, my Annie.' There was a note of pride in Jack's voice that Mossy entirely agreed with. It was as if light shone into the room. You are so right, he thought, nipping back to the safety of the easel as Jack picked the landscape up and headed towards the door.

Hang on, where are you taking that?

Jack was heading for the car. You can't take her paintings! Mossy wanted to call out. But there was nothing he could do.

Pausing briefly to wrap the picture carefully in a blanket on the back seat, Jack jumped into the car and headed off down the drive. Mossy stood flabbergasted. Surely Jack wouldn't steal Annie's paintings? He hadn't locked the house. He hadn't even shut the studio door. Seconds later the roar of the car returning down the drive broke into his thoughts. Maybe Jack had had a change of heart. The car swirled into the drive, crunching to a halt, and Mossy stared in amazement as Jack raced into the house. Hot in his wake, Mossy was just in time to catch a glimpse of him in his study, as he copied something out of the telephone directory before heading back to the car and driving off once and for all.

Mossy climbed onto the desk with a heavy heart. OK, so

Annie hadn't been into her studio for weeks – months even. But taking her work without mentioning it? She was bound to find out at some stage, and then what would happen? He almost wished Jack was back in the despondent state he had been in. At least then he hadn't done things that were just bound to make trouble.

The telephone directory lay open on the desk. Mossy stared gloomily at the lists of businesses on display:- Pet Shops, Pet Supplies, Petrol Stations, Pharmacies, Photocopiers, Photographers. Which one was it that Jack had been looking at? 'Is your copier giving you a headache?' he read.

'No,' he groaned, 'but you are, Jack. Just bring it back safely,' he pleaded.

A couple of anxious hours later Mossy was still pacing about the drive when he caught the sound of the car's engine again. Jack was home!

Lurking under the rose bush by the studio door, Mossy heaved a huge sigh of relief as Jack opened the boot and carefully carried the painting back into the room. He leaned against the door jamb to watch him slip it carefully back into place.

I know what you're doing, thought Mossy. You're checking no one will be able to see what you've been up to, that nothing is out of place. Suddenly he understood. You are keeping this secret from Annie. He shook his head as he gripped the edge of the wall. This doesn't look good at all, he decided.

As Jack left the studio he looked down at his watch. Time you went to fetch the children from school, Mossy agreed. But the thought cheered him too. He'd hang around. Maybe, during their news swap, Jack would tell the children what he was up to. Despite his ears almost waggling as they strained to catch every word, Mossy never heard any mention of paintings though.

Jack was in school with the children the following day, but the next time he was home alone he went back to the studio and carried on with his measuring and writing. Again he left everything looking as it had been when he first entered. He never touched the painting on the easel, and to any casual person there was nothing to show he had been there at all.

At the weekend, Rollo, Cissy, Jon and Jack packed picnics and set off on their bikes. JJ stayed at home with Annie.

'Mum?'

'Mmm...?' Annie was reading some papers she had brought home from work.

'Mum, can we do some painting?' She looked up at JJ and smiled. Mossy was perched in his usual spot on the dresser. Clever fellow, he thought.

'Right now?' Mossy and JJ both nodded their heads.

'Why not?' Annie got to her feet. 'This can wait, and I would love to feel a paintbrush in my hands again. All I seem to do these days is other people's work, nothing that comes from me. Let's see what we can conjure up, shall we?'

JJ, chattering non-stop, danced around as they went over to the studio with Mossy in their wake.

'So if I mix the right blue with the right red I can make black? Really?' JJ's eyes were alight with excitement. Mossy looked on in delight.

Annie worked magic with paint, but this boy worked his with people. Somehow he understood what they really wanted. And here he was about to achieve what no one else had managed – taking Annie into her studio again. As they opened the door, she took a deep breath.

'Smells good, doesn't it, Mum?'

'You're right. It is just the most perfect smell; a mixture of linseed oil and turpentine. Oh, how I've missed this.' Neither of them noticed a slight unevenness in the store of completed works.

In no time the two of them were immersed in their creations. Paint spread all around JJ as he mixed and splashed. There was a red streak across his hair and a green splodge over one cheek. Annie put a new canvas onto her easel and, glancing frequently over at her son, mixed her own colours on her palette.

Mossy watched, entranced. Slowly the image of a boy engrossed in his work appeared on the canvas. That's JJ's nose and the spark of his eye! thought Mossy. And there's the hint of a frown that he gets when he's really concentrating.

JJ looked up from his work.

'Mum, can we have lunch in here? I don't want to stop what I'm doing.'

'Fine with me,' said Annie. There was a light in her eye that Mossy hadn't seen in ages. The place simply buzzed with energy. My feast is already here, thought Mossy as he basked in it all. In no time they were back with big chunks of bread and cheese.

By the time the others arrived home, Annie was putting the finishing touches to her painting. Mossy felt there was something particularly special about this work. Somehow this was more than simply a painting of a boy. It showed how it felt to be that boy, and it carried all the love of the mother who had painted it too.

At the sound of the others' chatter JJ ran to the door.

'We're in here!' he called. 'Come and look at what we've done. I've painted everything that matters here.'

'Hey, JJ!' exclaimed Cissy as she burst into the room. 'That's brilliant! Those are my courgettes.'

'And that's your bottom sticking up when you're planting things.'

'And that's a fish in the stream.'

'And there's your hide, too,' added Rollo. 'And me on my bike.'

'Yup.' JJ stood back, proudly admiring his own work. 'It's everything, see? Mum and Dad as well.'

Jack stood silently behind Annie, looking over her shoulder at the picture on the easel. Mossy looked up at him. Ah, he thought, you can see it too.

'Annie.' He paused. 'That's...' There was real wonder in his voice. 'That's perfect.'

'I don't know about perfect,' said Annie with a shrug of her shoulders. 'It just seemed to flow out of the brush.' Now the others were clustered around them too.

'Cool, Mum. You've done JJ,' said Cissy.

'Looks just like him, too,' added Rollo.

'Wow.' Jon seemed to have run out of words. 'Are all your paintings as amazing as this?'

'Funny,' said Annie, turning to Jack. 'Dirk was telling me to concentrate on my work with him and to forget about my 'daubs' as he calls them. He says that I shouldn't waste my time.'

'Has he ever seen them?' asked Jack.

'No, but I was saying how much I missed it, and he said that a talent like mine should be channelled into productive work.' Mossy frowned and wriggled his nose. She keeps talking about Dirk, but what does he know?

'What does he know?' echoed Rollo.

'Multi-millionaire, head of a world-famous advertising company, looked up to by everyone in the profession…' Annie's words hung in the air.

'But if he's never seen these, then he still doesn't really know,' Jack pointed out.

'And he's not going to.' Suddenly there was a sharp edge to her voice again. 'I can't risk losing my job, and it's supper time now, anyway.' She flung her brush down onto the table and left the room.

## CHAPTER 20

# Wonderings

'Last two weeks of term!' sang JJ as he danced into the kitchen.

'And lots to get done before the holidays come.' Jack looked at the children sitting round the table.

'Like what?' asked Cissy.

'Never you mind,' laughed Jack. 'Grown-up stuff you needn't worry about.'

But Cissy did worry about it.

'What do you think they mean by 'grown-up stuff'?' she asked Rollo that night as they were brushing their teeth.

'Could be work, could be money, could be all sorts.' Rollo gave a shrug. Could be selling paintings, could be doing things behind each other's back instead of together, grumbled Mossy, propped against the bath taps.

'And why isn't she home yet?' Cissy was worrying at him like a dog at a bone, thought Mossy.

'She said she had to work late, remember?' Rollo wasn't going to be riled.

'What if they're getting divorced?' Cissy rinsed out her toothbrush, jammed it into the rack and turned on him.

'Who's getting a horse?' asked JJ, sticking his head round the door.

'A horse?' echoed Jack as he arrived to read JJ and Cissy bedtime stories. 'No chance of that, even if we had the space to keep one!'

Divorce?, thought Mossy, sighing heavily. He'd never had a divorce in his Dwelling. Puddle had, and he said all the anger and sadness wreaked havoc on him and the house, let alone on his Dwellers. His heart sank into his boots as he imagined the chaos he'd have to sort out, let alone all the aches and pains he'd suffer. If arguments could bring cracks to a house, what might divorce do?

He was so preoccupied in his thoughts that a spider, drifting down from the ceiling on a long thread, had landed by the plughole before he had time to warn it that baths were dangerous. Checking briefly that everyone was busy, he lifted it onto the rim of the bath, but Cissy caught the movement from the corner of her eye.

'Dad!' she called. 'Come quickly! An enormous spider has just jumped out of the bath.'

'Spiders don't jump,' Rollo tried to calm her.

'Yes, they do,' interrupted JJ. 'They jump. We've been doing them in school, and there are jumping ones that don't make webs. They just jump on their prey and gobble them up.'

'Dad! I don't want to be gobbled up!' shrieked Cissy. Mossy mouthed a silent apology to the spider, who had never jumped anywhere in its life. Instead it drew in its legs, rolling all its eyes at Mossy in horror, as Jack wrapped it in a towel before shaking it out of the window.

'When's Mum coming home?' asked JJ later, as Jack stood at the door after turning his light out.

'Any minute now.' Jack smiled at him. 'D'you want me to ask her to come up?'

'Mmm. I want to give her a kiss goodnight.'

Mossy hung about outside the children's rooms. He could feel the tension in Cissy's room leaking onto the landing. Despite Rollo's calm words, she was still fretful. Peeking into JJ's room, he could see the little boy lying in bed, his wide eyes glinting in the light that fell through the open doorway, his hand tucked under his pillow.

*'You hold onto that talisman. It'll keep you grounded,'* he projected. He caught the crunch of a car on the gravel outside.

'Mum's back!' called Cissy from her room, the tension seeping away. There was a break in the sound of Jack's tidying, followed by muffled voices and then footsteps on the stairs.

'I'm glad you're back,' said JJ, as he wrapped his arms around his mother, pulling her down into a hug. 'You'll always come home, won't you?'

'Of course I will.' She ruffled his hair. 'How could I miss my hugs from you?'

'Or from Dad and the others,' JJ reminded her.

'It was just a late meeting. Remember, Dad used to be late sometimes? You never worried then. No need to worry now either.' From JJ, Annie went to check on Cissy, where she turned out the light as she left the room.

'Sleep well, buggins.' Mossy was glad to see her spending time with each one. She lingered longer in Rollo's room. Their voices rose and fell gently through the conversation, and Mossy smiled broadly at the sound of Annie's light laugh. Rollo was good at keeping things even and relaxed.

But still he lingered, even after Annie had gone downstairs, leaving Rollo reading quietly in his room as the others settled down. He stationed himself on guard against any nightmares.

JJ soon drifted off, and Mossy sat quietly beside him, gently stroking the hair away from his eyes, easing deep, restful sleep over him. Tonight he was calm, the talisman doing its job. All was well there. It was Cissy's voice that broke the silence.

'Rollo?' A pause. 'Rollo, you awake still?'

'Yeah. I'm reading.'

'Rollo, you never said.'

'Never said what?' Rollo came and leant against the doorway to her room, his arms folded. Similarly propped against the top banister of the stairs, Mossy looked over at him.

'Whether you think they're going to get divorced.'

'It's like Mum said. Sometimes she has to stay late for meetings the way Dad used to. She was telling me about it. Some of the people she works with sound really dumb, and Dirk needs her to sort them out.'

'Yeah, but Dad wasn't cross at Mum when he came home, not the way she is with him. Whatever they say, it's different now, and I don't like it. I don't want things to go wrong.' Her words hung on the air.

Mossy knew what she meant. He didn't want it either. Rollo gazed around the landing, as if looking for an answer. Don't worry, thought Mossy, I'm here, and so long as you're here I'll look after you, no matter what.

'Cissy, feel the house. Feel how safe it is. Think of all the hundreds of years that it's been here, of all the good things it's seen happen inside its walls. I don't think it will let anything go wrong. Not that kind of wrong. It's never has here; you can feel it. That isn't going to change now.' Mossy smiled broadly. He couldn't have put it better himself.

During those last weeks of term Jack seemed to be in school almost every day. When he was at home, he rushed about making phone calls and scribbling things down on paper.

'Why is he hiding everything?' Mossy mused, dabbling his toes in the water as the duck paddled by. 'He never tells Annie or the children about any of this.' The youngest of the ducklings gave a loud squawk.

'But it **is** my business. They're my Dwellers, and I don't want any of them getting hurt, or upset. When things go wrong, I'm the one who feels it. It's alright for you,' he protested. 'You can just potter off down the stream without a care. I'm the one who carries the aches and pains. It's me and the house.' Under the water a trout swished by, blowing a trail of bubbles.

'Huh!' laughed Mossy, "Chill out!' That's all very well for a fish!'

Then a man arrived laden down with equipment – shiny

silver umbrellas, large black bags, snaking leads and folded metal spiders.

'Brilliant!' exclaimed Jack as he led him into the studio. 'Thank you so much for fitting it in so quickly, Dan. I want to get it all done before the holidays, so that we don't have to cope with awkward questions from the children.'

We? Awkward questions? thought Mossy. What you're really worried about is that the children will tell Annie what you're doing.

Keeping close on their heels, he nipped up the steps into the studio behind them.

'Wow!' exclaimed the visitor as he entered. 'That's amazing!' He was staring at the picture of JJ that was still standing on the easel.

'It's not dry yet,' explained Jack, as he headed over to the other paintings. But the visitor was entranced. He moved closer.

'*Don't you dare touch it,*' projected Mossy, his teeth gritted. The man stopped and inspected the painting closely. 'This is really good!' he said. 'It's more than just a picture. It's full of feelings too; love, concentration, what it is to be a boy. If they're all of this quality, I'm going to have a great time photographing them.'

Mossy breathed a sigh of relief. Photographs! That was fine. I'm sorry I thought you'd do something wrong behind Annie's back, he wanted to apologise. I should have known you wouldn't steal her work.

'The gallery need to see the photographs in order to be able to decide whether they'll take them or not.'

No! Mossy was aghast. His hands covered his face as he

sank in a heap to the floor by the book case. He hadn't been wrong! How could Jack be doing this? Just because they were short of money... How could he so calmly set about taking Annie's glory away from her? The tiniest of squeaks made him look down. A small pink nose and two dark eyes peeked out from between two books. Mossy stretched down a hand and stroked the light brown fur.

'Thanks for the company,' he sighed. 'I just don't know what to do.'

By the time Jack headed back to school, the two men had worked their way through over half the paintings. Jack lifted them onto the easel. The man waved things at them, shifted umbrellas, flashed lights which he'd attached to the unfolded spider legs and took photographs. Carefully Jack replaced each canvas exactly where it had come from. Mossy watched like a hawk, the mice on hand in case of emergencies.

'Not sure what we can actually do though,' Mossy had to admit.

Eventually the photographer loaded his lights, umbrellas and spiky stands back in the car, and the studio looked as if nothing had happened there. But the next day the two men returned and set about photographing the rest of the paintings. Mossy sat glumly on the steps at the studio door.

'I know you meant well,' he told the mice. 'But nibbling them isn't the answer. True, it would stop them being worth stealing, but Annie wants them as they are, not with holes in.' At the sound of footsteps behind them they all leapt for shelter in the rose bush by the door.

'I'll get the discs to you in a couple of days,' said the

photographer as he struggled down the steps with his equipment. 'I'd imagine the galleries will be fighting over the chance to sell them.'

'That's what I'm hoping. Annie had a bad experience when she first tried and has always stuck to commercial illustration since then. She hardly lets **us** see them, let alone a gallery. And it's not helped by her boss telling her she shouldn't be painting at all these days.'

'She's too good to waste,' agreed the photographer. 'Good luck.'

'Good luck, humph,' grumbled Mossy that evening as he sat on the chimney, the white owl perched beside him. Her soft reply surprised him.

'Just wait? Surely I ought to be doing something more than that? If he's stealing her…' She turned her head, her great golden eyes piercing through him. Mossy's shoulders slumped.

'OK. OK. I know I said I'd listen, but…' Again the soft hooting call rang through the twilight.

'Oh.' Mossy paused as her suggestion sank in. 'I hadn't thought of that. Maybe you're right.' Above them a star shot silently across the darkening sky. 'But if you're not?'

The owl lifted one foot and flexed her talons. She gazed out across the fields, then spread wide her wings and launched herself towards the last streak of red that glowed on the horizon.

'Mind you,' Mossy pondered. 'I can't remember a time when you have been wrong.'

## CHAPTER 21

# Expedition

When the summer holidays started, Jack lost interest in the studio. Mossy couldn't decide whether it was because everybody was around and he didn't dare do things they might see, or that the Barn Owl had been right all along and that it was just a matter of 'wait and see'. Meanwhile the children were constantly busy with one thing or another.

'We may not be having a going-away summer holiday, but we can still have fun,' Jack announced over breakfast. 'Who's up for a bike ride and a picnic?'

The children were keen, and Mossy had to leap out of the way to avoid being scooped up with the remnants of breakfast.

'Do you want to ask Jon if he'd like to come too?' Jack suggested, as he made sandwiches.

Mossy dug a long finger into the peanut butter, while his back was turned, and sucked it slowly. I don't need to go with them, he thought, and JJ is so much better at looking after himself these days… But I do like bike rides. While JJ filled water bottles and Rollo packed it all into backpacks for them to carry, Mossy snuck out to the pond.

'This will be so much easier to carry than the bag with all the newspapers,' he heard Rollo's voice through the open doorway.

'You're right. The change of scene would do me good,' Mossy told the moorhen as she peered up at him from behind a fine crop of watercress. She cocked her head on one side.

'Don't worry, we'll be on bikes,' he laughed. 'I can't get locked in those. I just need to get myself in position before they set off.'

By the time everyone was ready he was wedged firmly between the handlebars and the light-bracket at the front of Rollo's bicycle. He clamped his teeth down hard to stop them chattering as they bumped along the drive.

Don't shake me to pieces, he thought, grabbing the light as Rollo swerved round a pothole, swinging him first one way and then the other. Maybe this wasn't such a good idea. I hope I'm not going to be sick. Jon was waiting at the end of the drive.

'Up onto the downs first,' called Jack. 'Follow me!'

That's better, smiled Mossy, as the smooth road flashed by beneath them. With the wind in his hair and the sun shining down warmly he felt ready for anything. This is the life, he decided. You do the pedalling, and I'll sit back and take it easy. On the country lanes there were few cars, and they could easily hear any coming their way.

Rollo and Jon rode at the back of the pack, which gave him a perfect view of the others ahead. What could be better?

Pity Annie's not with us too, he thought. She likes bike rides.

Sometimes JJ dropped back to chat with them; at others it was Cissy who slowed down.

'Look!' she called, waving her left hand and pointing. 'Two magpies! That's lucky.' She wobbled towards the middle of the road.

'Try two hands on the handlebars. That'll help you to be lucky enough not to fall off,' Rollo reminded her.

At a meeting of roads a big oak tree made shade under its wide spreading branches. Jack had already stopped, his bike propped against an old letterbox.

'Who'd like a morning snack?' he asked.

'Me! Me!' called JJ, leaping off and letting go. Oh no! thought Mossy, preparing himself for a rather abrupt halt. Quick as a flash he unwound his arms from the light, ready to jump.

'*Stop slowly,*' he silently begged Rollo. '*Please!*' Rollo whirled round to the far side of the oak, swinging a leg over whilst still moving, and bumped onto the grass. Mossy was jolted from his seat, with one hand hanging onto the light-bracket but the other waving perilously close to the spinning spokes. He grabbed at the brake flex to stop himself from falling right off.

'Whoops!' laughed Rollo's cheery voice from somewhere above him. 'That was more of a bash than I expected.'

You're not the only one, thought Mossy, as he pulled himself upright again. Rollo left his bike beside Jack's, running to join the others, who were already sprawled in the grassy shade. Mossy checked himself for scrapes and scratches.

'Next stop we'll be at the top of the downs,' Jack told everybody. 'But we've got a very steep hill to cope with first.'

'No worries!' Cissy grinned broadly. 'We'll wait for you if you can't manage it.'

'Huh!' Jack's eyes flashed at her. 'We'll see who's waiting…'

Mossy stretched himself out in the sun, lying back with his hands behind his head as the others munched apples. Basking in the warmth, he feasted on their chatter, allowing their laughter and teasing to wash over him, easing away his aches and pains.

As they set off again, he was in high spirits. Jack was up at the front with Cissy and JJ close behind him.

'…so after that he said that I'd be able to do the red one,' Cissy's voice drifted back on the breeze.

'The red one already?' Jack sounded impressed.

'I'm only on blue.' JJ sounded envious.

'Your time will come,' Jack reassured him, glancing back over his shoulder. 'You're two years younger than her.'

'One and three-quarters,' JJ reminded him. As Jack dropped back briefly to ride beside his son the sound of laughter tickled Mossy's ears.

'You're doing your best. Nobody can do better than that.' JJ looked up and winked at his father.

Jon was riding beside Rollo.

'The auditions are right at the beginning of term,' he was telling Rollo. 'I'll show you where to sign up.'

'I glad I'm going to be in your school now, not going away any longer.' Mossy could hear the smile in Rollo's voice. Happiness flooded through him. He looked ahead to where

Jack led the way again. His back was straight, his head held high. Gone was the man who had looked so despairing a few months before. His time helping in school had given him a fresh lease of life. Delight in the day brought a song to Mossy's mind and he swung his feet in time to the silent melody, conducting an imaginary orchestra with his arms.

'Woah! There's something up with my bike!' exclaimed Rollo. 'It's got a wobble on the front wheel.' Mossy froze.

'Ah! That's better. Panic over.' Oops. Sorry, thought Mossy, and concentrated on keeping still again.

Slowly the road started to rise. Chatter ahead faded as more effort went into pedalling. There were fewer trees beside the road now, though the hedges were still thick, bustling with unseen life.

After another bend the lane became yet steeper. Mossy felt even more pleased that he was a passenger rather than the peddler. Now even Rollo and Jon had stopped talking. They passed a barn and the road levelled out.

'Well, that wasn't so hard,' Rollo called out to his father.

'You wait. We aren't there yet,' Jack's warning came back to them. 'That's where we're aiming for.' He pointed to where the mass of the grassy down still towered over them.

Around the next corner the road rose really sharply. Three-quarters of the way up the hill JJ ground to a halt.

'It's OK,' said Jack as he stopped beside him. 'I'll keep you company. You lot wait at the top,' he instructed the others.

'Race you,' said Jon.

'You're on,' agreed Rollo. Mossy could feel Rollo's grip on the handlebars tighten as he put even more effort into the pedals. They quickly slipped past Cissy. There was a rhythmic sound to the wheels now as the bikes powered on.

'I'm coming too,' Cissy's voice called from behind.

'*Come on Rollo, keep it up,*' encouraged Mossy as the two boys rode neck and neck. Rollo was panting. Jon's breath, too, came in short bursts. Mossy glanced over at him. His face was strained, every bit of effort going into the wheels. He didn't dare turn round to look at Rollo in case it unbalanced him.

'*Come on my Dweller,*' Mossy focused his strength into Rollo. Still the road curved steeply upwards, rising towards the blue sky. Nearly there, thought Mossy, as he rocked in time with the surges of the bike.

'*You can do it.*' Inch by tiny inch Rollo edged forward through the final curve. Suddenly the road flattened as it joined another.

'Phwoa!' called Rollo. 'Made it!'

'*Yes!*' Mossy clenched his fists in triumph. '*You did it!*' Rollo swung his leg over the saddle, cruising to a halt at the top of the lane, jumping from the bike as he let it collapse against the hedge.

The sudden, unexpected stop flung Mossy sideways into the air, cartwheeling over a bramble and landing with his arms about his head to protect himself from the prickles of the hawthorn. There was a loud squawk beneath him as a startled pheasant struggled out of the undergrowth, running off to the shelter of the ripe corn in the field.

'You beat me this time!' admitted Jon, still panting as he flung his bike down on the grass. 'But only by half a bike's length. I'll win next time.'

'You hope!' gasped Rollo.

By the time Mossy had extricated himself from the hedge, both boys were spread-eagled on the grass, recovering, so he was the one who spotted Cissy arriving, rather red-faced, as she cycled up the final slope.

'Made it!' she exclaimed, beaming with pleasure. 'Rode all the way!'

'Well done, you!' Jon propped himself up on one elbow. 'Sophie would never have managed without having to get off and push.'

'That's 'cos Cissy's my sister. Sister of the chap who beat you! Hey, don't! No! I take it all back,' yelped Rollo, as Jon landed on top of him, rolling him over in the grass and pummelling his shoulder.

By the time JJ and Jack arrived, Mossy was installed on Cissy's bike, ready for the final phase of the journey. Now it was the boys who led the way and Jack who brought up the rear.

'Bet you manage it next time,' Cissy said as she rode alongside JJ. 'I thought I was going to die, and Jon nearly killed Rollo for beating him. But I reckon Dad wanted to get off anyway; keeping you company was a good excuse.'

'D'you think Mum'll come next time?'

'We'll have to get Dad to do it again at a weekend, when Mum's here.'

'*Good idea*,' agreed Mossy.

'Is that the sea?' asked JJ, pointing at the shimmering horizon.

'Yup, and look the other way. See that dip in the far hills? That's where the road goes into the tunnel,' Jack explained.

'But that's miles and miles away! It takes hours in the car.'

Cissy was completely flabbergasted.

'We're on the highest part of the Downs here. That's why there's a beacon,' Rollo told her. 'Must have been cold up here, keeping watch in the pitch dark, knowing it was an enemy you were looking for.' Rollo shivered.

Mossy remembered previous Dwellers who had manned the beacon; something to do with a Narmada if he remembered rightly. 'Chilled to the core' was the way they'd described it. But the celebrations, when the safely-passed message led to a huge victory, had warmed them all again.

After the picnic, Mossy sat back and watched the others as they flung themselves about chasing a Frisbee. JJ could throw it huge distances, even if he couldn't always catch it. A lark dropped out of the sky, landing lightly on the saddle.

'Just thought I'd come out to see the world a bit,' Mossy explained in hushed tones. The bird dipped its head, hopped sideways and glanced over its shoulder.

'Goodness no! I wouldn't walk all that way. Caught a lift with them.'

'Look at that lark,' said Rollo, not seeing the Frisbee fly past his head. 'You'd almost think it was talking to someone.'

'Not your fault,' Mossy reassured the bird hastily. 'He's a Place Reader. Very little skips his attention. Almost spotted once, but not quite. I have to be careful. Wish me luck.' As the lark rose into the air, he let a song fall, a cascade of blessings sparkling about them.

'I'll stay here and look after the bikes,' said Jack as he flopped down beside Mossy. Go with them or stay here? wondered Mossy lazily. A bee hummed by. Well, if you think they'll be safe, I'll take your word for it, he decided, stretching out his toes so that a line of ants, marching briskly through the grass, had to clamber over him to keep to their route.

'Grass hide and seek!' announced JJ. 'I'm hiding first!'

Mossy lay back and watched the clouds drift by above him.

'...twenty-four thousand elephants, twenty-five thousand elephants. Coming!' The children's voices wafted in from somewhere over to his left. He caught the click of Jack opening his backpack and the scraping sound as he pulled something out of it.

Funny, he mused. I thought they'd all finished eating. But the rustle of a page turning told him it wasn't food. Ah, reading, he thought. I can't be bothered to read just now. There was more scrabbling behind him as Jack dug about for something else.

'Your turn, Cissy,' came Jon's voice, now somewhere beyond his toes.

Mossy's ears pricked up at the sound of a pen on paper. I've never seen you write in a book, thought Mossy. Quietly he flipped himself over and snaked through the grass until he was level with Jack's shoulder. He knelt up and peered at what lay before him. A magazine was spread open on the grass, bright pictures of landscapes, a photograph of a bronze horse straining at ropes. Jack had put a circle round the landscape. Slowly he turned to another page. Lots of writing this time, but instead of reading, Jack kept going until he came to more photographs. This time it was a picture of a woman sitting at a window. Once again he drew a circle round the picture and then underlined the writing beneath it.

Mossy edged closer. What did the writing say? It was too small for him to read from that distance. He was puzzled. He watched for a while as Jack continued until several pages had circled images on them with underlined sections.

Jack paused, looking down at a beautiful picture of a wild grassy landscape. Mossy could almost breathe the mist that seemed to swirl out of the page.

'That's it. That's the one,' Jack muttered under his breath. I've got to see what it says, Mossy decided, edging closer, until his nose was almost touching Jack's left ear. *Richard Glenville, Contemporary Fine Art, Bruton Street, London*, he read. A frown crossed his face. He had a sinking feeling that this was in some way connected to all those photographs of Annie's paintings.

Mossy was so preoccupied with his own thoughts that he didn't hear the sound of feet until they were nearly upon him.

'Hey there, Dad!' JJ landed beside them. Jack sprang into a sitting position, shoving the magazine behind him and knocking Mossy flying as he did so. By the time Mossy had disentangled himself from the dried campions in which he had landed, and had shaken their fine seeds out of his ears, Jack was standing up.

'Time to pack up, you lot!' he called. 'We've got another treat on the way back.'

Mossy looked around. Where was the magazine? Why had Jack hidden it? As the others came thundering over he hitched himself safely onto JJ's bike. Wait and see, his advisor had said. But if he waited too long, would he be too late?

# CHAPTER 22

# Brittle as Glass

Mossy spread his fingers wide, loving the sensation of air racing between them as they sped along the crest of the down. Far away and below, beyond the old windmill, beyond the distant town, the sea glittered, endlessly wide, always changing. Remember that, he told himself. Things change, but underneath life carries on, always adapting. If that is what is happening for my Dwellers, then I will just have to sail through it with them. I can only do my best.

'Turn right here!' called Jack's voice from behind. Mossy felt the incline of the bike change. 'And stop on the corner by the big barn!'

'Here we go!' called Rollo, as he and Jon gathered speed with Cissy close behind them.

'Way-hey!' JJ's voice sang out. 'This is better than coming up.' The thrum of tyres on tarmac sang a tune of its own as the wind beat against Mossy's chest and raked its fingers through his hair.

'Brake gently on the corner,' called Jack behind JJ's right

shoulder.

'*Back wheel only,*' added Mossy under his breath. Shadows flashed over them as they shot under the overhanging branches of a group of oaks, whirling down the helter-skelter lane. They rounded a corner to see the others, clustered together on the level part of the road beside the barn.

'That was so cool,' grinned JJ as he put a foot to the ground. Mossy squirmed round to look up at him. His eyes shone with excitement, and Mossy grinned too. He was so glad he'd come along.

'You're as good as any boy on a bike,' Jon said to Cissy. 'You just about kept up with us all the way!'

'Anything you can do...!' said Cissy proudly.

'So who's up for a cream tea?' asked Jack. 'We'll have to share, but...'

'Yum!' shouted JJ. 'Ace Dad!' Mossy decided to skip tea, preferring to wait out in the sunshine. He sat against the flint wall, letting the reflected warmth sink deep into him as the excited chatter of the others faded into the distance. Two rooks flew by, cawing loudly.

'Thanks,' he called back. 'I'll try to let them know.' It was good to rest, and the warmth made him sleepy. He remembered this place being built. What was his name? Bill Blackman? He'd built the house because...

He was jolted from his memories by the sound of Cissy's voice.

'But why Giant's Farm?'

'Haven't you seen the face?' asked Rollo.

'No. Where?' JJ looked about him.

'On the wall, muggins!' Jon chided him, waving a hand at

it. The children turned round to stare at the cottage beside the barn.

'Wow!' breathed JJ. 'It's huge, way bigger than me.' Mossy remembered when his Dwellers from that time had first seen the face. It had caused much discussion then, too.

'Well, you're not quite a giant yet!' laughed Cissy.

'But look,' said JJ. 'It's a sad giant.' Mossy looked over at the face. JJ was right, the stone eyes tipped down as if great stone tears were about to fall from them.

'Why d'you think they made it?' Cissy was intrigued. 'Was it for a giant? A real giant, and there was a man who fought him, and the giant died, and that's why he's sad?'

'I don't think so,' said Rollo. He paused, breathing in the place before answering her.

'Look how the house matches itself. The two sides are identical opposites. I think it was built as two cottages joined together. And the man who was building it...' Mossy could feel how the boy reached into the past. 'I reckon he found that big flint first, the one that makes the nose.'

'Stonking nose,' put in Jon.

'And that gave him the idea. See how the mouth smiles? I think when he started building, everything was fine and he felt positive, and then... then something went wrong.'

Mossy stared wide-eyed. This was the first time he'd ever seen a real Place Reader in action. No doubts about Rollo anymore.

'What went wrong?' asked Cissy, her face full of concern.

'I think the chap building it was making a home for himself, and for someone else – his parents, or maybe his brother? He and his family one side and the others in the other half.' Rollo stared at the house intently. 'And before he had finished the face, someone got hurt.'

'What, killed?' Cissy was hanging on his every word. Did he really know? wondered Mossy. He remembered the night of the accident so well.

Again Rollo paused.

'Not killed,' he said slowly. 'Hurt.' Too right, thought Mossy. Bill had always limped afterwards, and his right arm had hung useless at his side, but Beth had stood by him; they had married, and raised five children. The whole community had gathered together to complete the house. And his brother had lived in the other half with his own family so they could help with the farm.

'Come off it.' Jon's voice broke through the stillness. 'You don't really know, you're just making it up.' Oh, yes he does, thought Mossy. This is a first class Place Reader I've got here. He grinned with pride. Rollo laughed.

'You're right,' he agreed. 'I don't **know** for sure; it's just… a feeling I get sometimes.'

'But he's almost always right,' added JJ in his brother's defence.

'You should hear him when we go to visit places with guides. He tells us things that even surprise them,' Cissy pointed out. Now Rollo was blushing.

'Like you're going to be a mad scientist,' he told Jon, 'I'm going to be a crazy historian.'

Everyone was busy creating future lives for themselves by the time Jack came round the corner to join them.

'Sorry to keep you waiting, chaps!' he said as he climbed on his bike. 'Who wants to lead the way?'

Mossy scrambled onto the back of Jack's bike. He had been so caught up in the conversation that he had completely forgotten the rooks' advice. He had to warn them, but first he had to get into position. Balanced unsteadily on the rear mudguard he reached for the straps of the backpack and hauled himself up to Jack's shoulder.

Jack reached back with his right hand and shifted the strap that Mossy was clinging to.

'You OK, Dad?' Rollo checked.

'Yup; must have twisted a strap, it tweaked my shoulder. All fine now.' Fine for you, thought Mossy, squatting uneasily on the top of the pack and hanging onto Jack's helmet.

As Rollo, Cissy and Jon set off, he focussed on Jack.

'*Harvesting tractors,*' he projected. '*Warn them.*' Jack was still waiting for JJ to sort out his bike.

'*Tractors on the road.*' Mossy brought the picture vividly to mind, sending it through as strongly as possible.

'Ready, Dad?' checked JJ.

'Harvest time,' muttered Jack. 'I'd forgotten that it's harvest time. And I've let the others go ahead. There could be tractors on the road. Come on JJ, we've got to catch up with them.'

Message delivered, thought Mossy, but am I in time? His foot slipped on the smooth fabric of the backpack, and he found himself flattened against it, clinging on with both hands, his legs being shaken from side to side as Jack pedalled frantically to catch up.

Ahead the others were beginning the race down the next slope.

'Slow down!' Jack shouted, but they couldn't hear him.

'*Come on,*' urged Mossy. Jack didn't need any encouragement. Standing on the pedals, he put every scrap of energy into forcing the bike faster and faster. Hold on, Mossy told himself as he was flung about with each surge. His fingers ached from gripping so tightly.

As the slope increased, so did their speed. Mossy peered over Jack's shoulder. They were gaining, but there was a corner ahead. Glancing back, he saw JJ doing his best to keep up but slipping further and further behind. At least he's safe, he thought.

Gripping with his knees, Mossy pushed himself forward as they swung into the corner. Oh no! There was the tractor, huge, in the middle of the road. Where were the children? Desperately his eyes searched the lane. Rollo was on the left, his bike lying on the grass. Jon, his bike abandoned on the other verge, was running to join him. Jack slewed across the road as he braked to a sudden halt, leaping from his bike. As Mossy flew through the air he heard Jack's voice echo his own thought.

'Where's Cissy?'

Mossy struggled to his feet, checked that he was all still in one piece, and saw the driver of the tractor climb down from his cab.

'She alright?' he was calling out to Jack. 'They were in the road, coming so fast, she swerved...'

'Cissy! Cissy!' Jon and Jack were both crouched down in the dry ditch beside the lane. Mossy could feel a sharp pain in his ankle and knee. Serve him right, it was his fault for not warning them in time. JJ arrived, flinging his bike to the ground beside his father's and rushing over to Rollo.

'Is she OK? She hasn't done a me, has she?'

'I'm not that daft!' protested Cissy, her voice rising weakly from the hollow. Mossy almost laughed aloud with relief.

'I should have been in front,' said Jack as he scooped her up in his arms, hugging her to him, looking over at Rollo. 'I should have thought. I'm so sorry.' Jon looked at Cissy, his hand reaching out to touch her shoulder.

'I'm sorry, Cissy, it's my fault. I should never have suggested the race.' Cissy looked up at him.

'I just wanted to show you that I could beat you too. That'll teach me.'

'Dad, it's OK,' said Rollo, putting a hand on his father's arm. 'She's OK, we're all OK.' He looked over at the tractor driver. 'We shouldn't have been in the middle of the road.'

Lying Cissy gently on the grassy verge, Jack checked her over.

'Wriggle your fingers. Now your toes.'

'My ankle really hurts,' said Cissy, a slight catch in her voice. I know, thought Mossy, I can feel it too.

'*Check her knee,*' he advised.

'Let's have a look at that,' said Jack, pushing up her trouser leg.

'Ow! Ow! My knee too!' exclaimed Cissy.

'Blood on her knee,' JJ pointed out.

'Oh no!' moaned Cissy as she looked at the wound. 'I'm going to have a wooden leg.' Her face brightened. 'We'll have to get a parrot!' Mossy laughed with relief.

Mrs Blackman, from Giant's Farm, looked after Cissy, wrapping her ankle in a bag of frozen peas and cleaning up the blood.

'I think that might need stitches,' she said of the gash on her knee. 'You stay here and rest while your Dad fetches the car.' Mossy stayed too, deciding that the others would be fine without him.

'It's my fault,' he told Jigger, the Holder of Giant's Farm. 'And I'd better look after her. Serve me right if I have to walk home.'

'We can all make mistakes,' Jigger reassured him. 'After all, the first thing I ever did was let an accident happen.'

'You weren't even properly finished. We can all get things wrong at that stage,' Mossy reminded him. 'I should know better, I've had centuries of practice.'

He needn't have worried, however. When Jack returned with the car he brought Rollo and JJ with him.

'I'm coming with you to the hospital, 'cos Dad says I know my way round it at least as well as he does,' announced JJ proudly.

'And I'll take your bike back for you,' said Rollo. Mossy's ears perked up. I can ride home with you, he thought with relief. His left leg was very sore, and it would have been a long limp back.

'Be very careful on the ride back. And then go straight round to the Raitata's until Mum gets home. We'll fetch you if we're back first.'

They weren't. Annie arrived home at her normal time, discovered Rollo's note and went to find him. Mossy could hear her quizzing him as they came into the kitchen.

'But why wasn't Dad in front?'

'There'd been no cars, tractors or anything on the way, all day.'

'But the harvest is in full swing and he knows…'

'We were having such fun, Mum, and I guess we didn't think…'

'You didn't think…?  **He** should have been thinking.' Mossy looked at Annie.  Her voice was still calm, but it was the kind of calm you saw in the sky just before a major storm blew up, the kind that was full of thunder and lightning.

'Mum, don't be too cross.  We're fine, we're all OK.'

'Rollo,' she said, turning to look at him, her voice low and quiet.  'That's not true, Cissy's in hospital having her leg stitched.  She's not fine.'  Mossy drew a deep breath and let out a long sigh.  This was going to be bad.

'Look, Mum, huge bandages!' Cissy was delighted with her repair as she limped through the door.

'She was dead brave,' said JJ.  'Not a squeak when they stuck the needle in!'

'But no parrot,' lamented Cissy.  Mossy watched closely, his eyes darting between their faces.  Although nothing was being said he could still feel that storm brewing.  It didn't come to a head until the children were safely in bed.

'How could you!' Annie spun round to face Jack.  'You can't even look after the children properly.  What were you thinking of?'  Mossy, too, was looking at Jack.  He looked distraught.  But before he could answer, Annie flashed on. 'And cream teas?  You waste money on cream teas; money we haven't got to waste.  I'm earning that money, don't you dare waste it.'

And then the storm broke.  Her voice rose.

'You're useless. No job. No trying to get a job. Any work you do do, you don't bother to get paid for. Being a lollipop man at a road crossing would be more use than that. And you can't even keep the children safe. What is the point of you? I'm working so hard. I've given up time with the children, as well as the one other thing I care about, to keep the family going, and you just swan about, letting them get hurt.' Tears streamed down her face, her voice broke into a sob. 'She could have been killed.' Mossy caught a sound outside the room and crept through the door.

JJ stood on the staircase, his face as white as a sheet, with Rollo beside him, bending down to put an arm round his young brother.

'Come on JJ, come back up to bed.' His voice was low and gentle. That's right, thought Mossy.

*'Take him away from this.'* He followed them up the stairs.

'But Dad **was** looking after us,' protested JJ. 'We had a great day. I loved it.'

'I know, and we swerved out of the way ages before the tractor. It was the gravel that made us skid. Mum just won't listen. I tried to explain, but she didn't want to hear me. It's something about her work. It makes her so tired that she doesn't think straight any longer.'

'Rollo? JJ?' Cissy's voice called through her open door. The two boys went to join her, sitting on her bed. Mossy hovered in the doorway. Below them they could still hear Annie and Jack's raised voices.

'Is it our fault? I thought Mum would be OK when she saw I was fine,' said Cissy. 'It's sore, but you've done things much worse than this, JJ.'

'Yeah, and that was when Mum was looking after us, and Dad didn't shout at her.'

Tears spilled over, running down JJ's cheeks.

'Come on; it'll get better,' Cissy tried to reassure him. But Mossy could see that even her lip was wobbling now. 'Come and have a hug.' She put her arms round him, wrapping him in her duvet as he snuggled down.

Mossy stayed by them as they talked on, sitting close at hand until JJ's tears had dried and the two younger ones had fallen asleep. Quietly Rollo tiptoed back to his own room, Mossy in his wake. Silence had fallen over the rest of the house too.

As Rollo climbed into his bed and pulled the duvet over himself he looked over to where Mossy stood, carefully shrouded in the deepest shadow. His voice was barely above a whisper when he spoke.

'I can't see you, and I don't know who you are, but I'm sure you're there and that you are looking after us. Please keep it up, 'cos we really need you now.' There was a pause.

'All of us,' added Rollo.

Was it time? Mossy wondered. He shook his head. Not yet.

'*Don't you worry,*' he projected, knowing that Rollo would catch it. '*I'm here, and I'll never stop looking after you. Every single one of you.*' Rollo sighed, pushed the pillow down under his head and slipped into exhausted sleep.

Mossy stayed, guarding his sleeping Dwellers, pondering. What was it Rollo had said earlier? He sighed.

Something about Annie, and work. '…think straight …' That was it. Hmm, I wonder, he said to himself, tugging gently on his right ear.

## CHAPTER 23

# Secrets

By the time the sun rose, Mossy felt as stiff as a plank. He stretched his arms and wriggled his fingers to ease them. He spread his toes out wide. Pride comes before a fall. Maybe that was where he'd gone wrong. Had he been too proud of looking after his Dwellers well? He knew there were Holders who couldn't be bothered, and it just served them right if they tied themselves in knots. But maybe it was simply time to admit that not everything was under his control.

And yet he'd felt so sure about this family. They had done Annanbourne so much good. More than that, something deep inside him knew it was really important that they stay, that it truly mattered to the place. He shook his head. How could that be?

But here I am, he sighed, stiff and creaky, with the children sad and the parents fighting. I need to get rid of these aches and pains, concentrate on here and now. He wandered down to the pond and dabbled his feet in the cool water.

Mist shrouded the field beyond the stream, sheep

appearing to float through a grey mantle that swept out from the base of the trees. Above them a clear blue sky promised a fine day to come. On the far side the heron looked over at him, shrugged its shoulders and stepped daintily away from the water's edge. Mossy waved in greeting.

'If you were trying to find the source of a problem,' he asked, 'where would you look?' The heron dipped her head and looked down her long beak at him.

'Apart from me. I just don't like you eating my friends, so you can hardly blame me for warning them.' The heron stretched out her neck and lifted one long leg, elegantly balanced on the other. She shook her head.

'Thank you for saying that. But if the trouble isn't here, where is it?' She stretched her huge wings and leapt into the air, circling the pond, her heavy wing beats lifting her slowly towards the rising sun.

'Elsewhere?' muttered Mossy. 'What did you mean by elsewhere?' But she was already far over the fields, heading towards the fishing lake.

Mossy sat on, watching the trout emerge from under the lily pads to blow a line of bubbles at him. He shrugged his shoulders.

'You're welcome. At least you know when to stay put. So where d'**you** reckon I should be looking?' The trout scooped up some of the mud and gravel from the bed of the stream, spitting it out again in a dark cloud.

'Outsiders?' Mossy was puzzled. 'What outsiders?' But a flick of his tail had taken the trout upstream.

A light quack broke across his thoughts.

'Out without your Mum these days?' he laughed in

surprise. The youngest duckling uptailed, waving his feet in the air. Mossy flicked water at him as he righted himself.

'You were only an egg a few months ago, and already you think you can dish out advice.' The second youngest duckling swam up behind him, waggling her tail and waving some pond weed at him.

'You too? So what about Jack?' Now the quacks rang out like laughter. The moorhen popped her head up out of the far watercress to see what all the fuss was about.

'You're sure about that – he's on her side?' Mossy sighed, shaking his head. 'What am I doing? Listening to ducklings!'

Shy eyes peered round the hawthorn. Mossy smiled.

'No, of course I don't mind, so long as you don't eat the flowers or the vegetables. That would upset Cissy.' The deer stepped forward, quietly cropping the grass by the bank. She lifted her head and looked at him from under her eyelashes.

'So you agree too. It's to do with…'

A banging door sent the deer springing out of sight behind the bushes and the ducklings scurrying off in search of their mother.

'See you later, Mum!' It was Rollo heading off to his paper round. Time had flown by and the sun had already burnt off the early mist, but everyone seemed to agree and he was beginning to think they might have a point.

Slower footsteps crunched across the gravel. Mossy turned to watch as Annie got into her car. Jack stood by the door, his hand lifted in a farewell wave, but she wasn't looking.

For a while life moved at a gentler pace. Cissy was bright

and cheerful, although she still limped if she walked any distance. Mossy remained aware of her soreness because his knee still hurt, but it didn't seem to stop her. Gradually the pain faded, and by the time they returned to the hospital for the stitches to come out, he'd nearly forgotten about it.

Cissy was thrilled with her scar when she came home.

'Look, Mum, it's really neat!' she exclaimed as she pulled up her trousers to show her mother. 'And now I don't limp at all!'

It's good the way humans mend, thought Mossy. I wish houses just grew better, but once they've been hurt they take rather more work to put right. The arguments were taking their toll, and he had noticed a place where the some of the flints were working loose. He had a rash on his elbow too.

A couple of days later, as they were finishing breakfast, Mossy was in his usual perch on the dresser.

'Remember that Sean is arriving at about ten thirty, JJ. And Sally's mum said she'd be here at eleven, Cissy,' said Jack as he put some fruit on the table.

'I'm going round to Jon's after lunch,' said Rollo. 'Sophie's got a recipe we want to try out.'

'Cooking?' Jack was busy at the sink, scrubbing a saucepan, and not really asking seriously, thought Mossy.

'Er… sort of.' Mossy caught a wink between Rollo and the others, as Rollo held a finger to his lips. Cissy waved her hands in huge arching circles through the air.

'That's nice,' said Jack, as he propped the saucepan to dry. JJ clapped both hands over his mouth, his eyes sparkling in delight. He's shutting in a laugh, thought Mossy. What are they up to?

'What time will you be back, Cissy?'

'Oh! Um, teatime, I think. Sally's Mum's just taking us shopping.' She was busy mouthing something at Rollo. Mossy watched like a hawk. What was that? 'Way, ill, time, back'? She was waving her hands about again and pointing at herself. As Rollo nodded his head, Jack turned round from the washing-up.

'You alright, Cissy?'

'Oh! Yup! Erm, I was... erm... just being a ... a... windmill,' she finished in a rush.

You're a lousy liar, Mossy decided. It's a good thing you don't do it often. And you may be waving your arms round like a windmill now, but before it was more like... What was it like? he wondered. I'd better keep my eyes peeled at teatime.

Long before that, however, he spotted something going on. Cissy had left with Sally and her mother; JJ was busy in his hide with Sean, and Rollo had gone over to Jon's house. Seeing Jack head into his study, he followed and watched from a stack of papers and books next to the computer. Jack reached towards him, and Mossy ducked out of the way. As he righted himself, he read the title of the magazine Jack was holding. I remember that one, he thought. He had it on the bike ride.

Jack turned to one of the marked pages and, once the computer screen had whirred into action, typed briskly on the keyboard. *Clover Street Gallery*, Mossy read on the screen as a variety of images flashed up. Some of them were clearly paintings, others looked like sculptures, and there were yet more that seemed to be strange splashes of colour, without form, but nevertheless rather pleasing to look at. Mossy scrutinised each one carefully, stepping back in order to see better.

Then Jack grabbed the phone, punched in some numbers and waited. Mossy couldn't make out what the voice at the other end said, although hearing Jack was easy. The problem was understanding him.

'I'm Annie Breeze's agent, and I was wondering if I could talk to someone about submissions.' What's an agent? And what are submissions?

'Email them to you? Not a problem.' There was another pause as the voice the other end rattled on.

'Separate attachments, with details, that's fine.' Jack put the phone down, scribbled some notes on a sheet and turned to another of his marked pages.

A series of similar conversations left Jack with several pages of notes. He looked at them and then drew a big star at the top of one.

'That's still the one I want for my Annie,' he said under his breath. Mossy frowned, folded his arms and moved to a more comfortable position, on top of a pile of books.

Jack was busy with the computer again. A new set of images flashed up on the screen. Annie's pictures. These must be the photographs that Dan had taken. Mossy liked them. They were clear and strong. They really caught the feel of the paintings. Then Jack was writing letters, flipping the screen between the writing and the pictures. For the first time Mossy wished he understood more about computers.

'Dad!' JJ's voice floated in through the open window. Jack grabbed the magazine in one hand and the books with the other. For a brief moment Mossy thought he'd be alright, but there was no way he could hang on without grabbing at Jack's thumb in the process. As he slid to one side he glanced behind him and hoped that he was destined for the wastepaper basket rather than the sharp desk corner. He struck lucky; crumpled paper cushioned his fall.

'In here!' called Jack.

'What's in the bin?' JJ asked his father as he and Sean came through the door.

'I thought something fell into it,' replied Jack, 'but I must have been mistaken.' Mossy hardly dared to breathe, let alone shift his head from where it was wedged between a small box and an old ink cartridge. He hoped his knee would still be working properly when he did get out.

'Can we have a bit of rope?'

'It depends what for,' said Jack. Mossy heard the sound of the chair scraping back.

'You know in my hide, where we've built the ...' The voices faded as footsteps left the room.

Once Mossy was quite sure he was alone, he wriggled into an upright position, pulled a small plastic envelope off his left ear and brushed some pencil sharpenings out of his hair. Hooking a leg over the top of the bin, he levered himself out, straightened his clothes and glanced up at the screen.

'*...writing in response to your job vacancy in the accounts department...*' He remembered that letter. It was one of the dozens that Jack had written when he had first lost his job. Why was that up on the screen? What had happened to the letter he had been writing before? And where had the photographs of Annie's paintings gone? Mossy climbed back onto the desk, where the corner of the magazine still poked out from beneath the book heap. He shook his head. It looked as if Jack was still hiding things. Mossy decided he'd better hang about. Searching round the room he chose a safer lookout position and climbed up the bookshelf. He settled down to wait.

It was sometime later that Jack eventually reappeared.

'Now then…' he muttered under his breath, as he seated himself at the desk. Mossy watched as his hands rattled over the keyboard. The old letter vanished, to be replaced by the one he'd been working on before the two boys had burst upon them. I was right, thought Mossy, he was hiding that, too!

This time it was the sound of a car crunching down the drive that disturbed them. At the flick of a button the old letter bounced back to cover up Jack's writing. It was like watching Annie drape an old sheet over her paintings to protect them when she had to stop before they were completed.

Odd words of Cissy's excited chatter drifted in through the open door, and Mossy caught hints of pizzas and bungees, as well as smatterings of 'bright pink' and 'really shiny blue'. Another car rattled to a stop, and Cissy and Sally were dispatched to find Sean and JJ. By the time all the rightful occupants were installed in the appropriate cars Mossy was beginning to wonder if Jack would bother to come back to his study that day.

'Is Rollo back?' asked Cissy. 'Only they said to come over if we were free around teatime.'

'Oh yes,' said Jack. 'They've been cooking, haven't they?'

'Well… he… um…' came JJ's voice. Mossy craned his head round the corner of the bookshelf. Although he could see the back of Jack's head, he couldn't see either of the children.

'They've been making something,' said Cissy, 'and… we wanted to see.' Suddenly Mossy remembered all the windmilling over breakfast. Should he be checking what they were up to, or should he finish seeing what Jack was doing? The decision was made for him.

'Make sure you're back by suppertime. It's Friday, and I want us to start the weekend well for Mum.'

'No problem!' said Cissy. 'C'mon, JJ.'

'See you soon!' Mossy heard their feet running down the drive.

They'll be fine there, Mossy told himself, remembering talk of Sophie's recipe. Cissy's always waving her arms about. Pushing thoughts of the children to the back of his mind, he focused instead on what was going on in front of him.

'Right. Time to get this finished,' muttered Jack as he sat down again. His hands flashed over the keys, and he kept jumping between photographs and writing.

Now Mossy wished he'd stayed closer. The writing on the screen was too small to read from the bookshelf. Quickly and quietly he climbed the back of Jack's chair. There was the finished letter. Jack sat back, and Mossy had to whisk his toes out of the way to avoid them being crushed.

*Dear Mr Glenville*, he read, *… for your consideration… commission… discuss prices… happy to arrange a meeting.* There was plenty he didn't understand, including a whole lot of information about Annie which might or might not be true; he didn't know. There was a section with names and measurements taken from the list that he seen Jack make in the studio. But the bit that really worried him was at the bottom of the letter. *Jack Breeze, acting as agent for Annie Breeze.* It seemed to imply that Annie knew what was going on. And that was one thing Mossy was sure about. Annie knew nothing of this.

The sharp shrill of the telephone broke into his thoughts.

'Hello?' said Jack. There was a pause. 'Oh, that's a shame.' Another pause. 'No, no. Don't worry.' Mossy rubbed his knee and wondered who Jack was talking to. It sounded like a woman's voice.

'Yes, they're fine. They're over with Jon and Sophie. Rollo said something about cooking, but they'll be back any minute.' Mossy decided it must be Annie.

'Don't worry. We'll all be here whenev...'

A sudden, crashing boom exploded through the still afternoon. Mossy had never heard anything like it. Everything shook, the ground, the walls, the windows, even the trees. He and Jack had both leapt to their feet, the phone dropping from Jack's hand. The air quivered with sound. Mossy leapt from the bookshelf, careless of who might hear him. He knew where the sound had come from – Puddle's house.

# Chapter 24

# Rock Bottom

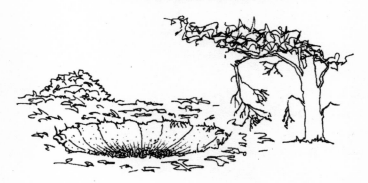

As Mossy raced through the door, he heard Jack's voice. 'I'll call you back. Don't worry.... Well, try. Trust me for once... If not me, trust them... Yes, I promise.' And then his footsteps were close behind as they both raced towards the Raitatas' house. A sound above them made Mossy glance skywards to see the robins and the rook flying in the same direction. They, too, had heard the explosion. Who wouldn't have?

At the end of the drive Mossy stooped to touch a hand to the ground. It felt shattered, trembling waves echoing through it, shivering under his fingers. Now he was chasing after Jack. As they turned towards the house, Mossy spotted Cissy and JJ. Where was Rollo?

'Wow! Dad!' called Cissy. 'You should have seen it!'

'Ker-boom!' shouted JJ, waving his arms in arching circles above his head. 'Brilliant!'

'Where's Rollo?' Mossy could hear the clear sound of panic in Jack's voice.

'I'm here!' called Rollo as he, Jon and Sophie arrived from the other side of some trees. 'No panic, it was just a bit bigger than we thought.' He grinned sheepishly.

'Thank goodness you're alright!' As Jack's shoulders relaxed, Mossy felt the panic seep out of him.

But what had they been doing? What had made the earth feel so stressed? As Jack reached for his phone, Mossy went to look further.

Beyond the trees he saw a huge hole in the ground. There were scattered leaves, grass and bits of wood all over the place. One of the trees had a raw gash where a branch had been damaged. Earth and pebbles had been flung everywhere. On the far side of the hole stood Puddle, peering into the depths with a forlorn look on his face. Mossy hurried round to his side.

'You OK?' he asked. 'What on earth happened?!'

'They've been working on it all day. Your Rollo's been helping them,' explained Puddle. 'It's supposed to be a surprise for their parents.'

'I'll say,' said Mossy. He could hear Jack's voice as he spoke into his phone.

'No... They're all fine. No one's hurt... Yup, I know... I know... **I know**. Look, can we talk about it later, when you get home?'

Mossy spotted signals between Sophie, Jon and Rollo.

'I'm really sorry, Mr Breeze,' said Sophie, approaching him as he turned to face them. 'It's my fault. I must have got the quantities wrong and it made a bigger explosion than I thought.' Jack ran a hand through his hair as he surveyed the chaos.

'Where are your parents?' he asked in a bewildered voice.

'They're out for the day. They left me in charge, and we wanted to help with the pond,' Sophie replied.

'Pond?' Mossy asked, nudging Puddle.

'They want to build a pond' explained Puddle, pointing at the hole. 'And the kids heard them talking about how long it would take to dig it out. I think that's what gave them the idea.'

'I worked out the recipe from a book at school,' Sophie carried on. So **that** was the 'cooking' that Rollo had been talking about, thought Mossy. And Cissy had known all along. That's what those windmilling hands had reminded him of – fireworks!

Jack rubbed a hand across his face and looked at the children ranged in front of him.

'Did it cross your minds that you might get hurt?' he asked. 'I mean, really badly hurt? And what about the younger ones?' He waved a hand in the direction of Cissy and JJ.

'Oh no, Dad,' burst out JJ. 'They made us stand miles away, and the fuse line went on forever. Look you can see where it burnt a line in the grass.' He waved a hand at a charred trail that led across the lawn.

Mossy walked along it, following the scorched grass until he came to a box of matches. Turning back to look at the now distant group of humans, he could see that JJ had a point.

By the time Mossy rejoined them, Jack had organised a tidying session. Rollo and Jon had rakes, and Sophie was fetching a wheelbarrow, while Cissy and JJ were collecting scraps of wood and leaves.

Mossy sat down beside Puddle, their feet hanging into the hole.

'The water will help to heal it,' he explained, 'but it'll take some time. Thank goodness it wasn't any closer to the house. You'd both have been in trouble then.' Puddle looked shocked.

'I never thought…' His voice trailed off in dismay.

'Look at it this way,' said Mossy, putting an arm round his shoulder. 'None of the Dwellers was hurt, you and the house are fine, and they're all learning a lesson. Making a hole is just the beginning of the hard work.' Cissy trudged by with an armful of leaves. 'You've probably got a bit of explaining to do to the worms. Maybe the moles and mice too, people like that.'

Supper was late that evening, and everyone was tired after the hard work. They had continued until Sue and Rajesh arrived home, when there had been much exclamation. Jon and Sophie's parents had been much angrier than Jack.

'You're going to have a fair bit of easing to do tonight,' Mossy told Puddle as they said goodbye.

'And probably for the next few days,' agreed Puddle glumly.

'It's what we're here for,' Mossy reminded him.

Annie arrived as Cissy put a big bowl of raspberries on the table.

'Mum!' exclaimed JJ, a beaming smile lighting up his face. 'Weekend!'

'I'm so sorry I'm late.' Mossy thought Annie looked exhausted, more so than usual.

'Dad said you wouldn't be home till after bedtime,' said Cissy. 'So this is much better!' Annie folded her arms and looked at the children. Mossy's heart sank. This didn't bode well.

'And what's this about dynamite?'

'Oh, you should have heard it! It was a mega boom!' JJ was still excited, despite yawning. 'Stuff went everywhere. Dad made us clear up, but there's still bits all over.'

'I did hear it. In London.' Annie paused, her face tight, and gave them what Mossy could only call The Look.

'*JJ*,' he projected, shaking his head, '*time to keep quiet.*'

By the time Annie had finished speaking, everyone was looking downcast. Even Mossy, on the dresser, sat with his hands hanging limply at his sides.

'I do not understand why your father can't simply watch out and keep you safe,' she finished.

'Mum, you can't blame Dad. It's not his fault, it's mine,' said Rollo. 'I didn't tell him the truth. He didn't even know. I let him think we were cooking, that 'a recipe' meant food. And I was the one who made Cissy and JJ promise to keep quiet. But we were really careful, and Sophie did all the right things to make it safe.'

'Apart from making dynamite and blowing up the garden.' Mossy had to admit that Annie had a point, but then so did Rollo.

No sooner had the children traipsed silently up to bed, than Annie turned to Jack.

'At the beginning of the holidays you neglected the children's safety so that Cissy could have been killed by a tractor. As if that isn't enough, now you are so caught up in your own little world that you have no idea what they are doing, and they end up blowing holes in the neighbour's garden.' Is this the time when he tells her what he's actually been doing? wondered Mossy.

'Annie, I'm doing my best. We've got a bright bunch of kids here. They're great. They think things through. They took all sorts of safety precautions. OK, so they overdid the quantities. And it would have been better if they had told us what they were up to first. But they haven't tried to get out of anything, and we've agreed that they all have to work until they have made things just the way that Sue and Rajesh would like them to be. And that another time they will tell us first.'

'Oh right, so you're planning on blowing up more things with them, are you?' Annie stood with her arms folded tightly across her chest like a barrier between them.

'Of course not,' Jack sighed. 'But Annie, try talking **with** them, not just **at** them. Listen to them. I know you're tired, and you had that extra meeting tonight, but you used to be so good at this. I learned to listen to them from watching you do it. Let them tell you about it, rather than simply thinking the worst of us all.'

Annie sank down onto one of the chairs, her elbows on the table as she rested her head in her hands. Mossy had to strain to catch her words.

'The meeting was cancelled in the end. Dirk had said that he wanted to go through the new proposal – could I stay late? So I asked Alice to stay on to help us, but when Dirk arrived, he changed his mind and said that we'd have to do it another time. I'd done a whole lot of extra drawings.'

Annie shrugged her shoulders as she looked up at Jack, and Mossy felt saddened by the exhaustion he saw on her face. She looked torn to shreds. 'I did say that I'd be glad to get back today after all these goings-on. You know what Dirk said? He called you a 'complete waste of space'. Sometimes I almost think he's right.'

Mossy stared at her, wide-eyed. Then his eyes narrowed as he looked at her hard. Dirk said that? What gave him that idea? He'd never met Jack. Mossy felt cross that an outsider should have criticised one of his Dwellers. He gripped the shelf, leaning forward.

*'He's a great Dad,'* he projected towards Annie. And the seed of an idea began to take root in his mind.

Now it was Jack who had his hands over his face.

'Annie, I'm sorry. Sorry that you have to cope with people saying something like that.' He shook his head.

'Oh, don't worry. That's not all. Usually he calls you The Loser. Or when you started doing stuff in school, The Classroom Prop. Or the Prop Backwards. And then something like this happens, or Cissy getting hurt, and… and I find it hard to disagree.'

Mossy had heard enough. It was time to go and check on the children, check that they were safely away from this. Carefully he climbed down the dresser, stopping briefly when his toe caught a cup and sent it swinging on its hook. He stilled it with one hand, but no one noticed, and he tiptoed quietly from the room.

# CHAPTER 25

# Better, or Worse

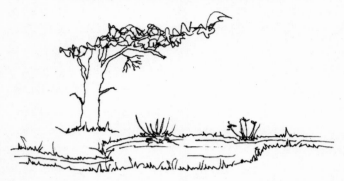

By Sunday evening Annie looked less tired. Although she spent very little time with Jack, she had helped Cissy in the vegetable garden for a couple of hours each day. Mossy watched as they pulled weeds from between the beetroots and picked a big basket of French beans for supper. Cissy knelt at her work, chattering to her mother as she filled her in with stories from the week.

'You've made a fine job of this, Cissy,' said her mother, brushing the earth from her hands as she stood up. Mossy frowned at the snail by his left foot.

'*Move on mate, it's not safe here,*' he warned him. '*Slug pellets.*' The snail waved his horns and sped off, millimetre by millimetre, towards the hedge.

'Well, Rollo has his paper round, and I wanted to do my bit. This was all I could think of. And now I really like doing it.'

'You're more than doing 'your bit'. You're great.' Annie smiled a smile that Mossy remembered from when the

Breezes had first blown into his home.

'I couldn't do it without Dad, though. He made all the difference during term time. And making the water tap and stuff.'

'I'd forgotten that,' mused Annie, resting a hand on the hurdles as she picked up the jersey that she had left draped over them. 'And I suppose you're going to tell me that if it hadn't been for Dad and the boys making these, most of the stuff would have been eaten by the rabbits instead of us!'

'You said it, Mum,' she laughed. 'I know that since Dad lost his job we've had to give up all sorts of stuff like holidays and having things just when we want them. And I know we're changing schools again, but that's OK, 'cos I'll be going on to join Rollo and Jon soon, and I'm looking forward to that. And although I miss you being around all the time, it's good having Dad here more.'

Well done Cissy, thought Mossy.

*'Help her to see it clearly.'*

Jack, Rollo and JJ had continued clearing up the explosion site. Annie and Cissy went to join them after they finished.

'Could have been much worse,' Mossy overheard Sue telling Annie, as he sat by Puddle on the branch of a low tree and watched proceedings. 'They were spot-on with the positioning, and the hard work's been done in a jiffy!'

'But think of the danger!' exclaimed Annie.

'And how!' exclaimed Rajesh, lifting his hands in dismay. 'Usually we count on Sophie to be sensible. She says she wanted to do some practical science. And believe it or not, she had gone through all the risks and planned how to do it safely. She had everything written down; she's shown us.'

Sophie came over to join them.

'I'm really sorry, Mrs Breeze. We should all have told our parents. It's my fault. I just wanted to prove that I could do it right without help. I seem to have spent so much time working to pass exams about all this sort of thing, and I've never done it for real.'

Mossy turned to Puddle sitting beside him.

'She wants to be an engineer?' he asked.

'Yup, that's right.'

'One of my previous Dwellers was an engineer. He didn't blow things up!'

'OK. OK. No need to rub it in. I'm just not very good at projecting yet.' Puddle looked down at his toes as they hung limply in the air.

'Early days,' comforted Mossy. 'You've only been at it for a hundred years or so. Keep practising. You'll get there in time.'

'We've done a lot of talking, all of us,' continued Sue. 'Including making it quite clear to Jon that he is in no way to try out any of his chemical experiments without asking us first.'

Mossy was pleased to see that they were echoing what Jack had said. They had listened as well as talked to their children.

'Bright kids! Who'd have 'em?' laughed Rajesh. 'You must thank heaven that your Rollo is into historical stuff. At least that doesn't lead to explosions!' Even Annie ought to agree with that, thought Mossy.

Later on, when he came into the kitchen, he found Cissy in full swing over the supper table, telling them about her visit to Giant's Farm.

'Bill Blackman was Mr Blackman's great-great-great-amillion-times grandfather, and Mrs Blackman showed me their Bible with all the names in it when I went to give her the thank-you vegetables. And it was just like Rollo said – half-built when something went wrong; two houses, not one, and loads of people living there, all together.' She launched into a fine impression of Mrs Blackman, and JJ moved to sit in his mother's lap where Annie's arms wrapped round him, everybody caught up in Cissy's dramatic retelling of the building of Giant's Farm.

You're doing fine, all of you, thought Mossy. You're the other things that she misses, as much as her painting, even if she doesn't realise it. Annie's face had softened, and there was a warm glow to it in the evening light.

After the children had gone up to bed, Mossy stood by the nearly empty bowl of fruit salad, helping himself to a final strawberry while Annie and Jack did the washing-up.

'Thank you, Jack,' Annie's voice broke through the sound of running water. 'You reminded me of something I was at risk of forgetting. It's good to listen to them. There are more important things than work.' She paused. 'And work isn't always good either. You know, there are times when I think that Dirk would swear that poison was good for you, black was white and water flows uphill, if he thought it would make a sale, or get him what he wants. He has no scruples, that man.'

*Take the hint, Jack,'* projected Mossy. *'She's listened to you. Now you need to tell her something else, too. Remember, you **do** have scruples.'*

'No need to thank me,' said Jack. 'Like I said, you showed me how in the first place.'

'*And whilst we're talking,*' prompted Mossy.

'And whilst we're talking…' Jack continued.

'Mum! Dad! We've run out of toothpaste,' shouted Cissy from upstairs.

'Tell me later,' said Annie, glancing over at him. 'I'll go and find it for her.'

Mossy listened hard, but he never heard Jack mention anything about the paintings. Twice he thought he might be about to say something.

'*Go on,*' he encouraged, but the moment seemed to pass. And there I was telling Puddle that projection was just a matter of practice, frowned Mossy crossly, as he stomped up the stairs at the end of the evening.

A couple of days later his Dwellers were still busy working on the surprise pond.

'It's called puddling,' Jack explained to all the children. Puddle grinned widely.

'So maybe it was meant to happen,' Mossy said, patting him on the back. 'We don't get our names for nothing. What do you expect with a stream to either side of your house? You were practically born in a puddle!' he laughed.

'Where did your name come from?' asked Puddle.

'My Starting Stone. When they first found it, it was so covered in moss that it looked like a mossy mound apparently. So I heard them say. I wasn't there – wasn't born till they laid it as the hearthstone. But it's a good one. Where's yours, by the way?'

'By the front corner, but I never heard anyone talking

about it,' Puddle said, slowly shaking his head.

'It's one of the problems with newer houses,' Mossy commiserated. 'They're often built by builders rather than your first Dwellers. I was lucky. I've heard,' he muttered darkly, 'that some of the really new Holders have concrete slabs as their Starting Stones. Imagine that!' Puddle stared at him with round eyes.

'That would be some Starting Stone,' he murmured.

While the two Holders went off to inspect Puddle's Starting Stone, the others settled to work.

'The smooth clay stops the water seeping away,' Jack explained, and by the time Mossy and Puddle returned they found everybody busy. Rollo, Jon, Sophie and Jack were working from the inside, their heads just visible above the edge, while Sue, Cissy and JJ worked from the outside.

'Do you think this was how our pond was made?' asked Cissy, lying on her stomach, reaching over the edge as she whacked at the clay with a mallet.

'Maybe, but the stream has always flowed through ours,' said Rollo, as he slapped and pummelled the heavy clay with his feet. 'It's how they've been made for donkey's years.'

'And now we're making a brand new pond in the same old way,' declared JJ. Sometimes things never really change, agreed Mossy.

By teatime the children were muddy and tired. Mossy and Puddle admired the results of the hard work. The stamping of feet and the smacking of the clay had produced a smooth, if uneven, surface.

'The idea is,' explained Sophie, 'that we break that thin wall of earth between the stream and the pond, so that it falls into the stream and changes the flow to come through here, filling it as it goes.'

'Can we do it now?' asked JJ, jumping about excitedly.

'Are you sure you're not getting too tired?' asked Jack. 'We don't want to overdo it.'

'No! No! We're fine,' chorused the children.

'We want to finish it!' Cissy beamed at Sophie.

'Tea first?' asked Sue.

'Yeah!' chorused the boys.

'I'm ravenous,' added Cissy.

Puddle and Mossy examined the pond thoroughly, while Sue brought out drinks and cake on a huge tray.

'Would you like another bit of cake, JJ?' asked Sophie.

'And try keeping the earth on your hands rather than eating it with the cake,' suggested Jack.

'I think you're going to have a fine pond there,' mused Mossy, as he and Puddle ambled over to the trees beyond it. 'Put your hands in the ground. It's already feeling much better.'

The two Holders were still bent over, their hands in the earth by the trees, their backs to the pond, when they felt the first shudder run through the earth.

'Don't panic,' said Mossy as Puddle spun round in alarm. 'It's Sophie attacking the bank to allow the water in.'

A couple of minutes later a cheer went up as the first trickle of water squeezed its way into the pond. In no time the trickle turned into a gush, and then a torrent, as the bank collapsed into the old streambed and water churned into the new basin.

'Wow! Look at that!' exclaimed JJ.

'It worked! Well done, Sophie!' Cissy gave Sophie a big congratulatory hug. Mossy spotted Jack looking over at Sue.

'All's well that ends well,' he said as he firmed the soil down in the old stream bed, carefully replacing the grass turfs on the top and ensuring that the outflow was still clear.

'See, Dad? She worked it out fine,' Rollo grinned at his father.

'But even so, any more grand plans, and you'll talk to us first?'

Seated on the far side, well out of the way, Puddle and Mossy watched the water swirl around the bottom, already starting to rise.

'Feel the ground now,' Mossy urged his friend. Puddle dug his fingers through the grass and into the soil.

'It's as if it's sighing. The shivering has stopped.' Puddle grinned. 'You were right, it's starting to heal.'

Back at Annanbourne Jack issued instructions.

'OK, team? Baths before supper today. I want you clean and presentable before Mum gets back. She'll have a fit if she sees you like that!' Mossy looked at JJ, whose eyes shone out of a mud-streaked face.

'I've got mud gloves,' he announced proudly, waving his hands at Cissy to show her the grey sludge that rose to his elbows. Mossy spotted a place at the base of one of his fingers where the skin looked raw. What's that? he wondered.

'Not just mud gloves,' laughed Cissy. 'It's everywhere!'

'You're no better,' grimaced Rollo. 'And I can feel that my legs are quite stiff where it's dried!'

'Muddy clothes into this to soak before you go upstairs.' Jack dumped a big bucket on the ground by the back door.

Mossy beamed. It reminded him of the days before baths when everybody had to wash under the pump by the cistern.

'Look!' chortled Cissy. 'I've even got mud on my tummy!'

'Ow!' exclaimed JJ, as he dropped mud-encrusted socks into the bucket. 'My hand hurts.'

On closer inspection it turned out that all three children had blisters. JJ had two.

'Don't worry, I've got some great cream to sort that out,' Jack cheered them up.

*'Just be careful when you put your hands in the bath,'* Mossy projected.

'Will it hurt when we wash them, Dad?' asked Rollo.

'Probably,' replied Jack. 'Be gentle. The pain will soon go.'

'Ow, ow, ow!' complained JJ. Mossy sat close by, a long finger gently resting on his arm to give him courage.

Just as the last hand came clean, the bang of a car door announced Annie's return.

'Scoot, you lot. Go on, up to your baths!' Jack made shooing movements. 'Give yourselves a good scrub!'

'What's this?' asked Annie, looking at the bucket.

'We got a bit mucky,' replied Jack, indicating his own knees as evidence. 'But the pond is finished and it's all been made good. Why don't you relax, and we'll be ready for supper in no time.'

'Isn't it getting rather late? What needs doing?' Annie's looked about the kitchen and sighed.

Mossy couldn't see any sign of any food. He looked over at Jack.

'It's fine.' Jack looked around hopefully, as if supper would emerge, suddenly ready, from somewhere. 'As soon as I've changed, I'm on top of it.'

'Really?' Mossy didn't like the look of that raised eyebrow, or the wary note to her voice. Hmm, he thought, pointing his nose at her, wondering if he could smell the cause. She recovered over the weekend, but a couple of days back at work and it was almost as if she was looking for something to be wrong.

JJ's eyes drooped over supper. He dropped his fork with a clatter onto the plate.

'What's up, JJ?' asked Annie.

'I'm really tired, Mum. It was so cool doing the pond, but I ache all over.' She put an arm round his shoulder to give him a hug.

'A good night's sleep will sort that out,' she said. 'Hang on! What's that plaster on your hand?' she added.

'Dad put it over the cream on the blister!'

'Blister?' she asked, her head coming up with a jolt.

'We all got them, even Dad,' said Rollo, showing her one on his thumb. 'Workman's hands,' he added proudly. 'That's what Dad says.' Annie glared at Jack

'I should have known,' she sighed. Mossy turned to look at her. 'Dirk asked me what had gone wrong over the weekend and I said 'nothing'; that it had been lovely. I should have known it was just a matter of time. You just can't do anything right, can you?'

'No, Mum. No!' cried Cissy. Mossy could see tears welling up in her eyes. 'Don't say that. It's not Dad's fault. We just didn't notice 'til it was too late.'

Mossy nodded his head. OK, he thought. You've told me everything I need to know.

## CHAPTER 26

# Prepared for Trouble

Catching nightmares, and checking on his Dwellers, made for a tricky start to the night. Mossy found JJ tossing and turning, despite holding his talisman tightly under his pillow. He sat guard by the bed, his eyes as sharp as a hawk's.

'Ha! Spotted you!' he chortled, reaching out a long finger to pin it down. The nightmare twisted and turned as he grasped it and flung it into the dark night through the open window.

'Don't you dare.' He glared, his eyes glowing yellow in the darkness. Returning to the bedside he gently soothed the boy's forehead, drawing pictures of clear flowing water, rainbow colours and sparkling fish sliding by. A smile crossed JJ's sleeping face, his breathing slowed and he slipped into restful sleep.

A muffled cry from Cissy's room called Mossy to her side, to find a different nightmare trying to attack her. Her white feather was tucked into the top of her bedstead, curled protectively over her, but the nightmare had managed to slither by, disguised as a dream. Now it was preparing to let rip. He was almost too late. She flung an arm out.

'No! No!' she cried, her breath coming in gasps. 'That's not fair!'

'Oh no, you don't!' Mossy grabbed it with both hands, pulling it away from her. The nightmare fought back, shooting out a tentacle, lashing at his face angrily. Cissy sighed, her body relaxing as the nightmare lost its grip. Shaking it fiercely until it hung limply in his hands, Mossy gritted his teeth as he strode over to the window.

'And don't you even think about trying to come back,' he glowered after it.

Even though Mossy had left visiting Rollo until the moon was high in the sky, he found him still awake. Somewhere over the dark woods that lay beyond the fields, the Barn Owl hooted, a lone cry as she hunted, and Rollo looked to the window as if searching for an answer somewhere in the darkness.

He sighed heavily as Mossy crept into the room, then turned over, hunched a shoulder and pulled the duvet close about him. Mossy stationed himself by the pillow, reaching his arms over the rigid form, careful not to touch him. Taking the greatest of care he blew gently into Rollo's face, the softest of breezes, filled with warmth, carrying memories of carefree summer days, the smell of ripe apples, full of light and laughter. Slowly the start of a smile lifted the corners of Rollo's mouth, and his eyelids closed at last as sleep took his worries away.

Mossy stood guard.

Only once he was sure that all his Dwellers were safely

asleep did he venture onto the roof. He sat with his back against the chimney stack, gazing up at the stars, a leg hanging down on each side of the house. The Milky Way arched overhead, as the moon began its descent towards the western hills. There would soon be only the starlight left for them to see by.

'I feel that I'm losing my way,' Mossy admitted, as the Barn Owl glided to his side, curving in on silent wings. She turned to look at him.

'Kind of you to say so, but I'm beginning to wonder if I've lost my touch,' he sighed. She blinked slowly.

'I think I know where the trouble is coming from, but I'm not sure what I can do about it,' Mossy told her. She stepped sideways, looked out over the still fields and let out a loud call, which echoed back at them from the woods.

The sky was beginning to lighten, though the sun had yet to rise, when Mossy finally rose to his feet.

'You really think that's the only way to keep them safe and make sure that they'll stay? What if I can't get back?' The Barn Owl didn't even look at him this time. Mossy flexed his fingers. The chill of the night emphasised the ache in them.

'Then I shall have to do it.' He shook his head slowly. He had never tackled anything as hazardous as this before. He turned to face his friend and adviser.

'I may need your help. I shall do some planning and let you know in a few days.' The Barn Owl turned to face the woods, stretched her wings wide and launched herself silently onto a morning breeze that lifted her into the air as the first spark from the sun burst through the trees. Mossy climbed back down the chimney, yawned, settled himself on the hearth and fell instantly into a deep sleep.

'Dad!' JJ's shout jolted Mossy awake. 'I can't find my swimming towel!'

'No towel, no swimming!' came Jack's voice from the kitchen. Feet raced by as Mossy rubbed sleep from his eyes.

'I'll help you,' called Cissy, grabbing JJ and shoving him in front of her up the stairs. 'No way I'm missing my first swim since the stitches came out!'

The telephone rang.

'Can you get that, Rollo?' Jack was still busy in the kitchen. Mossy ambled through to see what was going on.

'Hello?.... Oh!... Fine, thanks!' Rollo sounded surprised. 'Yup, I'll just get him.' He held out the phone to his father. 'It's for you Dad. Mr Goodman?' Jack took the phone as Cissy and JJ, with a towel draped round his neck, clattered back into the kitchen.

'Fill the water bottles,' instructed Jack, heading into the garden with the phone. 'Hello?'

Silence fell in the kitchen as four pairs of ears strained to catch what was being said.

'No, I'm sorry I can't,' Jack's voice came through the open window. 'Not until later... No, all day... I don't see why not... That would be fine!... See you this evening then!'

'Mr Goodman, coming here this evening?' Cissy sounded quite put out as she turned to her brother. 'But it's the holidays,' she protested. 'And anyway we've changed school.

I'm going with Rollo, aren't I? He can't tell me off at Rollo's school, and I'm not even there yet anyway. I can't be in trouble during the holidays!'

'Who says it's about you?' asked JJ.

'Dad, why's he coming?' asked Rollo when Jack reappeared.

'Didn't say. Wants to ask me something, but not on the phone. Can't think what, we've still a while to go before the beginning of term, so there's nothing really for me to do. Anyway, how's that picnic coming along?'

Mossy was glad to have the house to himself. He'd never taken this kind of step before, never left his home without knowing he would shortly return. For that matter he'd never met any other Holder who'd done it either.

The only time he'd ever heard of a Holder going missing had been connected to the ruins on the far side of the downs. No one knew why he'd gone in the first place. Had he been forced to leave? Or had he left of his own free will? Had some terrible accident damaged him beyond repair? Whatever the reason, it must have been agony for the Holder. Stories of torture, murder, missing children and finally the slow destruction of the house.

If he was doing this to help his Dwellers, would that make it alright? All he knew was that the more he thought about it, the more he had no choice. For the sake of Annanbourne, he had to keep these Dwellers.

He knew that just a day away from the house left him tired and weak, that the house was open to trouble without him there to protect it. He'd only done it once and that time The Travelling Holder had been there to look after things for him.

No sign of him this time, though.

Still, there were precautions he could take, things he could check. Doing it before his Dwellers came back, not having to dodge round them, would make it easier. If there were any possibility that he might be stuck away from home, he needed to make sure that Annanbourne had all the help he could find.

'First things first,' he told the trout who looked up at him from the water. 'If I look fine, the house is fine.' He scrutinised his reflection. 'Hang on, what's that smudge on my nose?' He twisted round and looked equally carefully at the chimney.

'Hey you!' He called out. A thrush popped its head over the top of the pot. 'You can't roost on there! You'll get smoked rigid, and anyway, you're making a mess of it! Go and find yourself a tree!'

He dipped a hand into the water.

'Flow calmly and keep them steady when I'm away.' Carefully he carried a handful of water over to the house, sprinkling drops of it onto the threshold and printing two wet handprints onto the hearthstone.

'Remember me in my absence, knowing that I always return.' The house sighed gently, aware how much he hated to be away, even for a few hours. He lingered by his Starting Stone, the strongest and safest place of all.

'I wish I didn't have to do this,' he sighed, 'but it's for all of us. They looked after us, now it's our turn to look after them.'

Pushing his worries to the back of his mind, he hurried into the garden, where he plunged his hands deep into the earth, wriggling his fingers into the soil.

'Drink in all things and keep them growing strong and straight while I'm away.' His hands brought up two fistfuls of earth which he poured into his pockets. Even far away he would still have some part of Annanbourne with him.

In the copse new shoots were sprouting strongly from the coppiced hazel. The robin hopped over from investigating the log pile. With his back resting against the old oak, he reached out his hands to the fresh growth.

'Lift your leaves high, spread your branches wide and keep them sheltered and safe in my absence.'

In the field beyond the stream he climbed to the top of the tumulus. Once these fields had belonged to Annanbourne, and he still took strength from them. The sheep had moved to higher pastures on the down, and the grass was scattered with wild flowers. The robin sailed in, landing gracefully by his feet with a short burst of song as he looked up at Mossy.

'No, no, I'm not going anywhere immediately, but I want to be on the safe side, be well prepared.'

A breeze wafted down from the hills, rippling through the long grasses that waved their heads in greeting. Turning into it he smiled.

'Blow softly or blow strongly. Keep all troubles away from here until I come back.'

And then, finally, he turned his face to the sun, lifting his arms in greeting as it burst from behind a cloud.

'Bringer of life and defeater of darkness, keep their vision clear and light my path home.'

In a neighbouring field a lark was rising, its clear song trickling down to the stubble of the harvested corn. A couple of mice looked up, pausing in the midst of collecting winter food stores, and turned to run towards the house, passing Mossy as he headed to the back door.

'Busy, I see,' said Mossy as they scurried by. They couldn't reply, their mouths were too full.

Now Mossy checked all the other inhabitants of the house.

'I'm counting on you to spin webs to catch bad dreams if I miss a Nightwatch,' he told the spiders. They waved their legs at him. 'No, it's windows only. Keep out of the baths,' he reminded them. 'And no bandages needed, thanks!' he called over his shoulder.

'Find your red cousins if there are any intruders,' he told the ants. They waved their antennae at him. 'They can only bite invaders, not the Dwellers. You'll have to watch carefully. They can get a bit carried away.'

Out by the pond the ducklings gathered round.

'Make sure you keep their spirits up.' The eldest quacked at him, whilst the second youngest hopped from foot to foot. 'You'll think of something, I'm sure,' he laughed, and set off for the stream, his eyes darting about as he looked for those others whose help he could count on.

He was basking on the threshold in the early evening sun, his back resting against the warm door, when the car came bounding back down the drive.

'Peg out the towels to dry,' called Jack as he headed towards the house. Mossy leapt to his feet and hurried off to the washing line, nipping through the hedge so that he arrived at the same time as the children, who had had to take the long way round.

'Can you do mine, Rollo?' asked JJ, passing his towel over. Mossy looked at them all carefully. They looked as if they'd had a good time. Flushed from the sun and the wind, their faces beamed in good humour.

'Oh, I do like to be beside the seaside!' sang Cissy. 'You know, it would be even better with Mum, too.'

'Well, if Dad's plan works out...' began JJ. Cissy span round to face him.

'You're not to breathe a word.' She waggled a finger at him. 'Dad said.'

'I won't. I said I wouldn't,' JJ grinned. 'I can keep a secret, too.'

'He doesn't want her to be upset if it doesn't work out,' Rollo reminded him.

Mossy was perplexed. What had Jack been telling them? What plan? Whatever it was, it sounded as if the children thought it was exciting. He watched them run back to the house, then lay on the warm grass, watching the damp towels flap above him, flinging memories of the seaside into the air.

Another car pulled into the drive. Annie back, thought Mossy, getting to his feet in time to see JJ erupt from the house.

'Mum! Look! I've brought back a weather forecaster from the seaside! Dad said I could hang it by the back door.'

'You've been to the seaside?' asked Annie. 'Lucky you! Are you sure we really want seaweed by the back door?'

'It was fantastic. We swam miles, and found rock pools and crabs and am-nemonies and made a sandcastle. I wish you had come, too.' JJ gave his mother a big hug, wriggling back out of her arms to dig a hand into his pocket. 'And I found a present for you!' He pulled his hand out with a flourish. 'It's specially just for you!'

'Well, what could be better?' asked Annie, taking the stone and holding it up to the light. 'It's perfect!'

'And I have the necklace for it,' Cissy announced as she joined them, waving a thin blue ribbon in her hand. 'Dad says it'll match your eyes!'

'Does he?!' laughed Annie. 'I'm not sure about that!' Carefully Cissy threaded the ribbon through the hole in the stone and then, while JJ held it in place, knotted it firmly at the back of her mother's neck.

'A special one for you, just like my talisman, to bring good luck and make you smile again,' said JJ standing back to admire his gift. Mossy admired it too. He had never seen such a small stone with a hole in it. You're right, he thought, if that doesn't bring luck, then I can't imagine what will. He followed them into the house.

Supper was already on the table as Mossy climbed into his place on the dresser.

'Water, Mum?' asked Rollo as he lifted the big jug.

'Such service!' exclaimed Annie as she held out her glass. 'Just what I need after the day I've had! The client decided to turn the scheme upside down. Dirk wanted this, then that, and then goodness knows what and then changed his mi...' She was interrupted by the sound of another car pulling into the drive. Everybody turned to look in the same direction.

'Oh, goodness!' exclaimed Jack, clapping a hand to his forehead. 'I'd completely forgotten.' Mossy spotted Cissy tugging at Rollo's sleeve. She pulled a face.

'It's Mr Goodman.'

## CHAPTER 27

# Surprises

'What's going on?' asked Annie, looking from one person to another.

'Your guess is as good as mine,' said Jack with a shrug. 'He just said he wanted to ask about something.'

'I didn't do it!' Cissy flung up her hands. Mossy's head whipped round in her direction.

'Didn't do what?' asked at least three voices.

'I don't know,' pleaded Cissy, 'but if Mr Goodman asks to see you, you're usually in trouble.'

'Unless he's telling you you've done really well,' Rollo pointed out quietly.

'And anyway, it was me he wanted to see, not you,' Jack reminded her.

'Well, just say you didn't do it!' Cissy told her father, resting a comforting hand on his arm as he stood up. Everybody laughed. Mossy looked out of the window. There was Mr Goodman, striding up the path to the front door.

'Ian! Good to see you. Come in!' Jack greeted him. 'I'm

afraid we're a bit chaotic. We were just about to have supper.'

'I'll be as quick as I can, then.' Silence fell in the kitchen as all ears strained to catch the conversation in the sitting room. Mossy clambered down to the floor and tip-toed to the door.

'We've had some tricky news at school. If you remember, last term you covered for Sally Arnold several times. Unfortunately the doctor has now told her that she'll have to stop work completely, with immediate effect.'

'What does 'immediate effect' mean?' JJ mouthed at his mother.

'Shh, sweetheart, I'll tell you later,' she whispered back.

'I'm sorry to hear that. She seemed like a lovely person.' Jack sounded sympathetic.

'And a good teacher, too,' continued Mr Goodman. 'However, it means that we have a job vacancy, and before I put it to anyone else I wanted to ask if you might be interested.' Cissy grabbed Rollo's arm, her eyes wide. Mossy saw Rollo lift a silent finger to his lips.

'I... Erm...' Looking round the edge of the door, Mossy saw Jack step back as he looked cautiously at Mr Goodman. 'What exactly do you mean?'

'We need a full-time teacher to take her place. A Geography specialist, with maths skills too. I've enjoyed our conversations, and you mentioned having a Geography degree. I've seen you working with the children at school, and I've seldom seen a more natural teacher. Some struggle to do it, others learn quickly. But just occasionally you come across someone who is naturally outstanding. You have a real gift. The children enjoy your lessons, and when I've dropped by to see how things are going there's a great feeling in the room. All the staff have commented on it. I don't need an answer right now. I expect you'll want to talk with the family. But if you are interested, then we'd love you to join our team.'

Mossy turned his back on the sitting room, looking at his Dwellers gathered round the table. Rollo's eyes were shining as he looked at his mother; JJ was bouncing in his seat, his hands clapped over his mouth; Cissy was sitting, her fists clenched tightly, her elbows tucked into her waist, her mouth clamped shut on a silent squeal.

Confusion and surprise were battling for a place in Annie as she looked in the direction of the sitting room and the front door. Mossy could have laughed in delight. At last, he thought, all that voluntary work has paid off.

'I've an information pack in the car if you'd like to have a look?' Mr Goodman's question hung in the air.

'That would be great. I'll walk out with you now,' Jack replied, and Mossy heard the front door close as footsteps and voices faded away down the path.

In the kitchen a riot broke out.

'Mum! Did you hear?'

'He said Dad was 'outstanding'!'

'So cool! No more disappearing Dad. He'll be home for all the holidays!' JJ could hardly contain himself.

'Hang on.' Cissy held out a hand. 'Dad, a teacher? We'll never get away with anything, ever again.' She grimaced as she spoke, squirming round in her seat to look out of the window. 'Thank goodness we're going to be in a different school!'

'Everybody in my class always said that he was the best,' Rollo told Annie.

'Cissy, sit down, please. It won't help Dad if you're pulling faces at him through the window. And it might make Mr Goodman change his mind.' Annie spoke quietly, but there was a light in her eyes that Mossy hadn't seen for months.

And I know why, thought Mossy. For the first time in ages you've heard someone talking about Jack as if he were a person you could feel proud of.

'Dad! Wow!' JJ flung himself across the room and into his father's arms. Jack ruffled his hair as he smiled at his family.

'It looks like you all heard?' He looked round at them. Mossy, back on what he now thought of as 'his shelf', could feel the excitement vibrating through the room.

'I'll say!' Cissy leant towards her father. 'And just as we were getting used to you being at home all the time.'

'How about you?' Jack turned to Annie. She shrugged her shoulders.

'I've never really thought of you as a teacher. I just need to get my head round the idea.' Mossy frowned. How come Annie wasn't as pleased as the others? Wasn't this what she'd always wanted? Jack with a job.

As the evening carried on, the children's enthusiasm built pictures of Jack's future life.

'… will be head of geography…'

'… football coach…'

'… head of the school…'

'… no more disappearing to America…'

'Dad hasn't said he'll definitely do it yet, has he?' Annie reminded all of them.

'But you will, won't you?' Rollo turned to look at his father.

'I need to talk it through properly with Mum before I tell Mr Goodman one way or the other,' Jack said quietly. 'And meanwhile, who's going tell her what we did at the beach today?'

'Apart from finding my lucky stone,' agreed Annie, her fingers lightly touching the threaded pebble resting against her neck.

Mossy sat back to enjoy the stories from the beach. Cissy performed impressions of an Italian ice-cream seller, her whole being full of expressive shrugs and grins.

'… wonderer fulla ice creama… justa for a yooou!' She followed it up with the photographer who had been turning people into pirates.

''Ow about you then, li'l lady? Fancy yerself as a pirate hen?'

Rollo described the sand fortress that he and Jack had created, and JJ explained everything he had discovered in the rock pools. It was almost as good as being there, Mossy felt, possibly better. At least he didn't have to worry about being trodden on, left behind or washed away by a wave. But he had to admit he'd have liked the ice-cream.

'Dad said we might be able to have one another time,' said Rollo.

'Well now that he's going to be a teacher and rich, we can go back and have one tomorrow,' decided JJ.

When it was time to head up to baths and beds Mossy leaned forward, preparing to climb down the dresser. Hang on, he thought. My back? He stood up, taking care to keep his head away from the jug hanging above it. No, he decided, I'm right. Some of the ache has eased. A broad smile spanned his face as he nodded his head. That's a good sign.

Mossy lingered by the children, checking all was well. JJ hummed quietly in the dark, passing his talisman from hand to hand. He held it up in the beam of light from the landing that washed through the open door.

'I did it right, didn't I?' Mossy jumped, drawing back into the shadows. It was bad enough that Rollo kept trying to talk to him without JJ starting too.

'Giving Mum her own stone, just like you. It **has** brought us luck.' Mossy relaxed as he realised that he wasn't the one to whom JJ was talking. Although the boy's fingers were closed tightly round the stone in his hand, Mossy could see the faintest glow shining between them.

Across the landing Cissy was doing a bed dance, her duvet slipping sideways to the floor.

'Rollo?' she panted, pausing for breath. Rollo appeared in the doorway. 'Rollo, d'you think Dad'll do it?'

'I can't see why not.' Rollo leaned against the doorframe.

'So then Mum can relax, stop being so uptight, and Dad'll be fine again too.'

'I told you not to worry,' Rollo grinned at her.

'Do you think you'll go to Dardens after all?'

'I hope not. I'd rather stick as we are. I wasn't wild about being a boarder. And anyway,' he added, as he turned towards his own room. 'I need to hang around to sit on you when you go hyper.' Mossy ducked to avoid the flying pillow.

Rollo stood and gazed out of the window at the dark sky. Far to the west, beyond the hills, a streak of lighter blue showed where the sun had disappeared. He drummed his fingers on the wooden sill and sighed a sigh that came from deep within him.

'I wish I were as confident as Cissy that everything was fine.' Mossy wasn't sure if he had heard Rollo speak, or if he had just received a projection fired at him. Rollo climbed into bed and picked up his book. That's a good idea, agreed Mossy, distract yourself with something else.

Annie and Jack talked late into the night. There were a lot of questions for Jack to handle, but Mossy could feel that Annie was pleased by some of the answers. Mossy perched between them on the back of the sofa, one hand resting on Jack's shoulder and the other on Annie's. Jack felt so much stronger.

He has found his path, Mossy realised. He knows what he should be doing, where his strengths are and where he can do his best. I don't need to worry about him any longer.

Annie was another matter. Her energy came in waves. It was turbulent, swirling about, sometimes almost disappearing, as if she was being pulled in too many directions at once. Still he felt an aching loss in her.

'*Listen to the children,*' he projected. '*They understand what he's doing. You too need to find your path, but I'm coming to help you.*' Once again her hand crept up to the stone on its sky blue ribbon.

'Let me sleep on it. How long do you have to give your reply?'

'A couple of days…'

Time to get cracking then, decided Mossy.

# Chapter 28

# Seeing or Hearing

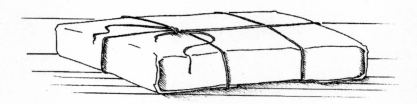

No sooner had Annie raced off to work the following morning, than Mossy spotted Jack hurrying into the studio barn. Running in pursuit, he nipped in through the open door to be greeted by two mice scurrying over, their noses a-quiver.

Jack hauled out a large roll of bubble wrap, then headed over to the stack of paintings and started looking through them.

'I've no idea,' Mossy told the mice in response to their whisker shake. They all watched, wide-eyed, as Jack carefully pulled one of the paintings out of the stack, laid it on the table and started wrapping it.

Mossy and the mice retreated behind a cupboard.

'Have you seen him do anything like this before?' Mossy asked them. The mice shook their heads. The elder gave a small squeak. Over by the table Jack looked up, stopping briefly in his task, glancing round the room, before he continued, reaching out for a roll of brown paper. Soon the parcel looked nothing like a picture. It was large and bulky. Mossy watched carefully as Jack started to write.

*Richard Glenville.* Mossy racked his brains. He'd seen that name before. But where? And what did it mean? *Bruton Street, London,* continued Jack. London! Mossy clapped his hands to his head. What was Jack thinking of? Just as things were beginning to go right again he was spoiling it. Annie would never forgive him if he got rid of one of her paintings.

But there was no time to think. Jack was already gathering up the parcel and heading for the door. Mossy darted out of his hiding place. The mice were ahead of him, going like the wind as they streaked across the room, bounding towards the steps in full sight.

'I thought I heard a squeak,' said Jack, pausing briefly on the threshold as they leapt over his shoe. It was just enough time for Mossy to race to the door, slipping through as Jack hooked a foot round it and pulled it shut.

Mossy found the parcel on the kitchen table. He sat disconsolately beside it. The mice had offered to chew it open, but he had turned down their offer.

'You've done enough for today, I think. That was a close shave! And I'd never have made it without you. But they don't need any more reminders about mice for a while. If I were you,' he warned them, 'I'd steer clear of the studio barn. And avoid cheese anywhere. Mouse traps...' The mice shuddered and headed off for safer quarters.

'Is that it?' asked Cissy, waving a spoon at the parcel as she plonked a bowl on the table beside Mossy.

'Yup.' Jack passed her the milk.

'What time is the man coming?' asked Rollo, returning

from his deliveries.

'Which one are you sending?'

'Me?' suggested JJ. Mossy eyes widened in alarm. Surely Jack wouldn't be sending him anywhere!

'No, not you,' laughed Jack. 'You're only just dry, and I think Mum wants to hang on to you.'

'Mum's always got real me,' said JJ, his mouth full of toast.

Quietly Mossy rose to his feet, stepped carefully round the sugar bowl and delicately reached towards Cissy's hand on the table. One little touch should do it. Very cautiously he brushed her little finger with the tip of his. She picked up her hand and shook it. Mossy ducked out of the way, reversing slightly until his bottom bumped against something.

'Watch out for the cereal!' warned JJ.

'Oops! Sorry. Funny tickle in my finger,' Cissy explained, stretching a hand across Mossy's shoulder to catch the box before it fell. 'I didn't think I'd knocked it.'

Hmm, that was interesting, mused Mossy as he crawled behind the Shreddies. She felt still and calm, not a worry in sight. Edging round the milk and skirting the toast, he decided to tackle Rollo next. But, just as he reached out a long spindly finger in his direction, Rollo jumped to his feet.

'Look! Is that the van?' He pointed out of the window.

Mossy trailed the family as they headed down the path. His mind was in a whirl. It looked as if everyone, bar Annie, were in on this. If that were the case, then he had to re-think.

'So – one parcel to collect,' said the man, looking towards Cissy.

'Here you are!' She held it up.

'My Mum's going to be a famous painter,' announced JJ. Mossy looked over at him.

'Really?' said the driver, fishing the in van for something.

'And we're all secret agents. Helping as a surprise!' Rollo reminded his brother. 'You still can't tell Mum.'

'I know,' protested JJ. 'I'm not telling Mum,' he explained, pointing at the van driver. 'I'm telling him. So he'll be careful with it.'

'Don't you worry. I'll look after it all right,' smiled the driver. Mossy fixed his eyes on him. Could he be trusted? 'If you'd like to sign here?' He held out something towards Jack. 'And here too?'

As Annie's painting disappeared into the van, and it and the man rattled off down the drive, Mossy stood with his hands on his hips and sighed. If Jack has told the children, then I'll just have to trust that it's alright, he told himself. They wouldn't do anything to hurt their mother.

Jack and Cissy headed back into the house, but Rollo and JJ lingered outside. Mossy hung around, hoping to gather more information.

'Come on, JJ,' said Rollo. 'Let's go down to your hide. I'll help you with that wall you wanted to build.' Mossy stomped along in their wake, listening as Rollo asked JJ to collect some of the hazel sticks from the coppice, while he cut willow to weave into it. Perched in the branches of the alder, he watched as the two boys busied themselves.

'Make sure the next bit weaves the other way to the last one,' advised Rollo. JJ frowned as he concentrated on weaving the springy cane between the upright hazel.

'*In front of this one, and now behind that one.*' Mossy was concentrating too.

'Rollo?'

'Mmm?' Rollo stood up from behind the new wall, a dirty smudge on his cheek.

'He will bring it back, won't he?' JJ bent the willow wand, twisting it into place.

'Who'll bring what back?'

'Mum's painting.' Mossy's ears pricked up. This was what he wanted to know.

''Course he will. Dad said the ultimate decision is Mum's. He can only set it all up with the Gallery. In the end it's up to Mum to decide whether she wants to work with them or not. They asked to see this one so that they can check something, not really sure what exactly. I think Dad said that it would be back in a couple of days.'

Mossy could have sung with delight. So Annie **would** be told. The Barn Owl had been right all along; it was a matter of wait and see. Or, as it turned out – Wait and Hear.

It felt as if a huge burden had been lifted from his shoulders. He should have known he could trust Jack, though he still didn't understand why it needed to be a secret. Be patient, he thought. It's paid off so far. Sitting on the branch, he swung his legs in pleasure, setting it bouncing, the leaves rustling. Rollo glanced up towards him. Oops! Mossy froze. But he couldn't stop a broad grin spreading across his face.

'Want to come and see where I've put the mud into it?' asked Rollo. You bet, agreed Mossy, gently easing himself along so that he could look down on Rollo's side. Both he and JJ admired the mud plaster. Trust a Place Reader to get it right, even if it could do with a bit of horsehair to be perfect.

With the two boys busy, Mossy decided it was time for his final preparations. He was worried about going away, but what option did he have? Annie needed him to help her see clearly, to stop the confusion that was taking her over. Bite the bullet, he told himself. You have no choice.

He strode briskly over to Puddle's house, pausing to admire the new pond as he passed it. That looks good, he thought, spotting two dragonflies hovering over the surface.

'I like those water iris.' He pointed at the spires of blue. 'Got any fish yet?' he asked Puddle, who had appeared at his side.

'Not yet, but we've had some visiting ducks already.'

'You'll be surprised how quickly they'll come,' Mossy reassured him, nodding his head sagely. 'Wait and see,' he grinned. 'You always do in the end.'

Puddle shook his head as Mossy explained his plans.

'London?' he checked. 'Rather you than me. It's bad enough going into town, let alone somewhere so far away. My last Dwellers spent lots of time there. And then they moved to the depths of the city. Good riddance, as far as I was concerned, though I feel sorry for the Holder who's got them now. They were a troublesome lot.

'They used to tell terrible stories about the place, bicyclists killed in passing every day it seemed to me. Fire engines and police racing around all the time. Non-stop trouble. Anything could happen to you. You could be hideously injured. Think what that would do to Annanbourne. You might never recover, either of you.'

Mossy shuddered at the thought.

'Still, they did some good work on your house,' he reminded him, changing the subject. Puddle patted his rather round tummy.

'Turning the garage into a kitchen? I s'pose so, but look at the shape it made me! Remember when I got stuck in the cat flap, and you had to pull me out?' Both Holders laughed at the memory, although a chill lingered in Mossy's mind.

'Your friend going to poll up to look after things?' Puddle continued. 'I haven't seen him in ages, but you said he usually comes when you need help.'

'No, no sign of him. Bit of a free spirit. Comes and goes as he pleases.'

'Has it ever crossed your mind how like him your eldest Dweller Child is?' Puddle scratched his head.

'Yeess, but Rollo's human, not one of us,' Mossy pointed out. 'And look at the size of him.'

'You're right enough there!' Puddle laughed. 'And rather too visible. Still, have you put out a call?'

'That's not how he works. He just turns up, out of the blue. Not just when there's trouble. It could be any time. Sometimes he's only here for an hour, or maybe a day, other times for a week or even months.' Mossy shrugged his shoulders. 'But I shouldn't be too long anyway. I'm hoping only a day.'

'Travelling by…?' checked Puddle.

'Handbag,' declared Mossy firmly. 'It's one of the good things about women these days, they're forever carting handbags about the place, and Annie's is the right size to take a passenger.'

## CHAPTER 29

# Getting There

Mossy was up long before anyone else the following morning. There was no sign of the Travelling Holder, but he knew that he had done his best to leave the house in good hands while he was away.

The evening before, when Annie came home, he had sensed an even greater confusion in her. During supper she had snapped at Cissy when she was telling them about the play that she had made with a friend during the afternoon. JJ had been given the part of Robber Bandit.

'Life isn't about making plays about stealing things. Stealing is wrong, you know!' she exclaimed. 'You have to give up fun and work hard at things if you want to make any kind of success.' Cissy had looked crushed.

'Mum, she's only eleven!' Rollo pointed out.

'As if you'd know about hard work!' Annie turned on him now. Mossy was aghast. Rollo was up every morning, off to do his paper round without any complaint, and without asking for help once. 'You've always got your head in a book, dreaming about the past. You can't live there, you know.' Rollo said nothing, but he looked hurt.

Mossy was puzzled. This wasn't fair, and fairness had been one of Annie's great qualities.

'For goodness sake, JJ! Can't you do anything quietly?' she had demanded, when he had let the cutlery fall with a clatter into the sink after clearing the table.

'It's OK, Mum, nothing broken,' he told her cheerfully.

'Not this time, but you're so careless.' Now that really isn't fair, thought Mossy. JJ hadn't broken anything for ages and was far less accident-prone than before. These days he took much more care.

When the boy opened his mouth to protest, Mossy spotted Rollo shaking his head, holding a finger to his lips behind his mother's back. JJ's hands dropped silently to his sides. I shall have my work cut out tonight, thought Mossy as he flexed his fingers – the stiffness was back.

'I mentioned your job offer to Dirk,' Annie told Jack that night as they tidied the kitchen. Mossy paused on his way to start the Nightwatch.

'He pointed out that I'd still need to keep working. You won't be that well paid while you're training still, and teaching isn't the highest paid work anyway.'

'For the first year, maybe, but Ian thinks that I may well be able to do more than simply classroom teaching. I have other skills that would be useful if I want to go further up the career ladder.' What have ladders got to do with it? wondered Mossy, as he turned to sit on the step.

'Big words from a small man,' commented Annie. Mossy winced. That really hurt. Small man? he thought. I may be small, but Jack is nearly as tall as the doors. He folded his arms across his chest. *It's a good thing I'm coming with you tomorrow, before it's too late.*

He was ready and waiting when Annie came down in the early morning light. As she collected her keys, he climbed into her handbag, neatly positioning himself at the side with something to hold onto, keeping himself upright and able to look out. She grabbed the strap, swinging the bag round onto her shoulder, Mossy hanging on tightly and landing with a thump against her side.

'Mum?' Rollo stood in the doorway.

'What is it, my love?'

'Nothing. Just hope you have a better day.'

'I'm sorry.' Mossy turned to look up at Annie's face. 'I was really crabby last night,' she continued. 'It's not that the work's hard, it's just that I… Oh, I don't know. There are all sorts of things I can't do because of it. I get frustrated.'

'Don't worry, Mum. We're OK. You'll see, it's all going to be fine.'

*'And you were the one telling JJ not to say anything,'* projected Mossy.

'Got to go,' said Annie, 'or I'll miss the train.'

'Love you, Mum.'

I'm glad I sat and stroked her head last night, thought Mossy. Some of the tension had eased, and she seemed more relaxed this morning.

Having been flung onto a car seat and nearly squashed by a briefcase dumped on top of him, Mossy was greatly relieved when they got out. Holding on tightly to the strap of the bag, he peered out as they stood on a wide station platform. Other people were gathered around them, milling about aimlessly, some reading papers, others simply staring vacantly into the air. Mossy shifted to the side as Annie dipped a hand in beside him, fishing about for a book.

Bells clanged, and then another rang as even more people hurried to join them. A roaring racket drew Mossy's attention. He craned his head round Annie's arm. There was the train! He gritted his teeth. There's a first time for everything, he reminded himself, and she does it every day. Perfectly safely. As Jack had before her. He shut his eyes tightly.

By the time he opened them again he had to admit it wasn't half as bad as he had imagined. He and the bag were dumped on Annie's lap, with the book balanced to one side of him as Annie read in silence, both of them rocking with the movement of the train. Opposite were three men, packed tightly together, rather like hens roosting. One of them had fallen asleep, his mouth open wide. Would anyone notice if I threw something into it? Better not, he decided, reluctantly.

When the train stopped, no one moved. More people got in. A woman with a large, black curly-haired dog came and sat next to Annie. The dog looked at Mossy and panted. Mossy winked back.

'D'you do this often?' he projected. The dog blinked, resting her head on the woman's lap, still looking at Mossy.

'Every day?!' Mossy repeated. 'This is my first time.'

'Good girl,' said the woman, gently stroking the dog's head. Nobody else said anything.

Each time the train stopped, more people climbed aboard. Soon there was standing room only. Mossy was glad to be safely stowed on Annie's lap. He rested his head against her, looking out of the window, as she turned another page of her book.

Outside he caught a glimpse of a massive wheel, far too big for any cart, bigger than a building. He moved his head to see better, admiring the huge structures. Would the Holders be as big too? he wondered. Annie tucked a hand under her book, and Mossy felt its warmth as it brushed against him. Hang on, she felt different! The relaxation that he had worked so hard to regain for her overnight was gone already, replaced by that unpleasant tightness again.

Loud squeals from outside made Mossy almost jump out of his skin. All around them people were shifting. Mossy squeezed to one side as Annie shoved her book back into the bag, pinching his foot between it and her purse. He gritted his teeth, carefully wriggling free. Ah, that was better.

He grinned at the dog, which was standing up again, having lain on the floor for most of the journey. It panted back at him.

'Watch out? What for?'

Suddenly Annie was bending over to reach something by her feet, crushing Mossy and the bag into her lap, knocking all the breath out of his body. And then he was swinging through the air as the train jolted to a stop and Annie rose to her feet.

People swarmed around them, Mossy looking back from his vantage point, catching a last glimpse of the dog. He reached out a hand for a farewell lick.

The march of a thousand feet tramped through the building, magnified by the vaulted glass roof. What kind of Holder lives here? wondered Mossy, ducking out of the way of a man who pushed past them. A voice echoed overhead. Something about 'Platform 15'. Mossy hung on tightly as he looked around for a kindred spirit. Was that a glimpse of a Holder he caught, far away at the other end of the building? He couldn't be sure in the crush.

The people flowed like a vast river, all headed in one direction. It reminded him of grain being poured into the mill, and he hoped there wasn't a grinding wheel further on. With another surprise jolt he felt himself being swooshed round to the front as Annie thrust her hand into her bag again. He whisked his feet out of the way, glad that there were so many people jostling them.

Hang on. What was happening now?! Annie had stopped walking, but they were still moving! He was sure of it. They were going down! Frantically he looked around him. Behind them the people were higher. He twisted round and squinted past her elbow. The people in front were lower. They seemed to be on some kind of terrible staircase that led down into the ground.

No wonder Annie was in such a state when she came home each day. He'd thought that Advertising was something to do with drawing and making pictures. It looked as if it was more like mining. What on earth had he let himself in for?

Bright lights and heat wafted up from the depths. Mossy wrinkled his nose. There were an awful lot of people down there in Advertising. Metallic odours mingled with the squash of humans, and then he caught a familiar smell too. There was a Holder down there! Mossy smiled; a friendly face at last, someone who could help.

Annie was on the move again. Barriers clanged, and then

came another of those terrible staircases. They went deeper and deeper underground. The flow of humans trudged on through the tube-like tunnels. The heat rose. Mossy told himself not to panic. Somewhere there was another Holder: it couldn't be all bad. When Annie eventually stopped, they were packed in the midst of a throng of people. Mossy kept very still, only his eyes roving about.

'*What are you doing here?*' The projection hit him out of the blue. He looked carefully to the left, across Annie. There he was, an ash-pale Holder, perched on the edge of a waste bin.

'*Helping my Dweller,*' he sent back. '*Is this Advertising?*'

'*No way!*' The Holder grinned at him. '*We're Waterloo Underground Station. I'm Walt. I guess you missed Stan up in the top station. He's pretty frantic in the mornings.*'

'*I didn't see anyone up there. Too many people.*' Mossy wasn't sure what he felt, relief or fear. If this wasn't Advertising, would that be even worse?

'*I can see you're not local,*' Walt rattled on. '*You'll be passing through, like everyone does. No Dwellers here, just Lingerers.*' A wistful look crossed his face. '*It must be good to have real Dwellers, like yours.*' He paused again. '*Train coming,*' he continued. '*I'll look out for you on your way back.*'

Mossy had never realised that humans could pack themselves so tightly. He had thought the train was full, but that was nothing compared to this. The elbow of the woman standing next to Annie stuck into his chest, and he had to dip his head to stop his nose being bent sideways against a man's arm. The corner of another man's paper tickled his ear as they lurched off, rubbing and swaying against each other in a noisy hush. And to think he'd been worried about the first train! Mossy felt in his pocket. It was alright; he still had a little bit of earth from home with him.

The train squealed and screeched, rattling and rocking through dark tunnels, until suddenly Annie spoke.

'Excuse me!'

Mossy looked up at her. The man in front of them eased sideways, allowing Annie to squeeze past and out of the train. Oh, it was good to be able to breathe deeply again, even if it was this rather stale air.

Mossy didn't mind the bumping and jolting and, as Annie strode forward again, he waved at the Holder he glimpsed standing by the tunnel entrance. Another staircase, only this time they were rising. He strained his nose forward. There was fresh air ahead.

Suddenly they were in daylight. Mossy blinked his eyes. Looming buildings tried to block out the sun. Three storeys above them Mossy spotted a Holder on a windowsill. He waved and got a thumbs-up in return.

Thunder rattled by, drawing his attention, and he saw two red buses chase each along the road. Crowds of people swarmed around, buzzing ferociously on their way somewhere. Annie walked with determination too, past a pizza restaurant, a newspaper stall and some other shops. She stopped by a set of lights, where a tiny red light man glared at her from the far side of the road.

Mossy looked at the hoarding that surrounded the building behind them. A small window had been cut into the wooden frame and he saw a thin Holder sitting disconsolately, staring out of dark-ringed eyes at the world that passed him by.

'*Don't worry,*' Mossy projected. '*I've had extensions, too. You'll be fine.*' He waved his spindly fingers in encouragement. The Holder sighed, a tear washing a track through the dust on his hollow cheeks.

'*If only it were an extension. They've already dismantled our plumbing and wiring.*' There was a look of desperation in his eyes. '*We're due for demolition.*' Mossy gasped in horror.

'*Surely they'll leave your Starting Stone? You'll be able to rise again?*' He wanted to find some crumb of comfort for this wasted spirit.

'*They're building a basement – underground parking. I don't think we'll even be hardcore. Nothing will be saved.*' Mossy shuddered. Even in his worst nightmares he had never envisioned meeting such a terrible end.

'*I'm so sorry. I…*'

Annie was on the move again, carrying him across the road and straight towards another building. Mossy waved a hand in farewell. He didn't care who felt him; the vision was too terrible to worry about his own safety.

Annie pulled her handbag, and Mossy, to the front of her, as she walked towards a door with 'Dorkling, Phibber and Fikness' etched into the glass. It swooshed open as she approached.

''Morning Annie!' A young woman, with a scarlet gash instead of a mouth, bared her teeth at them. Another, sitting beside her, spoke to a tiny metal beetle that seemed to be suspended in front of her face by a thread that slipped round from her ear. Mossy was amazed at the calm way in which she addressed it.

'Dorkling, Phibber and Fikness! Advertising you can trust!

Raven speaking. How may I help you?'

Ah-ha! thought Mossy. **This** was Advertising. No wonder Walt had laughed at him. You couldn't find anywhere more different. Here everything was glass, steel and light, sparkling clean and hard, and yet dangerously soft at the same time. The beetle didn't seem interested in help, but that didn't stop Raven telling it she was going to connect it now.

'You OK, love?' asked the Scarlet Gash, adjusting a beetle in front of her mouth too. Love? thought Mossy. What do you know about that? Your smile doesn't even reach your lips, let alone your eyes. He wondered if she was going to eat the beetle.

'I thought I felt someone fiddling with my bag,' Annie replied. 'But it's fine.'

Their progress was muffled by deep carpet, and Mossy watched wide-eyed as Annie pressed a button on the wall. A slit slid open to reveal a small cupboard into which she stepped. He nearly groaned aloud. He had known that London would be different, but never in his life had he seen so many strange things all at once. And now Annie was hiding in a cupboard. He couldn't blame her. He felt like hiding too.

Suddenly there was a strange lurching feeling in his stomach. Mossy closed his eyes. He had a horrid feeling they were on the move again whilst keeping still.

'*Hello there, stranger,*' came the projection. Mossy's eyes sprang open, searching round the tiny space. '*Behind you. Don't move; she'll feel it. I'll catch you when you get out of the lift.*'

## CHAPTER 30

# A Guided Tour

A slight whirring stopped with a ping as the doors slid open. Annie stooped to collect her briefcase. As she stood up, Mossy felt her gather her strength. She took a breath, paused and then stepped forward into a large open space, flooded with light. People hurried about.

"Morning, Annie!"

"Morning, Alice."

'Hi there!'

'Hi!'

'Got a moment?' Voices seemed to come from all directions. Mossy didn't know where to look.

Suddenly he was being swung through the air as Annie slipped the bag from her shoulder, dropping it to the floor by a chair.

'With you in a tick.' He heard her voice high above him as he looked around. Legs and feet everywhere, all on the move. He was going to have to be very careful. Slowly he edged himself out of the handbag, lurking by the chair where he was sure no one would tread on him. Stiletto heels spiked past, leaving sharp imprints on the floor. You could lose a toe under one of those, Mossy warned himself, and there's no saying what that would do to Annanbourne.

'Made it OK, I see.' The soft voice surprised him. He whirled round to find a decidedly strange Holder shimmering at his side.

'Wow! Do you always look like that?' he asked.

'Glass and steel building,' explained his new friend, shrugging glass shoulders and raising shiny steel eyebrows. 'I don't have much choice. I'm Flik-cum-Addero.' He bowed in greeting. 'But call me Flik.' He held out a glistening hand.

'I guess it's what you're used to, either way,' said Mossy, shaking it cautiously. He didn't want to break him on first meeting. 'I'm Mossy,' he added.

'It's toughened glass, don't worry,' laughed Flik. 'We don't chip easily!' Although being invisible was necessary a lot of the time, Mossy felt deeply relieved that he wasn't transparent in his natural state.

'So what are you doing here?' continued Flik.

'Trying to help my Dweller,' replied Mossy, waving a hand in Annie's direction, but realising, as he looked over his shoulder, that she had vanished.

'Don't worry, they come and go,' Flik grinned. 'As long as their handbags and briefcases are here they'll be back.' Handy tip, thought Mossy. It was good to have Flik on his side.

'So tell me what it's like here,' he asked.

'Busy, mostly.' Flik beckoned Mossy to follow him,

launching off across the open floor, dodging racing feet with an expert wiggle or skip. Mossy kept close on his heels. 'Lots of people during the day, few at night. I'll give you a tour.'

As Flik guided him through the building, Mossy discovered that the moving cupboards were called lifts, that firedoors were best avoided, that red lights meant you had to keep quiet, and that people in the sales room all had beetles suspended in front of their faces.

'Do they ever actually eat them?'

'Eat them?!' Flik was enjoying himself. 'You really don't know much about this world, do you? They're telephones. Surely even out in the country you've heard about telephones!'

'Of course we have,' protested Mossy, blushing to the tips of his ears. 'We just don't disguise them as insects.'

The constant flow of people meant that they never waited long before a door was flung wide to let them pass. As they came round a corner, Mossy spotted a pale girl lingering by a notice board.

'She alright?' he asked.

'Not really.' Flik shook his head. 'Just been dumped by her boyfriend. But she was too good for him anyway. She'll be much happier with the new one I've got lined up for her.'

He gave a broad grin, lightly touching the back of her leg as they passed, and she sighed, ran her fingers through her hair, found a smile and followed them into another big room full of people.

'It looks like you've got a really good place here,' Mossy congratulated Flik as they came back to their starting point by Annie's desk.

Maybe he had been wrong. He'd felt sure that Annie's problems were coming from her workplace, but after all he had seen that seemed unlikely.

'We're mostly fine,' Flik agreed, nodding his head. 'There are a few tricky problems I could do without; the depressed woman I pointed out two floors down, for instance, and there's a young man with a serious illness he doesn't know about yet. And that person in the press office whose wife died.' He paused, sighed and drew a deep breath. 'And then, of course, there's Dirk.' Mossy's ears pricked up.

'Dirk?' he queried, doing his best to look casual.

'One of the bosses. Dirk Dorkling. Founded the business. Brilliant at advertising. But a really nasty piece of work.'

'In what way?' Maybe he hadn't been wrong after all, wondered Mossy.

'He's underhand. He's a bully. He cheats. He claims work is his, when someone else should be given the credit. Lies so much I wonder if he'd recognise the truth if it stood on his nose. And constantly chasing after women in the office. A few years back there was a major rumpus when one of 'his women' complained to a court after he turned her down for promotion. So then his wife found out. It was a right mess! I thought that would make him stop, but I've noticed recently that he's trying to get his claws into someone new. A lovely woman, she is. I don't think she realises what he's up to, but I do. I've seen the signs before.'

'What are the signs?' Mossy asked.

'He keeps popping down to check things with her. Tells her she's brilliant. Asks her to stay late for extra meetings.

Tells her that she's about to get a promotion – 'fantastic new client' for whom her work is perfect. The trouble is that I can see he's wearing her down. He's too used to winning, to always getting his own way. He doesn't care about her. He doesn't care that he might wreck her life the way he has so many others.'

'But surely this woman must realise what he's up to?' Mossy felt this was terrible. He'd had an uncomfortable feeling about Dirk from things Annie had reported, but had never realised he could be this bad. No wonder she felt confused. If she could see all this sort of thing going on around her with no way to stop it, she was bound to be unhappy.

'Oh, no. Dirk's a typical bully. Wouldn't ever dare to do something up front, out in the open. He'd only ever pick on someone who is basically kind and good, someone who wouldn't see what he was up to, because they don't think people are that bad.'

'Poor woman. And poor you, having to try to sort it all out,' Mossy put out a hand to comfort him.

'Poor me?' Flik frowned. 'I thought that was why you had come.' He pointed over Mossy's shoulder. Mossy turned round. Annie was walking towards them. 'It's your Dweller he's picking on this time.'

## CHAPTER 31

# Dining Out

Annie was seated at her desk again. Mossy was slumped under it, Flik at his side. Mossy shook his head. The Holder's words had quite taken his breath away.

'So he's trying to steal her work?' he checked. He could have kicked himself. All this time he'd been thinking it was Jack who was taking Annie's paintings, when in reality the thief was Dirk.

'Oh, he did that ages ago. Passed off one of the first things she did as his. No, what I'm worried about is that he's trying to steal **her**.'

'What? Steal Annie?' Mossy couldn't believe what he was hearing. But Annie belonged with Jack and the children. They loved her. They needed her. She loved them too. Thank goodness he'd come. And only just in the nick of time, by the sound of things.

'Watch out, this is him now.' Flik pointed at a man in an immaculate dark suit who was gliding towards Annie's desk.

''Morning, Ms Breeze.' Mossy took an instant dislike to

Dirk's somewhat treacly voice. Highly polished shoes stopped by the desk. 'Interesting suggestion you made at the morning meeting.'

'Thank you, Dirk,' Annie's voice sounded pleased.

'Quick, give me a hand,' Mossy whispered to Flik as he grabbed a shoelace and pulled gently. The bow unravelled.

'Having lunch with a client today. Like you to meet him. Think you'd be the perfect person to handle the account.' Dirk's voice oozed across the table above them, as Mossy pointed to the other lace.

'Thank you very much, Dirk. I'm flattered. What time should I be there?'

Mossy wrapped the lace round his hand, holding it firmly, and indicated to Flik that he should do the same with the other one.

*Don't pull 'til I wink, then hold really tight, and let go when I nod,'* he projected. Flik nodded back silently, his eyes bright with pleasure.

'Shall we say one fifteen at Marcel's? No need to be flattered. The pleasure's all mine, I can assure you.'

'Who's the client?' Annie asked.

'Don't you worry about that,' Dirk assured her. 'Just be there – I think you'll enjoy it.' Mossy felt sickened by the sticky charm in that voice.

The feet turned to leave, the two Holders trailing on either side. Only once Dirk was in an open space did Mossy wink at Flik. They dug their heels into the carpet and pulled for all they were worth, gluing Dirk's foot to the floor.

'What on earth?!' exclaimed Dirk, jerking his leg. Mossy nodded. His foot released, Dirk went flying forward, both hands stretched out to break his fall. Mossy and Flik admired their handiwork, broad grins on both their faces as several people, including Annie, rushed to assist their boss.

'Are you all right?' asked a young man. Annie stepped back.

'Fine. Fine.' Dirk brushed at imaginary dirt on his sleeves, his cheeks an embarrassed red as he straightened his jacket. 'You should keep your floor clear.' His eyes glared round the room, daring anyone to say a word. Mossy spotted another woman on the far side of the room covering her mouth with her hand.

'Nice one, Mossy,' murmured Flik.

Only once Dirk was well out of earshot did comments begin to fly.

"Keep the floor clear!' There was nothing on it!'

'Sight for sore eyes!'

'What on earth made him crash over like that?'

'It's a bit early in the morning to be drunk!'

Annie was back at her desk. She didn't join in the laughter. Mossy sat under her chair. He could feel her confusion. She was sorry for Dirk.

*'Come on there, Annie,'* Mossy projected. *'He's been passing your work off as his, gaining the credit that should be yours.'*

An older woman came over and stood by her desk.

'Be careful, Annie. Dirk's not always as straightforward as you think.'

'What do you mean, Meg?' Annie looked up from her work.

'When he invites you to join him for lunch…' The words hung on the air.

'He wants me to meet a client. That's all.'

'Well, don't say I didn't warn you. You've heard the stories. We all really like you, but that'll change if...' Meg paused. 'You know, sudden promotions, all that?' That made Mossy's mind up. If Annie was going off to lunch, he was going with her.

Installed in the handbag again, Mossy paid attention as she headed out of the building. He glanced across the road. Something had changed. His heart leapt into his mouth as he recognised what it was. The demolition had begun. He buried his face in his hands, shivering in horror. Only that morning he'd spoken to him. The memory of that pale, terrified face was still with him when Annie's voice broke across his thoughts.

'I'm meeting Dirk Dorkling?'

'Ah yes, Madam. Mr Dorkling told me to expect you.' A smooth young woman smiled placidly at them. 'Follow me.'

Mossy rolled his eyes in amazement at their surroundings. He had never seen anywhere so grand. Everything was immaculate, with perfect white flowers adorning the large tables, hushed voices and soft music.

'Ah! Annie!' Dirk's voice poured across the table as he rose to his feet. 'Nothing I like better than a woman who comes on time.'

'I'm glad I managed to get here before the others arrived,' Annie replied, gently dropping her bag onto the soft carpet by her chair. Mossy climbed out.

'Mmm...' There was a brief pause before Dirk continued.

'I'm afraid the others couldn't join us in the end,

cancelled at the last minute. I thought we'd just make the most of it anyway.' His mouth smiled widely, but Mossy realised that his eyes were full of calculation.

I don't like you, you're mean, he decided. Delicately he placed a hand on Annie's shoe. Her feet were itching to take her away.

'*Remember Meg's warning,*' he projected.

Mossy was still crouched beside Annie's bag when he heard a low voice by his shoulder.

'Haven't seen you here before. Visiting from out of town?' He looked over to see a rather portly Holder standing to his left. Immaculately presented in black and white, his cropped hair gleamed in the soft light. But, unlike Dirk, his smile filled his eyes, and a glowing warmth wafted around him.

'Yes,' Mossy nodded. 'Trying to look after my Dweller.'

'Thank goodness. I've seen that one tell too many women about 'last minute cancellations'. I'll check if you like, but I'm pretty sure this table was only ever booked for two. By the way, I'm Ricco.' He held his hand out. 'Anything I can do, just let me know.' Mossy clasped the offered hand gratefully in both of his.

'I'm Mossy, and thanks. I've a funny feeling I'm going to need all the help I can get.'

Above them Annie was still hesitating as Ricco slipped away to check the bookings.

'Well that's very kind, but I've a lot of work on – the launch of that new perfume?'

'*That's it,*' agreed Mossy. '*Get yourself out of here.*' But Dirk was prepared. He stepped towards Annie, taking the back of her chair in his hands.

'Yes, yes. I'd like to talk about that too, whilst you're here. Do sit down. Might as well make the best of it.'

Humph! thought Mossy – best of it? What do you mean by that?

Reluctantly Annie sat. Wine was poured into her glass.

'*Don't drink that, it won't help,*' Mossy warned, but Annie took a sip. The conversation turned to work. Maybe I've been hasty, Mossy decided, perched carefully on the back of Annie's chair where he could keep a close eye on things. Maybe it **was** just work.

'Psst!' Ricco was back. 'I was right. No cancellations, table only ever booked for two. He's lying.' Mossy's mind raced.

'Can you do anything about the food? Make it really revolting?' A look of horror shot across Ricco's face.

'This is one of London's top restaurants!' he protested. 'Chef would go bezerk if I did that. Some of my Dwellers might be fired. Really sorry – that's out of the question.'

'Well at least we can get rid of that wine,' Mossy decided.

'With you on that one. You look after your Dweller, and I'll sort her wine glass.'

Mossy returned to his perch on Annie's chair and watched in admiration as Ricco nimbly climbed the plush table cloth. Glancing round to check that none of his waiters were anywhere near, he crept across the table, skirting the plates and stepping daintily over the cutlery. As Annie reached her hand towards her glass, Ricco flicked a finger at the stem, knocking it out of her reach. Briefly it teetered before falling towards Dirk, wine splattering across his plate, leaping over the edge of the table and trickling down onto his trousers.

'Oh Dirk, I'm so sorry!' Annie clapped a hand to her mouth as a waiter rushed over with a napkin to help mop up the mess.

Mossy grinned and gave Ricco a thumbs-up. That ought to put him off, he decided. But Dirk wafted the waiter away.

'Don't you worry, Annie, my dear. Accidents happen, and I'm sure you'll find some way to make up for it.' Mossy's heart sank. Annie wasn't Dirk's dear. What if this made her feel indebted to him? That wasn't the plan at all.

'And thinking of people who make mistakes – how's that Loser of yours?' Dirk continued. 'What's he losing at these days?' Loser? Mossy thought. Who was he talking about?

'Actually he's considering a serious job offer, and I'm beginning to think he should take it.' Mossy laid a finger cautiously on Annie's shoulder. Somewhere deep inside her, struggling to make itself felt, he could feel a steeliness, a hidden strength.

*'Come on Annie. Stand up to him. He's just a bully. You wouldn't let your children be got at by someone like this.'*

'I think he might be right,' she continued. 'This could be the beginning of something new, something he might really enjoy.' Dirk laid a hand on Annie's as it rested on the table. Mossy wanted to grab a fork and stick it into him. You leave my Annie alone, he nearly shouted.

'I have a proposition I want to put to you. There's a conference coming up in Paris. I'm going to be speaking at it – Advertising for the Future, New Formats.' Who cares? thought Mossy.

'*Leave Annie alone, get your hands off her.*'

Annie shifted uncomfortably.

'I need an assistant.'

'Oh, Dirk,' Annie protested, pulling her hand free. 'I don't have the experience for something like that. I'd be no use.'

'*Just say no,*' projected Mossy. '*Say 'No!'*'

'Come on Annie, you know what I mean…'

'Dirk…' Annie's voice was firm. Mossy remembered it from times when she had been cross with the children. She spoke slowly and clearly. 'I only agreed to come to this lunch because you said there was a client you wanted me to meet. Then they cancel. Now you start talking about 'conferences'.'

'Annie, it's simple, a trip to Paris. My wife's busy. Your Mr Stay-at-Home-Classroom-Assistant is out of the way. You're a good-looking woman, with qualities he doesn't seem to recognise. And I'm a winner, looking forward to… recognising them. Don't you want your job?' Mossy could feel the shock shoot through Annie.

'*Stay strong, Annie,*' Mossy encouraged her as he projected images into Annie's mind; memories of JJ snuggled up against her during his bedtime story; Cissy prancing round the kitchen recounting some drama from school; Rollo looking up from a book to share some exciting discovery with her; Jack's beaming smile that welcomed her back after a hard day.

'Dirk!' she exclaimed. 'That's not fair. You know I need my job. But I'm a creative designer, not a 'conference assistant', whatever you seem to mean by that.'

Suddenly Mossy was furious. This Dirk was a bully. He was attacking Annie, trying to trap her into something. Flik was right, he **was** trying to steal her. It was time to step in.

Holding his breath, he let the fury build, knowing the changes it would bring in him. On the far side of the table he spotted Ricco giving him the double thumbs-up.

'*Go for it*,' came the message. And then, well, Mossy did.

Squatting on the back of Annie's chair, he pulled his knees up towards his ears, his long toes pointing down over her shoulder. He tucked his fingers into the corner of his mouth, pulling it as wide as he could. His elbows stuck out to the side; his nose quivered in fury; his eyes burned red in anger.

And then he made himself visible. Just for a flash. Just for long enough.

'Oh, my God!' Dirk exclaimed. 'What the...?' Snatching his hand away from Annie he rocked back in his chair, a look of horror on his face. Invisible again, Mossy leapt across the table, knocking over the flowers, scattering cutlery all over the place and launching himself onto Dirk's shoulder. He gripped the collar of his jacket firmly to keep himself in place.

'You dare to lay a single finger on her,' he hissed, careful that only Dirk should hear, 'and I'll be back for you.'

'No, no!' exclaimed Dirk, leaping to his feet, shaking his head as if trying to free himself of Mossy's threat. But Mossy hadn't finished yet.

'Dirk?' Annie sounded surprised. 'Are you alright? What's up?'

'I... You... On your... In my...' All the smooth oiliness had vanished from Dirk's voice as he gesticulated frantically at Annie.

'Say sorry,' instructed Mossy through gritted teeth.

'I'm sorry. I take it all back. I...' Dirk blurted out the words, still staggering backwards, looking frantically round the room, where several other diners were staring at him open-mouthed.

'Now, go,' announced Mossy, jumping free to land lightly on the abandoned seat. Dirk held up a hand in submission, sweat breaking out on his pale face.

'Got to go,' he said. He turned and fled.

Annie, standing by the abandoned table, put a hand to her mouth, but not before Mossy had spotted a smile creep across her face. She was stifling a laugh.

'I take it Mr Dorkling won't be coming back?' The young woman who had initially greeted them was at her side, calmly taking control, smoothing things out.

'I don't think so,' Annie shook her head. 'And I think I'll be on my way too.'

'Best entertainment I've seen in ages,' smiled Ricco, clapping his hands silently in appreciation, 'and more than time that one had his come-uppance. Well done.'

'Thanks for your help!' called Mossy as he dived between the waiter's legs, dodging hands that were scooping up the scattered flowers from the floor. He grabbed the handle of Annie's handbag as she lifted it onto her shoulder and dived in, head first.

'It was nothing,' said the waiter, not quite sure to whom he was speaking.

## CHAPTER 32

# Back In Place

Flik was waiting anxiously for them at the door to his building.

'You alright? What happened? Dirk the Dork came back in a real state!' Mossy unwrapped his arms from the strap and hooked one leg over the side of Annie's handbag.

'G'afternoon, Annie.'

'Afternoon Beth, Raven.' Annie nodded at the two wide-eyed receptionists who followed her progress across the entrance hall. Mossy wriggled the other leg free and launched himself towards the floor just as a ping announced the opening of the lift doors. Unfortunately his toe caught in the lip of the handbag, and he crashed head first at Flik's feet as Annie disappeared into the lift.

'Whoops!' Mossy winked at him, his eyes a shining blue once more. 'Thank goodness your carpets are soft!'

'Did you see her? Cool as a cucumber!' exclaimed Beth once the lift doors had closed, carrying Annie upwards.

'D'you think she did it deliberately?' Raven rested her

elbows on the desk, her chin in her hands, the beetle nudging her cheek. 'His trousers were a right mess.'

'Well, if you ask me…' But a phone rang and Beth spoke to her beetle instead. 'Dorkling, Phibber and Fikness! Advertising you can trust! Beth speaking. How may I help you?'

Another ping and the lift doors slid open again, releasing two men into the hall.

'… in an absolute fury. Never known him come back early from a lunch meeting before.' The speaker headed towards the street. Flik dived towards the open lift doors, beckoning Mossy to follow.

'Wouldn't want to be his secretary just now. He was absolutely bellowing at her when I passed his office,' said the other man, hurrying behind his friend, as Mossy slipped through the gap in the nick of time before the door shut.

'Boost my jump, can you?' Mossy clasped his hands together, bracing himself as Flik took a run-up, jumped onto his palms and leapt for the lift buttons. As they sailed upwards Mossy told him about the events at the restaurant.

Flik was holding his sides, tears of laughter running down his cheeks, when the doors slid open, ushering them onto Annie's work floor.

'I wish I'd been there. No wonder he looked grim. The story will be everywhere in no time, and he won't take it well.'

'Maybe he's learnt a lesson,' suggested Mossy. 'And if I have to come back, so be it. Advertising isn't as scary as I thought, thanks to you.'

'You'll have to watch out for your Dweller, though,' warned Flik. 'She won't get that promotion. He'll want to get back at her somehow.'

As the two Holders sauntered towards Annie's desk, Mossy remembered something else.

'Flik... Across the road?'

Flik shuddered, his face turning pale.

'It's terrible. Demolition. Poor Hubert, there's going to be nothing left.'

'Is that how you came?' Mossy hardly dared to ask.

'No, thank goodness. There was a bomb during the war, but my Starting Stone wasn't damaged. I rose again. I was Flik Furness originally, then a rubble car park for ages, but lots of us struggled after the war. I think the worst thing for Hubes has been the waiting, the slow disintegration. He's been empty for ages. And then there's going to be some new whippersnapper skyscraper, thinking he's the bee's knees because he's umpty floors high. Still, that's London for you. Always moving on. We have to go with the flow here. That's why I'm Cum-Addero now; my surname changed after the new build.'

'I wouldn't know all that,' Mossy admitted with relief. 'It's different where I come from. Though we've struggled with empty in our time.'

Mossy hung around Annie's desk for the rest of the day, watching her work, enjoying the concentration on her face as she conjured an image onto the paper. People came and went, asking for advice or an opinion. Alice asked her to check some writing.

She's good at this, he admitted, but still he felt that what she really needed were her paintings. These drawings were small-fry doodles by comparison. They didn't radiate the energy of her work in the studio at Annanbourne. But he was very pleased to notice there were no more visits from Dirk.

Annie glanced at her watch, stood up and stretched her back.

'See you in the morning!' she called to Meg, who waved a hand as she passed.

Annie slipped an arm through the strap of her handbag. Mossy, who was stretched out along the top edge of her drawing board, leapt to his feet. This was one ride he seriously couldn't afford to miss! As he scrabbled across the surface his foot slipped on a loose piece of paper. A pencil spun from under his toe and rattled across the desk. Annie turned back, frowning. That was all Mossy needed. He dived from the edge, his hands reaching for the strap.

'Whoops!' he muttered under his breath, as the force of his flight whisked the strap off Annie's shoulder, depositing both him and the bag in a heap at her feet. With a quick somersault he rolled himself inside as she picked it up again.

'Seems to be my day for sending things flying,' laughed Annie, dropping her book and purse onto Mossy's bottom. Seems to be my day for landing upside-down, he muttered to himself.

'And no bad thing,' he heard Meg reassure her.

There were plenty of people in the lift this time, so Annie was oblivious to Mossy righting himself. Nor did anyone but he notice Flik perched on the handle of the main door.

'*Good luck!*' projected Flik. '*You're welcome anytime. But watch out...*' Annie was hurrying onwards now, a mass of people crowding about her, as everybody flooded out of the surrounding buildings. The sound of Flik's projection crackled. Mossy tried to catch it, but it didn't make sense.

'*She sowing a bee via.*' What on earth did that mean? He racked his brain. It sounded like a warning, but he couldn't make head or tail of it. Sowing bees? And via where?

The trains were even more packed than they had been in the morning. Nevertheless, Mossy caught a glimpse of Walt as Annie left the underground train and headed for the moving stairs.

'*Was that you in the restaurant?*' came the pale projection. Mossy gave a surprised nod, receiving a broad grin in response.

'*Nice one!*' News travels fast in London, he decided. As a sharp whack from a determined elbow winded him, and another scrunched his nose, he decided it was time to take shelter at the bottom of the bag until they were closer to home. But even so he could distinctly feel that Annie was as keen as he was to get back to Annanbourne.

Tired after a busy day, weakened by the time away, but safe in the dark warmth of Annie's bag, he let the gentle rocking of the train lull him into restorative sleep, only waking when the car bumped down the drive to his Holding. He poked out his nose for a breath of country air again. His heart broke into song. Home, what a joy!

London hadn't been as bad as he had feared, and he was safely back within the day, but he was hugely relieved that he didn't normally have to cope with the bustle, all those people, that sticky dirt every day. It was good to be surrounded by the trees and the fields. The house smiled back at him.

'Mum!' JJ's call greeted them as Mossy stepped onto the

gravel of the drive. 'Mum, come and look. I've been helping Dad, and we've made a new path beside the stream.'

'And I'm Air Sea Rescue,' announced Cissy. Annie paused. Mossy looked over at her. This was the sort of thing that had sparked anger in her recently. She was looking closely at Cissy.

'Who needed to be rescued? Should I be worried about Rollo?'

'No, I'm fine, Mum,' Rollo reassured her, appearing from the back of the barn. 'It was JJ who fell in, and Cissy was brilliant.'

'Well, what a surprise!' Now Annie was laughing too, as she ruffled the hair on JJ's head, hugging him to her. This is different, thought Mossy. This is the way Annie used to be.

'Show me the path and tell me all about it. And then I'll tell you about what happened at work.'

Supper turned out to be a cheerful affair, with much laughter. Annie had been impressed by the new path.

'We got the paving slabs second-hand from the dump. Cissy spotted them when we took the bottles for recycling,' Jack explained as he collected plates from the dresser.

Mossy was in his favourite spot, his legs dangling either side of a mug, watching proceedings eagerly. Cissy kept them entertained with impressions of JJ cartwheeling into the stream and blowing bubbles of mud. And then it was Annie's turn.

Mossy was fascinated by her version of the events in which he had taken part.

'He went down like a felled tree. As if he tripped, but there was nothing to trip over. And you should have heard what people were saying!'

'But you said he's one of the best people at his job in the whole world,' Rollo reminded her.

'He is. But maybe he's not the best person in the world.' Her description of the glass of wine going flying, the flowers spraying about the place and the cutlery being scattered everywhere had the children falling about with laughter.

'But Mum, you never do things like that!' giggled JJ.

'Well, today was my Disaster Day. I stopped being The Creative Designer and turned into The Chaos Designer, and Dirk was so horrified that he leapt from the table and fled the restaurant.'

Hmm, thought Mossy, that's not quite how I remember it, and she's left out all the part about conferences. But he didn't really care. His Dwellers were happy and he feasted on that.

'Oh, and by the way,' Annie added, turning towards Jack. 'Have you told Ian Goodman that you're taking the job yet?' Everyone fell quiet. All eyes were on Jack.

'I... We said... we'd talk about it again?' Jack was hesitant. 'You were worried about it being the right thing to do.'

'I must have been crazy. If it's what you want, you do it. If you're doing what is right for you, then everything will be just fine.'

'Yay!' JJ leapt from his seat, rushing to his father's side. 'You're the best, Dad.'

It was only later, when Mossy came downstairs after watching the children settle for the night, that he heard Annie talking to Jack again.

'I had no idea he was such a smarmy creep. He was implying that my job might be at risk.'

'So what made you say no?'

'It was weird. Suddenly all I could see was all of you. That's what he was trying to put at risk. The children, you, everything that makes us a family. Remembering how brilliant you are with the kids. OK, so accidents happen, but they learn from them. They had accidents when I was looking after them. I know the inside of that hospital like the back of my hand.' She laughed softly, her head resting against his shoulder. 'It was as if, suddenly, I could see the way clearly. It was obvious, like it being obvious that you should become a teacher.'

Mossy relaxed, a gentle sigh settling him down, back in his proper place at Annanbourne, in his home. He curled up on the ancient hearthstone, his Starting Stone. There was no need for a Nightwatch. The happiness of the evening had wrapped the whole house in a protective glow that would keep any nightmare away.

## CHAPTER 33

# Letters in The Post

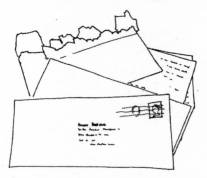

Mossy jumped from one slab to the next beside the stream as he trailed the children. He liked this new path, another improvement to his home. It made it much easier than battling through the coarse dried grasses at this time of year. No more seed heads tickling down his back.

Since his return from the city, he had noticed a suppleness returning to his body. The ache in his toes and fingers had gone. He ducked under the wire fence and pushed his way through the dry cow parsley. A shower of seed scattered down the back of his neck. He was still fishing them out when he joined the children lazing on the top of the tumulus.

'See that elephant?' Cissy pointed up at the sky. 'It's going to gobble up the man with the big nose.'

'I can't see a man with a big nose.' JJ squinted skywards.

'Or an elephant for that matter,' Rollo agreed with him. 'Giraffe maybe.'

'No, no,' Cissy insisted, waving vaguely at the fluffy white clouds. 'That's him. His nose is growing.' It's a fine nose,

Mossy noted with approval. Nothing wrong with long noses.

JJ sat up.

'Talking of things changing… Have you seen we've got Mum back?'

'We always get Mum back, every day,' Cissy pointed out.

'What do you mean, JJ?' Rollo asked, rolling onto his tummy, propping himself on his elbows to look at him.

'Proper Mum. Mum like she always is. Our Mum,' JJ insisted. 'She's stopped being cross all the time.' So I'm not the only one who's noticed, Mossy smiled to himself, his ears wriggling in satisfaction.

'You're right, you know.' Now even Cissy agreed. 'Last night when I dropped spaghetti all over the place, she laughed instead of going ballistic.'

'Yeah, I thought you'd had it, but she just said it was a pity we didn't have a dog!' He paused. 'I'd like a dog.' Me too, agreed Mossy.

'I could take a dog on my newspaper round,' said Rollo, rolling onto his back again.

'We could have an Afghan Hound,' suggested Cissy.

'Don't be daft. It'd have to be a fox terrier to chase off the fox. And then we could have chickens too,' decided Rollo.

'Or a St Bernard, so that it can rescue us,' countered JJ.

'Who needs rescuing?' Cissy sat up. Mossy sighed contentedly as he watched a ladybird scurry up a stalk. He felt confident that just now no one needed rescuing. They were all fine.

'I'm going to find Dad and tell him we need to get a spaniel,' Cissy decided, jumping to her feet and running down the side of the tumulus, the others in hot pursuit. She wriggled through the fence.

'I thought you said you wanted an Afghan Hound?' Rollo called after her.

A couple of days later Mossy watched as Jack bundled the children into the car.

'Going to school in the middle of the holidays?' protested Cissy. 'It's not as if it's our school any longer, anyway.'

'Hardly the middle of the holidays with only a week left. It's so that I can pick up some stuff,' Jack explained. 'I need to do some reading to prepare for next term.'

'Dad?' JJ paused, one foot still on the ground. 'Have you heard from the gallery yet? When's Mum's painting coming back?'

'They rang to say it had arrived safely, and they said they'd be in touch soon. Don't worry, I promise I'll let you know as soon as...' The rest was lost as the car door slammed. But Mossy wasn't worried any longer.

He watched as they left. They didn't need him. He could relax. He sat out on the staddle stone, swinging his legs. The kingfisher darted up the stream, skimming low, flashing blue, his shrill call bouncing off the water.

'Thanks,' called Mossy in return. 'I think they're fine!'

The ducks, no longer fluffy chicks but boldly patterned adults, wandered by, quacking loudly.

'Thanks for the offer, but I don't think I'm going to have to go again.' The youngest launched himself into the pond with a splash and waggled his tail.

'Cheeky!' laughed Mossy. 'This is where I belong, on my Holding.'

Two magpies danced round each other as they flew low

across the meadow towards them. Mossy grinned. Two for joy. It looked as though good news was coming.

On Saturday morning the whole family were together for breakfast.

'Jon said he'd be round later,' Rollo announced. 'They were out celebrating Sophie's results and her scholarship last night.'

'Sophie's done brilliantly,' Annie smiled at Rollo. 'She deserves to celebrate.'

'Post!' announced Cissy as she slid a handful of envelopes onto the table.

'Toast?' asked JJ, looking over at her. 'Looks more like letters to me. Mostly yours, Dad. And one for you, Mum. Where do you want it?'

'Bung it on the dresser. I'll get it after I've finished scrambling these eggs,' replied Annie. Mossy looked at the envelope that JJ propped up beside him. 'Advertising you can trust', it said on the postmark. Now where had he heard that before?

'Dad,' said Rollo, handing the mail to Jack, 'This one first.'

'Why?' Jack looked puzzled.

'Look at the postmark.' Now Cissy was craning over Jack's shoulder as well. Mossy wondered if Jack's letter was telling him to trust advertising too.

Suddenly he remembered where he'd heard that before – the women with telephones disguised as beetles. A shiver went down his spine. Oh, no. And just as he was beginning to think that everything was going well again.

'Is that it?' asked Cissy.

All eyes bar Annie's were glued to Jack's face as he opened the letter. Rollo, his back to Mossy, looked over his father's shoulder, reading with him.

'Dad?' he said. 'You're going to have to tell Mum now.'

'Tell me what?' said Annie coming over to the table with the saucepan. 'Who wants scrambled eggs?'

'Me!' Cissy held out her plate.

'Me, too!' added JJ. 'Sit here, Mum, next to me.' He pointed at the chair beside him. Annie sat, the saucepan still held in one hand.

'What's all this about?' A puzzled frown settled over her eyes. Mossy's heart sank. Please don't let this be bad news.

'A while ago now,' Jack started, 'I decided that I had to do something to help out.'

Now all eyes were on Annie. Mossy twisted his ears for good luck. 'I know that ever since you had that ghastly experience with the gallery just after you left Art School you've refused to show your paintings to anyone.' Annie put the saucepan down on the table. She looked intently at Jack.

'With good reason. I don't paint them for other people. My work, the stuff I do for the agency, is for other people. My paintings are my way of saying something for me. They are how I see life, the world around me.' JJ slipped a hand into hers and held it tightly.

'I know that, Annie,' Jack continued. 'But maybe it's time to let other people see your vision. Your paintings are wonderful. They make me see the world better, more clearly, with more hope, than I see it through my own eyes.'

'He's right, you know, Mum,' Rollo added. 'Even we hadn't

really seen them, not till you painted that picture of JJ.'

Annie shook her head.

'I haven't the time. And I don't think I could face it. I still have horrid memories of when I tried...' Her voice petered out. Mossy could feel the tension in the air, as Jack reached a hand towards her.

'Which is why I thought I'd try for you.' Silence fell across the room.

'You what?' Annie stared blankly at Jack, as if she didn't understand.

'It's alright, Mum.' Cissy came round to Annie's seat, putting her arms round her mother's shoulders. 'Dad wouldn't be telling you if it wasn't alright.'

'I spoke to all sorts of people, all sorts of galleries.' Suddenly the words poured out in a rush, as if Jack wanted to get it over with.

At least this way, thought Mossy, if it's going to make trouble it'll make it quickly. He curled his toes around each other. Cissy moved back to her chair, now slipping her hand into her father's.

'Eventually I decided on the Richard Glenville Gallery. It just seemed the best one. They've seen photographs and they still have one of your paintings. But this is their reply. It arrived this morning. The final decision is yours, whether you want to go ahead or not.' He handed over two sheets of paper.

Annie seemed frozen. Mossy decided it was time to help out again. Quietly he slipped down from his shelf, lowered himself to the floor and crept across to Annie. Climbing the back of her chair, he laid a hand lightly on her shoulder, pouring his strength into her.

'Go on, Mum,' Rollo urged her. 'Just look at what it says.' She picked up the pages.

'Richard Glenville? In Bruton Street? It's one of the best galleries in London.' She looked again at the letter in her hand. Mossy closed his eyes tightly. He could feel her all knotted up, fearful. There was a pause while she read. And then a sudden change. An energy, like a bursting fountain erupted deep inside her.

'Jack!' Now the fountain gushed forth. 'All of you!' Annie leapt from her chair, rocking it backwards and tipping Mossy onto the floor. 'It says… It says…' Mossy sat up, rubbing his elbow where it had bashed against the ground, to see Rollo grinning broadly at his mother.

'We know what it says. It says what we all know – what Dad's always told us – that you're brilliant.'

By the time Jack had persuaded everybody to eat their breakfast, Annie had read the letter several times over, and the news was beginning to sink in. Mossy had reorganised himself to the windowsill, away from any risk of being flung about the room. All tension had gone, washed away in the excitement.

'Even cold scrambled eggs are yummy,' said JJ, reaching across Rollo for more toast.

'Especially when they're cooked by a famous artist!' added Cissy.

'Not yet,' laughed Annie as she looked again at the price list in her hand. 'These prices!' she exclaimed, still waving her toast in the air. 'I would never have dreamt of asking this much for my paintings. It would take me years to earn that much through the agency! And a solo exhibition!'

'Can we all come to see it?' asked Rollo.

'You bet!' she replied. 'If it weren't for you lot and Dad, it wouldn't be happening. You'll be the guests of honour!'

'So you're pleased, Mum? Even though we didn't ask you first?' JJ wanted to check.

'You know, Dad was right.' Annie put an arm round JJ, giving him a warm hug. She looked over at Jack. 'Sometimes I think he knows me better than I know myself. If he'd asked me first, I'd have told him not to do it.' Mossy nodded his head. That was exactly what the Barn Owl had said.

'Oh Mum, you've forgotten your other letter,' Cissy pointed out.

'Maybe it's from the gallery too,' added Rollo. Mossy shook his head. He knew where the letter came from, and he had a horrid feeling it wasn't good news.

Annie was enjoying Cissy's impression of the queen knighting her for services to painting as she picked up the envelope from the dresser and opened it.

'Arise, Sir Annie' declared Cissy, carefully balancing an imaginary crown on her head as she waved a buttery knife in the air.

'Oh, it's from…' Annie broke off abruptly. Her face paled slightly. After a short pause, she turned to Jack. 'Well, now you're not the only one who knows what it's like to lose a job.'

'What do you mean?' Jack stopped in the middle of the kitchen.

'The project I'm working on has been 'terminated'. I'm being 'let go.''

Suddenly Mossy understood what it was that Flik had

been trying to tell him, that last-minute warning he had misunderstood. It wasn't anything to do with sowing bees, or going via anywhere. He'd been trying to warn him that she was 'going to be fired'!

'I told Dirk what I thought of his suggestion, and this is his response. I thought things had been a bit quiet at work, no little visits, no more 'aren't you brilliant'!'

'Oh Annie! I'm so sorry.' Jack looked at her anxiously.

'Mum!' All the children turned to look at her.

'I'm not sorry, not at all. Even though some of the people were fine, I hated working there. And there are certain people who I won't miss at all,' said Annie her eyes shining in delight. 'But even better than that – thanks to you lot it doesn't matter anymore!' Annie grinned at them. 'I'll be able to concentrate on painting full-time, being with you, preparing for this exhibition, and then the next, and the one after that and... Who knows what we'll be doing next? And who cares? As long as we're doing it together!'

## CHAPTER 34

# New Beginnings

The last week of the summer holidays disappeared in a whirl. Annie went to London a couple of times to visit the gallery. Mossy knew she didn't need him and stayed at home, poring over maps and charts beside Jack, watching as he prepared for his new job.

'Richard says that he thinks this exhibition will be a triumph,' Annie told the family on her return. 'I never thought that someone would have such complete faith in my work.'

'You should have asked us. We'd have told you,' Cissy pointed out. Mossy agreed. He could have told her any time. The ache in his back had gone; his sparkle was back; he was full of energy again.

On a bike ride with the children, whirring through the country lanes to the old quarry, he had scared himself rigid as they hurtled through the tracks, bouncing over the jumps and racing at dizzying speeds down the steepest slopes.

'Nothing broken, Mum!' announced JJ on their return.

Mossy shook his head in wonderment. Maybe not, but he was pretty sure there would be some bruises to admire soon, and JJ wouldn't be the only one to have them either.

And suddenly the holidays were over, and term was due to start the next day.

'You know what, there are times when I'm nervous and times when I'm just excited at the thought of this new term,' Jack admitted as they tidied up after supper.

'You're not the only one,' agreed Cissy. 'I know it was my idea to change school again, and I'm glad you agreed in the end, but now that it's happening I'm a bit nervous too. At least I won't have to worry about you watching over my shoulder now. And Bella and Tilly are starting there too, so it's not nothing but strangers this time.'

'And you've got Rollo and Jon there anyway,' JJ reminded her.

'You know it's funny, Dad – I always thought it was us kids that did all the work in school, but you've been doing quite a bit already, and it's still the holidays. I think you're going to be a weird kind of teacher.'

'I think he'll be a fine one,' said Annie, giving him a hug. Mossy smiled. Annie was back to being the person he had first seen when they arrived as his Dwellers. Her frowns had gone, and she shone with happiness in the evening light. She looked good with her Hole Stone strung round her neck, even with the smudge of paint on her ear.

As the children settled down to sleep, Mossy lingered on the landing. No need to watch for nightmares any longer, he realised. The house glowed again, keeping all anxiety and fretfulness at bay. The summer sun was setting as he looked into JJ's room.

'I just keep it under my pillow because I like it there,' he explained to Annie, snuggling down under the duvet.

'And where did you find it?' she asked, handing him his talisman. Only Mossy could see its gentle light, but JJ clearly felt it as he tucked his hand under his head.

'Here, in my room. It was waiting for me when we first arrived.'

Mossy went through to Cissy's, to find her propped up on the end of her bed, looking out of the window.

'I love it here, Dad.' She turned to look at her father standing beside her.

'That's good, because here is where we're staying,' he replied, looking up the hill to the far sunset.

'When I'm a famous actress, I'll still come home here and keep you and Mum company,' she assured him. Ah ha! thought Mossy, of course, that's what all that emotion is for.

'Don't you worry about us, we'll be fine, with or without company.' Jack tucked some stray hair behind her ear, letting his hand drop to her shoulder. 'Not that it won't always be great to have you here for as long as you want.'

Yes, agreed Mossy. You are fine. I had my worries. We all had our worries, but now they are gone. You and Annie have found your paths again. And then all we have left to keep us busy will be helping these three find theirs.

When the parents went downstairs, leaving Cissy and Rollo reading in bed, Mossy stayed behind.

'Rollo?' JJ called out.

'Mmm…?' Mossy heard Rollo's duvet flump off his bed, as he padded across the landing. He stuck his head round the door.

'Wassup?' asked Cissy joining them.

'Mum was asking about my talisman, and Cissy has her magic white feather. But you, you haven't got anything special, have you?' JJ seemed concerned.

'Haven't I?' Rollo sat on the end of the bed. 'You know, I think I have, but not something I can hold in my hand. For me this whole place is special. You know how there have been times when things were tough, and we all worried?'

'I'll say,' agreed Cissy. 'But it's better again now.'

'Well, I always felt that the house was looking after us,' Rollo continued. 'As if something was protecting us, keeping nightmares away, making sure that it all worked out in the end. It's something about the spirit of Annanbourne.' He sighed. 'I can't really explain it. And I certainly can't put it in my pocket, but I'm sure it's there. It's as if the whole place was holding us safely.'

'That's alright then.' JJ turned over, pulling the duvet snugly round his shoulders. 'I've got my stone, Cissy's got her feather, and you've got the whole house. So that's fine.' His voice faded as sleep washed over him.

You've all got me, thought Mossy. That's what he means. He just doesn't know it.

The bright, full moon lit the dark fields and woods almost like daylight. Long moonshadows stretched across the garden. Mossy sat on the roof ridge beside the Barn Owl.

'So it's not just me who thinks everything's recovered. You do, too, this time.' She turned her head slowly, looking deep into him with her golden eyes.

'I see what you mean.' Mossy nodded his head. 'On a clear night you can see forever.' He smiled. Forever looked good just now. The Barn Owl shifted her feet.

'Mustn't keep you,' Mossy smiled. 'And thank you for all your wise advice.' He watched as she spread her wings and lifted silently into the spangled darkness. Good friends make all the difference.

Silence fell, and Mossy revelled in the calm. Below him the stream glinted silver, the ducks floating on the still water of the pond, heads tucked under their wings. Was that the mice he spotted scurrying across to the back of the barn? He looked down carefully, so absorbed that he didn't hear the silent danger swooping low over him until the last minute.

In desperation he flung himself to one side as the sparrowhawk lashed out at him, her razor-sharp talons skimming his shoulder. Knocked off balance, he was suddenly slipping. He clutched at the roof tiles, but he was sliding down, his fingers scrabbling in vain to find a hold.

'It's alright, grab the gutter,' he told himself, reaching with his toes, trying to feel it as he gathered speed. There was a sudden jolt as his knee struck the curved run of guttering, his hands wildly flailing about him, grasping at thin air.

And then he was falling.

'Oh no, this is going to hurt!' Mossy clapped his hands over his eyes. Faintly he caught a pounding sound, or was he imagining it? Couldn't be, he thought, it's the middle of the night. It must be the sound of his heart. Did a door bang? Or was it his heart bursting? If he was seriously hurt, injured, what damage would it bring to the house? It was all his fault.

And then suddenly he was caught. And it didn't hurt. He'd landed on something soft. Cautiously he opened his eyes.

'Ah,' said Rollo. 'There you are. I was so worried I wouldn't be in time when I heard you falling. I've wondered for ages when I was really going to see you.' Mossy looked up into the smiling eyes that shone down at him. He shrugged his shoulders as understanding spread through him. In the terror of the fall he'd forgotten to turn invisible.

Ah well, he decided, with this one it was probably time to stop hiding.

'Hello, Rollo,' he said as he held out a hand in greeting. 'Edwin Mosstone, at your service.' It was impossible to bow, spread-eagled as he was all over Rollo's hands and forearms. Instead he winked. 'But you may call me Mossy.'

If you enjoyed reading about Mossy, find out what happens next in the Annanbourne series.

Mossy and Rollo have to discover if they can really believe in each other, and come to realise just how important their relationship could become.

But first, the Dweller children disturb something in the woods, a Holder so wrong it shakes their family again and threatens to take over their home. It doesn't care who gets hurt. Mossy knows the twisted Holder has to be confronted if they are to survive, but dare he ask the Place Reader for help?